Hei~~rs~~

Shayda KARIMI

Preface

2159, London.

"You have the worst timing ever," Kenneth said.

Celine didn't dare stop running, but turned her head just far enough to glare at her husband. He looked back at her and smiled; how he could be so infuriatingly happy in such circumstances was beyond her. His dark hair was matted with dirt and dust, and there was blood streaked across his face from a nasty cut on his cheek.

She paused as another contraction hit, leaning against a crumbling wall. A shower of plaster dust filled her hair. She brushed more off from where it had settled on her very pregnant abdomen.

"Are you sure you don't want me to carry you?" Kenneth asked.

"I'm nine months and two bloody long weeks pregnant- I doubt you'll be able to lift me." She struggled to catch her breath as the pain passed.

"You're probably right," he admitted. He took her sweaty, plaster- stained hand and they continued their run to the hospital wing. Ordinarily of course, when a queen went into labour there would be wheelchairs and assistants and pain killers, but these were extraordinary circumstances. They'd be lucky to find a doctor.

Someone - they suspected the rebellion but hadn't proved it yet- had planted a bomb in the castle. Parts of the ceiling had collapsed, there was smoke everywhere and

Celine's ears were still ringing from the blast. Worst timing ever indeed.

"We're here!" Kenneth announced, reaching to open the hospital door. He stepped back hastily as it simply fell off its hinges. "Hello? Is there anyone here? We need a doctor!"

"Your Highness!" The doctor exclaimed, stumbling out from a small office in the corner. His thinning brown hair was dishevelled and there was dust and plaster clinging to the knees of his scrub trousers. Celine suspected he'd been taking shelter under the oak desk. "You're hurt!" He made to examine the cut on Kenneth's face, but Kenneth pushed him away.

"The Queen is in labour!" Kenneth announced joyfully. But as he helped her lie down on a bed Celine could feel the tremor in his hands- he wasn't half as relaxed as he seemed. He made to sit on chair beside the bed, then immediately leapt up again when the doctor approached, a nurse following behind him.

"Is everything OK?" Kenneth asked, wringing his hands together.

The doctor looked as if he was suppressing a grin. Maybe all prospective fathers, no matter their rank, behaved in this same erratic manner.

"If you'll give me a second to examine her, Your Majesty, I'll be able to give you a better idea," the doctor said. He bent down to examine Celine and then looked round at both expectant parents. "I can see the baby's head already! Shouldn't be too much longer."

"Oh thank goodness for that! " Celine panted.

Twenty minutes later, the doctor was anxiously pressing a stethoscope to her abdomen. The baby's head was still visible but had made no further progress. Celine was on the verge of exhaustion, and though her husband was rubbing her shoulders soothingly and whispering words of reassurance, she knew that everything was not going to plan.

"I think I can hear- Reema, get me the ultrasound!" The doctor said, his eyes widening. The nurse looked alarmed but rushed away.

"What is it? What did you hear? Is there a heartbeat?" Kenneth asked, his face growing even paler under the layer of dirt and blood. The ultrasound machine was rarely used, even for a queen.

The nurse, Reema, rushed back in, pushing the machine in front of her on rattling wheels. Celine felt something cold on her stomach- the lubricating jelly- and turned her head so she could see the imagine on the screen. Reema gasped, though Celine couldn't see why. There was a head, limbs, two pulsing areas that looked like they could be heart beats….

"Twins." The doctor said in a hushed voice.

"Twins?" Kenneth croaked, sounding as if he were about to either laugh, cry or throw up.

"Not ordinary twins. They are conjoined- that's why the baby is stuck- see here." He pointed to an area of the screen, but all Celine could see were shadows and darker shadows.

"What can we do?" Kenneth asked. His fingers gripped her shoulders tightly.

The doctor shook his head, twisting the stethoscope around his neck over and over again until Celine feared it would either snap or strangle him.

"It might already be too late, the first twin's heart beat is slowing down."

"There must be something you can do. Anything!" The monitor attached to Celine's abdomen began to alarm shrilly.

"It's very risky. We can try an emergency C-section. But with one twin already so far into the birth canal…" The doctor trailed off.

"Do it," Celine said. Kenneth looked at her fleetingly, his expression torn. She squeezed his hand and gave him a fierce look. She wouldn't be able to live with herself if they didn't try everything they could to save their children.

"OK," Kenneth said.

"We're going to put the Queen under general anaesthesia. Then attempt the C-section." The doctor rushed around collecting equipment as he spoke, and his words were punctuated with the sound of various instruments clattering into a metal kidney dish. "Your Highness, we're going to put you to sleep now." The nurse injected something cold and achy into Celine's arm. Then the room exploded.

Kenneth woke up with his ears ringing. The room stank of smoke and he coughed heavily into the crook of his elbow. Where was he? He'd been having the strangest dream; Celine had gone into labour, the castle was under attack, something about conjoined twins… A nearby shriek brought him back to his senses.

"Celine!" He shouted, staggering to his feet and towards his wife. The doctor was bent over her, his face pale under streaks of smoke and blood. He looked stricken and Kenneth could immediately see why; Celine was grey and still the way no living person ever was. A piece of shrapnel had buried itself deep into her neck, killing her instantly. Had it been aimed purposefully the marksmanship would have been impressive. As it was, Kenneth wondered how unlucky a man could possibly be.

He swallowed hard and met the doctor's regretful gaze.

"And the babies?" he asked. His voice sounded cold and calm. Why wasn't he screaming, like the doctor was?

"Give me your knife!" he shouted, and pulled a dagger off Kenneth's belt. "There might be a chance…." The doctor plunged the knife into Celine's abdomen making a long vertical cut. Blood pooled out, already slow flowing and congealed. The doctor reached inside, pulling out a very oddly shaped bundle; two infants facing each other and attached by a wide strip of flesh across their tiny chests.

They were still and ashen coloured. The doctor wrapped them in a blanket, and rubbed them vigorously, but Kenneth couldn't look away from the mangled remains of his wife. He felt a sudden uncontrollable rage towards the doctor for slicing her open, and had the knife gripped firmly in his hand when he heard a high pitched cry. A second identical cry joined it a moment later.

The knife clattered to the ground as he turned to look at his children. They were wrapped in a bright blue blanket, tiny and wrinkled, but rapidly turning a healthy pink colour.

"Two boys, Your Majesty," the doctor said, glancing at the dropped knife and tentatively holding out the infants. Kenneth stroked Celine's hair one final time and then took his sons from the doctor. He expected them to be awkward to hold, attached as they were, but they moulded perfectly against his chest and the crook of his elbow. A strange calm came over him as he gazed at his infant sons.

"We need to get to the dungeons. The survivors will have gathered there. It's not safe here, there may be another blast." Kenneth said. His mind was working rapidly. "No one must know Celine had twins. Bring what you need-they must be separated as soon as possible."

"But-" the doctor protested, and then began gathering equipment into a bag as Kenneth glared at him. Kenneth made sure the infants were secure under one arm, and then checked on the nurse. She had been knocked unconscious but was now coughing and spluttering on the smoke fumes. Her left leg was obviously broken; it jutted out at an alarming angle, and she screamed in pain as Kenneth pulled her to her feet.

"I'm sorry, we'll fix you up as soon as we get to the basement, OK?" He threw her arm around his shoulders, taking most of her weight. "Doctor, are you ready?"

"Yes," the doctor panted, several bags of medical equipment tucked under his arms. Kenneth led them down the corridor. None of them did more than inhale sharply when they saw the destruction that had befallen the West side of the castle; three of the four towers had crumpled to the ground, leaving nothing but a pile of rubble and spirals of smoke rising lazily off the ground.

They reached the dungeon door and the doctor hammered on the wooden panels. It opened quickly and they were dragged inside, the door rapidly shut behind them. They were hurried down a narrow, dark staircase; Kenneth practically carrying the nurse and the doctor dropping two of his bags.

Kenneth winced as someone flashed a bright light in his face. It was lowered with a cry of surprised delight.

"Your Majesty! We feared the worst!" The speaker was Harry, the prison warden in charge of the dungeons. He snapped his fingers and two guards appeared, taking the nurse and carrying her carefully away to a corner where several other injured people had already been placed on blankets.

"Ken!" Kenneth's heart lightened at the sound of his best friend's voice. Tom would help him figure out what to do. He was a well-known figure at court, and people leapt out of his way almost as promptly and respectfully as if it were the king himself. He winced as he walked, one hand pressed to a wound in his side.

"I need a room," Kenneth announced, shocked by the paleness of his friend's face and alarmed by the small crowd that had gathered already. The bundle in his arms, though quiet, was already receiving unwanted stares.

"The East dungeon, your majesty." Harry said, opening a door. Kenneth dragged his friend inside, gestured for the doctor to follow and shut the door behind them.

"You look awful," Tom said, looking Kenneth up and down. The doctor gave a sharp intake of breath, there weren't many people who would dare speak to the King that way, but Kenneth ignored it.

"So do you," he said.

"I'm fine," Tom said. He leant heavily against the wall, his arms crossed across his chest as if he were simply being lazy. His shoulders were a bit too slumped to be convincing.

"Stich him up where he's standing if you have to," Kenneth said to the doctor, who looked startled but opened one of the bags he'd brought with him.

"What happened? Where's Celine?" Tom asked, reluctantly lifting his shirt so the doctor could see the wound. Kenneth shook his head. He couldn't say the words. Tom's face paled even further than it already was and he swallowed hard. He was staring at the bundle in Kenneth's arms.

"And the baby?" He asked with a grimace, as the doctor did something particularly painful to his side. Kenneth took a deep breath, bouncing the babies up and down as he paced across the room. His thoughts were scattered, jumping all over the place, driven by adrenaline and fear and grief.

"Babies," he said simply, and held the wrapped bundle out to his friend. The infants began to cry as they were separated from the warmth of their father's chest. Moving past the doctor, Tom peeled himself off the wall and took the bundle. He held the infants gingerly as he unwrapped the blanket. He stared at them and gently touched the thin strip of skin where they were joined together. They stopped crying at his touch.

"Well, thank god!" Tom said with a grin.

"What?" Kenneth said.

"They got Celine's looks," Tom said. "Congratulations, my friend." Tom's easy grin had turned into a small, sad smile. This wasn't how Ken had expected to share the news of his first born with his best friend; in a dungeon, with Tom bleeding and Celine lying dead somewhere above their heads.

"Ouch!" Tom said. He handed the babies back to Kenneth and glared at the doctor.

"It needs to be stitched, which would be a lot easier if you would lie down! Or at least sit! And stay still."

"Just get on with it," Tom said, through gritted teeth. The doctor swore under his breath and jabbed the next suture in with what Kenneth thought was probably unnecessary force.

"What am I going to do?" Kenneth asked, half to distract his friend. "I don't even know which was born first; I have no idea who the heir is…. Even if there is something left to inherit." He wondered if his friend would reach the same conclusion he had.

"It's simple." Tom said. "No one knows they are twins. We'll keep it that way, make everyone believe there is only one prince." He hesitated over the next sentence, but said it anyway, "If one is killed, the other will take his place. The perfect safety net." He looked sickened at himself for saying it, for seeing the two tiny infants as simply the next in line to the throne.

"You're right." He was condemning his sons to live a lie, but this way at least one of them would be safe. "It will never leave this room. Me, you, the doctor. No one else must ever know. "

"And the nurse," Tom reminded him.

"And Holly…. Nothing stays secret from your wife for long."

Tom laughed, but stopped abruptly, holding his newly bandaged wound.

"This will help," the doctor said, and handed him two tablets.

"Thanks," Tom said grudgingly, tipping them into his mouth.

"Right, let's get on with this," Kenneth said, and passed the sleeping twins to the doctor. The doctor took them. A look of uncertainty passed across his face.

"Before we do this, I think we should name them." Tom said. The unspoken phrase at the end of his sentence lingered in the air- *just in case.* Kenneth swallowed hard as he looked at his friend and then back at his sons.

"I'll give them Roman names. They had twin emperors didn't they? And they built a great empire. My sons will be named Cassander. Cas and Ander. One day they will be as legendary as Romulus and Remus."

Tom gave him a peculiar look.

"What? Too weird?"

Tom shook his head. "No. It's about time royalty had more interesting names. I was thinking about Romulus and Remus. Didn't one kill the other?"

Chapter One
England, January 23rd 2176

In the hour before dawn, the smog parted and London was bathed in a pale silver glow. The river slunk through the city, black as spilled ink, except for the perfect round orb reflected on its surface. In the long row of terraced houses by the river bed, mothers woke their sleeping children and pointed up at the sky- the full moon had not been seen for several years. In the middle of the houses stood a pub, and a handful of people spilled out, staring upwards with their arms around each other's shoulders and swaying on the spot. They started to sing, loudly and out of tune, an old millenial song about flying to the moon.

Unbeknownst to them, across the street, lurking in the entrance of what was once Embankment Underground station; the King of Britain cursed his bad luck. Cas was running late- his bicycle lay abandoned several miles away, one tyre demolished by a sharp piece of rubble. And now there were plenty of witnesses and a bright glaring moon to see him sneaking out of the underground tunnel.

Cas pulled his hood up over his head. It was now or never. Abandoned empty bottles and old newspapers littered the floor, bits of smashed glass glittered in the moonlight. He picked up a bottle and strode across the street, hoping he hadn't misjudged exactly how inebriated the singers across the street were. Hating himself vehemently, he began to sing-

"When the moon hits your eye like a big-" He pretended to stumble over a pothole. He heard laughter interspersed with the singing. A pair of beefy hands helped him to his feet.

"Thank you!" Cas said, much louder than he needed to. "I seem to have lost the pub!" More laughter echoed from the signers. Except for the man who'd broken away to help him up, who was looking at Cas wearily.

"You should go home son. Your parents will be worried." He was older than his group of friends, probably old enough to have grandsons around Cas' age.

"Nothing worries them, Sir. They're dead." Cas felt guilty using his dead parents this way. The man said nothing further.

Pretending to take a swig from his bottle, Cas stumbled past him and into the pub. A blast of warmth and alcohol hit him as soon as the door opened. Despite the lateness of the hour, it was packed. Cas made a beeline for the girl behind the bar. His godfather always teased him that his pretty blue eyes and long eyelashes could make a girl spill all her secrets. Cas kind of hoped he was right.

"Can I tell you a secret?" Cas flashed a grin at the pretty bartender as he sat on a wooden stool. Caroline, according to her name tag. She tucked a loose brown curl behind her ear, putting down the cup she was drying. A flush crept across her cheeks. Cas flicked his own dark hair out of his eyes- he had to remember to get it cut- and leaned towards her across the counter.

"I'm the king," he whispered into her ear. He was enticing and mysterious, she would surely tell-

Caroline rolled her eyes and scoffed.

"Sure, and I'm Tom Candler's sister." Cas frowned and sat up. His godfather's fame had reached even this small pub in one of the poorest London suburbs. Caroline resumed drying the glass. "How many of those have you had?" She nodded at the beer bottle in his hand.

"A couple," Cas said, and shrugged, picking at the label. He pretended to take a sip. "I needed some courage." He waited to make sure he'd piqued her interest. Her eyes flicked up towards his and he held her gaze. He kept his voice low enough that she had to lean in to hear him over the drunken shouts and clatter of bottles. "I'm looking for Grant. I want a job."

She burst into laughter. There were literal tears running down her cheeks.

"Don't be ridiculous, kid." She was only a couple of years older than him, nineteen or twenty at the most. It added extra sting to the word. But he got the message- flirting wasn't his strong suit.

"I need to see him," he said. "I'll make it worth your while." He straightened up and reached into his inside jacket pocket, pulling out a wad of bank notes. They were crisp, freshly-printed, and rustled pleasantly when he separated out half a dozen and handed them to the girl. Her brown eyes widened, but she took the notes without hesitation and tucked them into her apron pocket. At least he could manage to be enticing.

"He's in the back office. This evening's password is glomerulonephritis."

"Where does he come up with these passwords?" This one was another mouthful. Last week's had been almost as bad- astrocytoma. He pushed his stool back and stood, leaving his empty bottle on the counter.

"Be careful," Caroline said. She already looked as though she regretted giving him the password.

"I'm always careful." He threw her a wink. He had to get better at flirting eventually. She shook her head, but he caught the hint of a grin tugging at her lips.

He pushed his way through the crowded bar towards the back room. No one paid him much attention, except for the big, hairy drunk who ruffled his hair affectionately and told him he was a good lad. Cas ducked under his sweaty hand, smiling uneasily as he caught a snatch of conversation from the man's drinking buddy.

"We better start making a move if we want to make it in time for the fight!"

Cas glanced at his watch- he had time. Just about. He tried to move away but the man had tossed an arm around his shoulders. Cas stumbled under the weight- the guy was massive.

"I've bet three hundred on the challenger," someone else shouted.

"Disloyal bastard!" Cas' hairy friend lifted his arms in outrage; half his tankard of ale sloshed over the side and onto Cas' shirt front. Ignoring the uncomfortable wetness against his chest, he slunk away before the inevitable fistfight broke out.

A guard sat discreetly a couple of yards away from the back door, drinking from a large mug. A blue scarf covered his neck. His hands were steady- unlike almost everyone else in the bar he wasn't drunk. It was probably just water in the mug.

"Glom-el- ulonefitis" Cas said as he approached. He didn't think he'd pronounced it exactly right but the guard nodded curtly. Cas felt his steely grey eyes follow him the last few yards to the door. Before the guard could change his mind, he pushed the door open.

Grant was sat at a desk in front of him, with a woman he didn't recognise. She was well dressed, and judging from the large stack of paperwork and the pages and pages of numbers and tables piled in front of them, his accountant.

"You again," Grant sounded exasperated. He barely looked up from the document he was reading. "How did you get the password?"

Cas ignored the question.

"I've had an idea."

"Show me the money and maybe I'll listen." His green eye's flashed at Cas over square shaped spectacles. Cas pulled out the entire wad and dumped it on the table. The accountant looked like he'd just killed her horse- all her careful calculations would have to start from scratch. It was a lot of money. "Saleena, just pretend you didn't see a thing." Grant patted his accountant on the shoulder and nodded for Cas to continue.

"I think we need to find Bonnington. He's the answer." Cas said. He bounced up and down on the balls of his feet. If Grant knew where he was- maybe he could go see him right now, before-

"Kid, I don't think he's gonna be the answer you're looking for." Grant said. He put down the papers he was holding, finally giving Cas his full attention.

"Can you find him, or not?" Cas leaned across the desk, his fingers clutching the edge. This had to be the answer. He was running out of options.

"Fine. I'll ask around," Grant said. He picked up his papers again- a dismissal. "And next time come to my actual office. In daylight. A kid your age shouldn't be hanging around in bars at 6am."

5am? He was late. Crap.

"Do you mind?" He gestured at the big window behind Grant's desk- it would be faster than shoving his way through the crowd.

"Help yourself." Grant nudged Saleena, redirecting her attention to the papers in front of them. She had glared at the pile of money throughout the entire conversation.

Cas prised the window open, wincing at the gust of frozen air that hit his lungs. At least his shirt would dry in the breeze. It was still dark outside, but only barely, across the river and about half a mile downstream the sky above the castle was dark blue with pink tinges. The moon had disappeared. Dawn was minutes away.

He'd never make it back through the tunnels in time. He couldn't be late.

He sprinted to the riverbank, boots squelching in the mud. He stared at the filthy grey water; the current could carry him much faster than his own two legs. But if hypothermia didn't kill him, then disease would. Swimming was out of the question. A boat however...

There was a small rowing boat tied to a wooden pillar a few metres away. The wood was rotting in places, but Cas couldn't see any leaks. It probably belonged to a smuggler; criminals and thieves were the only ones desperate enough to brave the river's toxicity. It made him feel better about stealing it.

He unhooked the rope securing it and pushed it away from the bank, vaulting over the side. It swayed when he landed; a trickle of water sloshed over the bow and soaked his boots. He sat down quickly- he'd expected more stability. He picked up the oar and realised he had no idea what to do with it. Luckily, the river's current was pushing him in the right direction at an impressive pace.

He struck out against the bank with the oar; trying to get himself to the other bank. The boat tilted, almost capsized, soaked his boots again but moved no closer to the other bank. Cas took a deep breath- through his mouth, the river's stench was overpowering- and tried not to vomit. Flirting and sailing; not his strong suits.

He'd have to get off on this side of the river and cross the castle bridge on foot. Now the next problem- how to stop. Bathed in pink, the castle loomed ahead of him.

The little boat swept under the castle drawbridge. His breaths echoed hollowly as he stood, his arms held out to the sides for balance. The bank was only a metre away. He could probably make it. He had to. He braced himself and jumped.

His fingers scrambled for purchase on the muddy bank, his boots hanging out over the water, and he fought to stop himself sliding straight back into the river. Grasping hold of a particularly stubborn weed, he steadied himself and rolled to his feet. The little boat continued without him, quickly disappearing from view.

Briefly, he wished he were still on it.

He joined the throngs of last minute spectators for the fight. He shoved and pushed his way between them, running up the bridge steps. He pulled his jacket hood up over his head, suddenly glad for the mud caking his face. He could not afford to be recognised, not here, and especially not now.

Across the bridge, Cas peeled away from the crowd being diverted towards the main entrance and ducked into the courtyard. No one noticed him dart across the grass and leap into a disused garbage chute. He wiped his hands on his trousers as best he could and began to climb; his breathing harsh and echoing in his own ears. The mud on his skin began to dry, cracking and itching. If only he had time to wash.

He leapt out of the chute and into the corridor, boots squealing across the ground. He winced at the trail of mud he was leaving behind, but he couldn't do anything about it right now. He could hear the dull roar of the crowd, vibrating through the stone floors.

He slowed as he descended the steps to the arena. He had to catch his breath, steady his heart rate. A voice floated up to him through the preparation room door, shrill and angry.

"Where the hell is he?" Skye said. Cas could imagine his best friend pacing up and down, pulling out strands of her dark brown hair. "He agreed to this stupid fight, the least he could do is show up!"

Cas grasped the door knob and hesitated, the handle cold under his palm. If the challenger didn't kill him, then Skye probably would. He grinned and pushed the door open.

Chapter Two

When Cas walked in, Skye stopped pacing. She smothered her disappointment. Part of her, maybe a large part of her, had hoped he wouldn't turn up for this fight. What was the point of being king if you had to risk your life at the whim some power hungry nut job? The challenger, Spider as he called himself, had flounced into court and challenged the king to a duel for his throne using some pre-millennial law.

"Where have you been?" Skye demanded. His black hair was streaked brown with mud, dried clumps were on his arms and face, and he smelt like- "Have you been drinking?!"

"Of course not." He waved a dismissive hand. "I just went on an early morning walk to prepare." Liar- his eyes wouldn't meet hers. But his gait was steady when he strode past her to take the helmet his personal assistant, Tae, offered him. The helmet had been borrowed from the castle's historical museum; there was a dent in one side and it was so misshapen it took Cas a good minute to force it onto his head. Flakes of red rust and dried mud drifted to the floor. Tae handed him a freshly sharpened knife. It sparkled as Cas threw it in the air. It span several times before he caught it cleanly by the handle and tucked it into the sheath at his hip. Show off.

"How do I look?"

His eyes gleamed dark blue against the dull iron of the helmets visor; his voice muffled by the metal. Although he was athletic, he looked nothing like the hulking, metal encased ancient knights she had seen in pictures. Cas had refused the full set of armour the museum had offered. *It will only slow me down.* His hands were balled into fists at his sides, but Skye could make out a slight tremor. He wasn't as calm as he was pretending to be.

She caught Tae's eye. Always perceptive, he nodded at her and slipped out of the preparation room, past the heavy curtain that led to the arena.

"You don't have to do this Cas," she said.

"It will be fun." She could tell he was grinning under the helmet. Abruptly he stopped. "The law is the law Skye. I do have to do this." His gaze drifted, staring at something above her head. "Breaking any law, even one as out dated as this one, would just be fuel for the rebellion's fire."

"Be careful," she said. She wanted to hug him, or kiss him, or something, but it felt too much like goodbye instead of good luck. She kept her hands by her sides.

"I'm always careful," he said, taking a step towards her. Another lie, but he was smiling again. She caught the scent of rust and iron; Cas smelt like blood. How many people had died wearing that helmet? He gripped her shoulder fleetingly and she pushed the thought aside. Without hesitation, Cas pulled the curtain aside and stepped out into the arena.

Skye followed him out and listened to the crowd roar; clapping, cheering, stamping their feet. Hundreds, maybe thousands, had braved the ice cold morning and turned up to watch their king fight Spider. She was captured by the sight of the crowd; her breath froze in a white cloud above her head and for a long moment she couldn't hear the noise they were making. There was an odd expression on some of their faces, tense, hungry, like they didn't care who won. They just wanted blood.

She shook her head and redirected her attention to Cas, standing in his allotted corner. The arena floor had been set up like one of those boxing rings the gangs ran in the city outskirts; lightly padded floor, four posts joined by thick ropes. The referee stood in the centre of the ring; a large man with a bald head, but an impressive goatee. A whistle and a stethoscope dangled from his neck- this was a fight to the death.

Skye drummed her fingers against her thigh, her foot tapping up and down. She had no idea how Cas was standing so still, practically lounging against the post.

A hiss came from the stands. The challenger entered the ring from the opposite side, vaulting over the ropes effortlessly. Spider was a slight figure, like Cas, devoid of all armour apart from a helmet. The visor was down. He was dressed all in black, spotlessly clean down to his military style boots. All she could see of the challenger's face was the flickering of his eyes behind the metal.

Five days ago he'd arrived at the castle, alone and on foot, and issued his challenge. No one had seen him without the helmet. Rumours were flying around the castle; he was hideously scarred, he was actually a woman, he wasn't even human... But Skye could see goose pimples appearing on the challenger's forearms- that seemed human enough. He took his place in the corner opposite Cas without acknowledging the crowd.

The referee was speaking, though Skye couldn't hear the exact words. Spider nodded at the instructions, but said nothing. Other than to issue his challenge- a single paragraph recited almost perfectly word for word from the constitution- he had barely spoken. Within an hour, he or Cas could be dead. They didn't even know the challenger's real name; Skye refused to believe it was Spider.

"You may begin on three," the referee said. Now his voice sounded far too loud. "One." Skye's finger nails dug into her palms. Cas pulled the knife from its sheath. His hand was steady. "Two." He caught her eye and winked behind the visor. Skye stopped herself rolling her eyes. "Three."

Cas stepped forwards simultaneously with his opponent. They circled each other, like two wolves vying for the same piece of meat. Cas leapt forwards first. Knife in hand, Spider pivoted out of the way. The blade slashed across Cas' upper arm. Skye's heart leapt into her throat as blood welled up around the wound, but Cas didn't seem to notice the cut. He faced his opponent again. This time Cas attacked with a jumping kick. Spider blocked it, grabbed his foot and threw him to the floor. Cas leapt back up wincing but not seriously hurt. Thank goodness for the cushioned floor.

Cas was a good fighter, Skye knew that. He had been training since he could walk. This should have been easy for him.

Cas jumped over the low slash aimed at his shins. The knife sailed under him and he landed a kick on Spider's head on his way down. Spider shook it off and once again they were facing each other.

Skye tried to assess them impartially; it wouldn't do Cas any good if she broke down and started crying hysterically. They were both breathing hard; their chests moving in short harsh gasps. They well matched; same height, same build. More than that, their fighting style was so similar they could probably predict each other's moves. It was exactly what happened when she sparred with Cas herself. To win he had to do something unexpected. Something reckless.

Spider swung a left handed punch towards Cas' face. Skye waited for him to block with his left hand, the way they'd drilled a thousand times.

He didn't.

Cas ducked under the blow, tossed the knife to his other hand and slashed forwards. Reckless. It worked- the challenger's t-shirt was ripped open and a shallow wound from shoulder to hip made him gasp in pain. Cas didn't wait for him to recover; he launched forward and brought the hilt of his knife down on the challenger's temple. There was a clang and the metal of his helmet dented.

Spider crumpled to the ground.

Skye breathed a sigh of relief. It was over. Cas had won.

The audience roared their appreciation as Cas knelt beside his enemy, his knife, now stained red, clenched in his left hand. Cas had never killed a man before- Skye knew he wasn't ready to start now. He ripped the helmet of his head; his hair damp with sweat; his face flushed.

"Kill him! Kill him!" the crowd chanted. Several people in the front row stood; their thumbs held down like ancient Roman emperors. Cas looked back at them briefly, Skye saw him throat move as he swallowed.

Skye held herself back from screaming at the crowd. Couldn't they see the merciful thing, the right thing, was to-

Cas collapsed onto his knees, the knife he'd been holding clattering to the ground. Skye rushed forwards before she'd even decided to move, grabbing a bandage from the referee's bag. She pressed it to the wound on his arm- it must have been worse than it seemed. She looked him up and down, searching for other injuries, any damp patches of blood, but she couldn't see any.

"Skye," Cas croaked. His voice was almost unrecognizable. "Look." He pointed a trembling finger at the boy on the ground.

"It's OK Cas, you're the King, you don't have to kill him." She barely glanced at the fallen boy. She was fixed on Cas, on the cut on his arm, on his face, on his blood staining the arena floor.

"No, look at him. Look at his chest." Cas said again. He took the bandage she was pressing to his arm and pushed her forwards. What was he playing at? She bent forwards to look at the boy's chest. A long vertical scar ran down the centre. Her breath caught in her throat. It wasn't possible. She turned back to Cas, pressed her hand against his chest. Beneath his T-shirt, alongside his pounding heart, she could feel the raised edges of an old scar- identical to the one on the boy on the ground.

"Your Highness, are you alright?" This was Tae. He was wringing his hands as he approached them. His straight black hair stood up at all angles, as if he'd been tearing out clumps of it.

Skye turned around. The audience were muttering darkly, waiting for the killing blow. The referee stood with the whistle to his lips, frowning.

"Take him to my room. Have the doctor see to his injuries, but under no circumstances must anyone remove his helmet," Cas said. Tae raised his eyebrows at the strange request, but gestured to his men and whispered orders. A stretcher appeared as if from nowhere and five soldiers lifted the unconscious boy and carried him inside. The audience roared its disapproval. The noise was loud enough to make the ground rumble under Skye's feet. The referee blew his whistle but it was lost in the noise.

Cas faced the crowd. Skye stayed close by his side. She felt every eye in the stadium focus on the boy next to her.

"Rejoice, for I have won!" The audience cheered. "I have left him alive so that we may question him about the rebellion and so it may be squashed for good!" Only a few people looked disappointed.

"And now the King is injured and must rest," Skye said, taking him by the elbow. She dragged him away as the crowd made noises of sympathy.

As soon as they were out of sight, she stopped, pulling him round to face her. His eyes were wide, his pupils dilated in the dimly lit passageway.

"It can't be him. He's dead," she said. He had been killed the same day as Cas' father, King Kenneth, in a rebellion bomb along the East Corridor.

"You saw the scar."

"But-"

"We can easily find out," Cas interrupted and strode forwards again, towards his room. Skye's head buzzed. She could concentrate on nothing but the memory of that scar. The mottled pink on smooth skin. The raised edges under thin fabric.

Tae stood guard outside the door, efficient as usual. His eyebrows contracted when he saw them.

"Your Highness, interviewing the prisoner can wait. I can assure you he won't be going anywhere. You should attend to your injuries first," he said, and nodded at Cas' arm. He'd lost the bandage somewhere. Blood dripped down to his wrist and onto the floor- he'd probably left a trail on his way here. His face was the colour of ash. She could understand why Tae sounded worried. But this couldn't wait. They had to know.

"Let us through," Cas ordered, and Tae stepped aside.

Spider was sprawled on Cas' sofa. His T-shirt had been cut away and a nurse was applying a dressing to the wound on his chest. The challenger stirred, but through the slit in his helmet Skye could see the boy's eyes remained shut.

"I need a minute with him," Cas said. He held on to Skye's hand, gripping it tightly, he didn't want her to leave.

His hand was shaking. Or hers was- she couldn't actually tell.

"But-" Tae started to say.

"Now!" Cas barked. Skye flinched at his tone, but said nothing. She gripped his hand harder.

"Yes, Your Highness." Tae said and disappeared back out through the door, gesturing for the two guards and the nurse to follow him. The door shut behind them and the room was engulfed by silence.

"You do it," Cas said. Her heart was pounding so hard she barely heard him. She glanced at his pale face and let go of his hand. She took a deep breath and stepped forwards. She grasped Spider's helmet in both hands, braced herself, and pulled.

She recognised him instantly- the black hair, the high cheek bones, the curve of his jaw. The boy they had thought was dead, the boy who should have been king and the boy who had just tried to kill his own brother.

Ander.

Chapter Three

Ander's head throbbed, pulsing painfully in time with his heartbeat. His helmet was gone. The throbbing got worse as his pulse raced. The fight: what had happened? There were bandages across his chest and stomach. He'd been cut, he remembered, a moment when he'd been surprised, and then- nothing. Ander kept his eyes closed. He'd lost to the imposter King, but then, why wasn't he dead?

He could make out voices above him. A girl and a boy. They argued in hushed tones.

"He tried to kill you. He might not be the Ander you remember." The girl. They had seen his face- they knew who he was.

"He's my brother, Skye." The boy lied. A hand dropped onto Ander's shoulder.

"I know that, but-"

Ander opened his eyes. The boy, the imposter puppet king, was staring down at him. He almost flinched; it was like looking into a mirror. The castle plastic surgeons had done a fantastic job; if someone had handed him a photo of Cas, he may well have mistaken it for himself.

The girl stood beside him. Skye, the king's best friend, never left his side, reportedly an even better fighter than her legendary father. Her brown hair was tied in a messy bun; strands had fallen loose and framed her emerald green eyes. They widened with alarm as she noticed he was awake.

"Cas, we should-"

"Ander!" The imposter held out his arms. Really, he wanted to hug the guy who'd just tried to kill him?

"I don't hug," Ander said, holding up a hand. Cas held out a hand instead. Ander ignored it. The imposter had a glazed, ecstatic look on his face, as if he'd just sniffed some of that nasty white powder that turned up at the wilder barracks parties. "Why am I still alive?"

"I saw the scar- I knew it had to be you," Cas said. His hand dropped back to his side.

"It was a fight to the death."

"You're my brother, I could never hurt you." The imposter spoke slowly. He was eyeing Ander's head as if worried he was brain damaged.

"I think the more pertinent question is why would you *want* to kill your own brother?" Skye said. She was smart. Protective. Less emotional. He needed to watch out for her. Ander sat up- he didn't like looking up at the two of them. They both took a step back.

""Why does anyone try to kill a King? It was a fair challenge," he said. "I did nothing wrong. I want the crown, for General Laric and the rebellion."

"The rebellion?" Skye asked, "You mean the people who killed your parents? And almost killed you?"

Ander smirked at her. "Yep, they'd be the ones." Skye fists clenched at her sides. Ander decided he liked making her squirm.

"You know you have a right to the throne. The plan was always that we would be joint rulers. Had we known that you were alive-" Cas said.

"You've even got yourselves believing this ridiculous farce you've created." Ander scoffed, and shook his head. He hadn't realised- the puppet king really believed it. The whole nonsense identical twin story Tom Candler had cooked up to steal his throne.

"Look, you're tired. You've been through a lot today. Why don't you rest; you can sleep here, and we'll talk properly tomorrow." The fake king was anxious. Ander searched his face for signs of deceit but could find none. Cas really was that naïve.

The door opened and a man walked through without knocking. He was tall and dark haired, green eyes like his daughter's. Ander recognised Skye's father from the file photo General Laric had provided him; Tom Candler. The real enemy, the man controlling the puppet king. Ander took a deep breath to stop himself leaping at the man and slashing his throat.

"Cas, why have you brought-" Tom caught sight of Ander and froze. His face went from light brown to paper white in an instant- it was fascinating to watch. He swayed on the spot as though he might pass out. Cas went to grab him by the elbow but Tom pushed him aside, crouching beside Ander.

"Ander." Tom's voice came out as a whisper. "We thought you were dead." He reached out a hand, almost touching the scar along Ander's chest. He was a good actor- Ander had to give him that.

"Look I don't blame you, *brother*," Ander said to Cas. "You're just a pawn, a puppet king. He's the real culprit. He'll be the first one I execute when I come to power." He glared at Tom, still crouched in front of him, and Tom stared back.

"How dare you?!" Skye hissed. "My father has done nothing but support Cas. He loves him as if he were his own son." She looked like a wolf; elegantly ferocious. If she'd had hackles, they would be raised. If she'd had the big jaws and sharp teeth to go with them, Ander imagined he wouldn't have had a head anymore.

Ander looked at her and very pointedly yawned. Skye leapt at him. She was quick; her open palm connected with the side of his face and his head snapped to the side before he could block her. His cheek burned; the throbbing headache returned with full force. She lifted her arm again, this time ready with a closed fist, but before she could strike Tom grabbed her hand.

"Skye, why don't you give me a minute to talk to the boys," Tom said. She ripped her hand out of his grasp. She glanced breathlessly at Cas, as if hoping he would protest on her behalf. The puppet king didn't seem to notice. The door slammed shut behind her.

"Quite a lady you've raised there," Ander said, flexing his jaw gingerly. He was sure there would be an angry red handprint on his face when he cared to check.

"We thought you were dead," Tom ignored Ander's comment. "Clearly you weren't. Which begs the question, where have you been?"

Cas stepped in before he could answer.

"All that matters is that he's back." How sweet. Ander restrained himself from scoffing.

"No, Skye is right. He tried to kill you. We need to know why." The emotion had drained from Tom's voice. He was no longer acting as the shocked man being reunited with his long lost surrogate son- this was the ruthless fighter Ander had been warned about. Good. He didn't care much for soppiness.

Ander smiled and told the truth.

"The rebellion sent me to kill the imposter and take my rightful place as king."

"Imposter?"

"Him." He nodded at Cas. The imposter stared back at him, mouth hanging open. Ander hoped that expression had never appeared on his own face. Cas looked like an idiot.

"You think he's an imposter? The two of you are identical," Tom said. He spoke mildly, calm like the eye of a hurricane. Ander hated people who could hide their emotions so easily- it made them too good at lying.

"I'm sure a King would have access to a plastic surgeon." Ander shrugged. "Besides, I'm much better looking." He had been warned about this before he left. *Don't let them trick you,* General Laric had said. *Always remember, they tried to kill you. They're very clever. They stole your throne and no one even knows it.*

Tom shook his head, taking a physical step backwards.

"She's actually got you believing that crap doesn't she?" Tom couldn't hide the disgust in his voice. It seemed he hated General Laric as much as she hated him.

"I'm your brother. Don't you remember?" Cas broke in. Pathetic.

"No, I don't." This was true. Ander couldn't remember much of anything before he'd woken up in a sterile hospital bed with General Laric holding his sweaty hand. Just below his hairline, on the back of his head a thin scar ran along his scalp- the physical evidence remaining from the head injury that had stolen a large part of his early memories. All he had from his childhood were flashes- his father's face, the sound of a girl's laugh, even Tom. But nothing about a brother- he would have remembered a brother. "Now unless you're going to kill me, or throw me in a cell- please could I get some sleep? My head is killing me."

"Absolutely." Cas said, and grabbed Tom by the elbow, ushering him out of the room. The door shut behind them. Ander listened but there was no sound of a lock clicking into place. There would be a guard posted- Tom would insist on it.

They hadn't even searched him. The knife strapped to his thigh was still there, as was the smaller one tucked into the side of his left boot. It would be so easy- knock out the guard, slit Cas' throat whilst he was sleeping. Ander grinned to himself imaging the vacant smile that was bound to be on the imposters face.

But his head still hurt, his wounds stung, and he was bone weary. One more day wouldn't hurt.

He pulled out the other object hidden in his boot, a mobile phone, one of many millennial relics the rebellion had managed to get working again. He waited for the flashing lights to stop as it switched on and then typed a message, his fingers fumbling over the still unfamiliar keys. 'First attempt fail. Try again tomorrow. Am safe.' The message sent and he shoved the device back into his boot.

Chapter Four

"Good morning!"

Cas woke up his brother the way he had when they were children- by smacking him over the head with a folded up pillow. Ander's amnesia explained everything, the ridiculous duel, why he hadn't come home years ago, the cold stares. As of 5am that morning, Cas had read everything he could find in the castle library about amnesia and head injuries. *Occasionally familiar places and situations can help trigger a return of lost memories,* wrote Dr Ndoro, an eminent consultant of the twenty-first century. Cas took her advice to heart, ignoring Tom's dire warnings and Skye's bitter comments. Today, he would get his brother's memories back.

"Are you always this exuberant in the mornings?" Ander's voice was muffled by the pillow. He tossed it aside and stretched. He sat up and rubbed the sleep out of his eyes, before looking Cas up and down. Cas felt like he was being assessed, though what for he had no idea.

"Only when my brother comes back from the dead," he said. This wasn't strictly true; Cas had always been a morning person. He liked the way the dusky quiet before dawn transformed into the hustle and bustle of getting ready for the day ahead.

"You look like crap." Ander said. Blunt, but honest. Cas could live with that.

"I didn't sleep." Cas replied, and ushered his brother to move over so he could perch on the edge of the sofa next to him. Ander's hand twitched as he moved closer, as if itching to reach for a weapon, but his fingers simply curled into a tight fist beside him. *Amnesia patients may be prone to fits of aggression and violence, especially when adjusting to new environments. Safety is paramount, but carers must be patient with their loved ones.* Dr Ndoro was spot on.

"I'm going to help you get your memories back." Cas said, and unzipped the back pack slung over his shoulder.

"How do you propose doing that?"

"Put these on." Cas shoved a pile of clothes into his brother's lap. Ander shrugged on a new shirt. As he buttoned up the front Cas couldn't help staring at the scar on his chest, the jagged pink line that marked them as twins.

"You must be joking." Ander pulled a wavy blonde wig from the pile and gave it a look of utter loathing.

"You need a disguise. We both know we can't be seen together."

Ander's look of disgust deepened as he stuck on the fake moustache and goatee. Cas surveyed his work. They were still identical, and anyone looking closely at them wouldn't be able to deny it. But from a distance the costume would do its job and that was all Cas needed for the time being.

"Let's go," Cas said, and leapt to his feet. He held out his hand to help his brother up. Ander ignored it and stood, brushing imaginary specks off his fresh shirt.

"Lead the way, brother." The last word was laced with sarcasm. Cas ignored it.

Cas stuck his head out of the door and checked both sides of the corridor- he'd rather not have the costume tested so early on. He'd dismissed the night guard and most of the castle residents were still asleep. He stepped out. Ander followed behind him, as silent as a shadow. That was eery. Ander had always been the clumsier of the two of them; the one who'd accidently let the door slam behind them when they were sneaking out or knocked over a plant pot at a crucial juncture.

"Does anything look familiar?" Cas asked. They were in the main upper corridor. The wall was lined with red bricks, marking it as part of the newer wing of the castle. Off this corridor were all the largest bedrooms. Their father's old room was at the very end, empty and untouched for several years now. Cas didn't want to move in there; and neither he nor Tom could bare to have anyone else in there. The room still provoked a gut wrenching feeling when Cas was forced to enter it and he certainly didn't want that to be the first memory his brother regained. He led them the other way.

"No it doesn't." Ander's voice was a monotone, as if he didn't care one way or the other.

"Don't worry, it will." Cas felt the beginnings of pessimism but held it in check. Ander would recognise the ruins once they got there, he was sure of it. They were the oldest part of the castle, several thousand years old, derelict and abandoned. No one was allowed to enter. The two brothers had found a hidden passageway when they were seven and snuck inside. It was a perfect place for two young boys, full of hiding spots, walls to climb and obstacles to avoid. It was the only place they could play together without being seen. Even Skye had never known about their adventures in the ruins.

"Come in here." Cas said, and pulled open a door. He led his brother into one of the spare bedrooms. It was small by castle standards and had remained empty for years. It was sparsely furnished; an old writing desk sat in one corner and a moth eaten armchair in the other but little else. The room's only redeeming feature was a large fireplace, complete with marble pillars and a real chimney. Ander looked around.

"I like the wallpaper" he stated. The wallpaper was a pale pink colour with generous amounts of brown floral patterns. It was undeniably hideous. Cas hoped this was his brother's attempt at humour and not another side effect of brain injury. He gave a short laugh but Ander's expression did not alter in the slightest.

"Get in the fireplace," Cas instructed after a moment of awkward silence.

"May I ask why?"

"It's a surprise. You'll see." Cas said, and ushered Ander forwards.

"As Your Majesty orders," Ander said and stepped into the fireplace, ducking his head until he could stand again in the chimney chute. A cloud of ash and dust rose up around him, and Cas wondered how he kept from coughing.

"Don't call me that." Cas said. "Now start climbing."

"Why? Does it bother you?" Ander's voice echoed; he was making his way up the chute at impressive speed, scuttling up like, well, a spider.

"From you it does." Cas replied and followed his brother into the chute. It was an easy climb; the walls were close together and the gap between bricks was wide enough to provide decent hand and foot holds.

"Am I to take it I spent most of my childhood in a chimney?"

"We wanted to let you sleep in the cupboard under the stairs but it was already occupied." This was the kind of easy banter that Skye would respond to with a light punch or a witty retort. Ander just kept climbing. "What's the first thing you remember?" *The more you engage the amnesia sufferer, the more likely they are to reconnect with you and their surroundings.*

"Waking up in hospital." Ander said and didn't elaborate. He'd reached the top of the chute and vaulted out in one smooth motion. Cas followed him, stumbling slightly on his landing. Ander gave him a disgusted look.

"Still don't recognise anything?" Cas asked, ignoring the embarrassed squirm in his stomach.

"We're on the roof."

"You don't say…" Cas could be sarcastic too. This was a very small section of roof; surrounded on all four sides by taller walls of other parts of the castle. The Eastern wall was the outermost section of the ruins; the sun was not yet high enough to light this section of roof and you could easily miss the opening if you weren't looking for it. "Through there." Cas pointed to the Eastern wall; at the small gap near the bottom where a grown man could just about crawl through.

"This little adventure is proving rather strenuous." Ander said, though he did not look the least bit tired. He knelt and pulled himself through the opening, Cas close on his heels.

Cas stood up straight with a grin. The ruins were just as he remembered them; a sprawling playground of crumbling archways and pillars. The sun was still low in the sky and casting impressive shadows. There were lower levels as well; dark gloomy rooms complete with cobwebs and scurrying rats as large as rabbits. But the best part was an old observation tower, almost thirty feet high. Even parts of the windows remained- large arches right at the top. They had never managed to climb it as children, because although the spiral staircase inside the tower that led to the top was intact, a second structure had fallen against the entrance many years ago and they had been unable to get inside.

"What are you grinning at?"

"Care for a challenge?" Cas said. If Ander couldn't remember places, perhaps he would remember actions. Ander had been the clumsy one yes, but part of that had been because of his reckless abandon for rules. He had relished the danger of being caught. And he had never been able to say no to a competition.

Ander smiled, and Cas was certain it was the first genuine smile he'd given since he'd arrived.

"First one to the top of the tower wins."

"The entrance is blocked." Ander pointed out.

"I know." Cas met his brother's eyes and they reached an unspoken understanding. They may not have been able to scale the walls when they were seven, but they certainly could now. It was more challenging than the chimney chute, but again the uneven bricks would provide decent hand and foot holds. "Let's go!"

Cas set off for the base of the tower at a sprint. His brother kept pace with him easily and they began climbing at the same time, starting on opposite sides of the tower. Cas didn't have time to acknowledge how reckless this was, and he didn't dare look at how quickly the ground was getting further away. He couldn't see his brother, but for the first time he could hear him moving: the occasional scrape of his boots against the wall and the odd grunt of effort.

The climb wasn't technically very difficult, but it was tiring. His hands were slick with sweat and his grip was getting dangerously slippery. He paused to wipe one hand then the other on his trouser leg, clinging to the wall like a limpet. He glanced upwards before continuing- ten feet to go.

He listened again for his brother but couldn't tell if the noise was coming from above or below him. Then the brick under his left foot gave way and he sucked in a breath; his fingers tightening reflexively so hard they began to bleed. Skye's face popped up in his mind- full of righteous anger that he'd dared do something as stupid as getting himself killed. He lifted his left foot higher and found another foothold, testing his weight on it before allowing his aching fingers to loosen.

He climbed the final five feet steadily, no longer able to hear anything over the harsh sound of his own breathing. Sweaty, breathless and exhilarated he dragged himself over the ancient ledge and onto the observation platform.

"Looks like I win."

Ander had beaten him to it. He didn't even sound out of breath.

"I let you win, obviously." Cas said. "Welcome back from the dead present." Cold sweat trickled down his neck as he walked forward to shake his brother's hand. He couldn't help grinning. Ander stepped forwards, his hand outstretched.

"Seriously though, how are you-" Cas never finished his sentence. Quick as lightning, Ander thrust his other arm forward. Cas dived to the floor and the knife intended for his heart caught him in the shoulder. He ignored the pain and the sudden flickering of his vision, and forced himself to his feet, his uninjured arm outstretched; ready to fend off another attack.

"Ander, stop. I'm your brother." *Stay calm during aggressive episodes. A reassuring familiar voice will abort most aggressive episodes.* "Ander. Just stay calm."

"I am calm." Ander said. He didn't have a tremor, there was no uncertainty in his gaze. He looked like a lion ready to pounce. "I need you dead and you've given me a perfect opportunity."

It turned out Dr Ndoro had no idea what she was talking about. Cas leapt to the side again as Ander threw a punch at him. No, not a punch, he'd got another knife from somewhere. Cas assessed his chances quickly and didn't like what he found. He may have beaten Ander once, but this time he was fighting one handed and weaponless and when push came to shove he wasn't sure he could intentionally hurt his brother, not even to save himself.

"Ander, let's just think about this for a minute." He climbed to his feet again, fighting a wave of dizziness. His left arm and shoulder were damp with blood.

"I've been thinking about this for years." Ander said. Cas was concentrating on the hand holding the knife- he didn't see the kick coming towards him till it was too late. It connected with the centre of his chest and sent him flying backwards over the ledge. With nothing but air beneath him, he screamed as he began to fall.

"Ander!"

Chapter Five

Standing at the top of the tower, Ander could not believe how lucky he had been. The imposter had left him his weapons. He'd dismissed the guards. He'd led him to an abandoned set of ruins- a body could be easily hidden here and not found for years. This was even better than killing him in a duel. Once the imposter was dead Ander would simply take his place. Very few people knew he had an identical copy- he would deal with them. He would rule for the rebellion, for General Laric, and no one would know any difference.

"Ander!" The shout came again, urgent, desperate. It echoed around Ander's head again and again, becoming higher, shriller. A picture formed in his mind to go with the voice- a boy, no more than nine years old. Dark hair, blue eyes- he was seeing himself. Wasn't he? 'Don't let go,' the boy said. He looked terrified. Ander could see another identical boy reflected in his blue eyes. That boy reached down, hauling the first boy up onto a tree branch.

A flash of memory, they happened every so often. This one left him reeling and confused.

Ander ran to the ledge. The imposter was clinging on with one hand, his blood-stained fingers had turned white with the pressure. Ander had to decide. He could wait for Cas to fall- he wouldn't last long, his fingers were slipping, millimetre by millimetre. Or he could stamp on his hand, end it instantly. Or-

He could pull him up.

Ander grasped Cas firmly around the forearm and dragged him back onto the platform. As soon as was safe he released Cas' arm and staggered back. What had he just done? Cas collapsed face down, his breaths coming in short shallow gasps. Ander watched him; didn't dare get closer. If General Laric ever found out what an opportunity he'd wasted... *I told you they'd try to trick you!*

"Ander. What-" Cas paused to take another breath before he could continue "-changed your mind?" He rolled onto his back, clutching at the knife still embedded in his shoulder.

"I-" Ander hesitated, but he had no reason to lie. "I think remembered something."

"What?" Cas pushed himself into a sitting position. His face was pale but he was grinning like a maniac. "If all it took was me almost dying I would have done it hours ago. What did you remember?"

"Just a flash. We were climbing a tree. I was helping you up." Ander couldn't look at the imposter anymore. If the other boy were truly an imposter surely he wouldn't have thought twice about killing the boy who'd tried to kill him not once, but twice. And if Ander could remember Cas as a child then- it didn't make sense- but he had to conclude they were brothers. That meant that General Laric, the woman who'd raised him, who'd fed him and clothed him and taught him how to fight, had lied to him all his life. There had to be another explanation.

"Oh yeah, I remember, in the gardens. I fell and you caught me." Cas said. He wrapped his hand around the knife handle and braced himself.

"What are you doing? You need to get to a surgeon." He hadn't saved the imposter just to have him bleed to death.

"No one can know about this," Cas said, and yanked the knife out before Ander could stop him. Cas bit his own lip so hard a trickle of blood ran down his chin.

"You're an idiot," Ander said, shrugging off his jacket and pressing it to the wound. What was he doing? He was meant to kill him, not nurse him. But he couldn't, not with that memory unexplained in his mind.

"Nice knife," Cas breathed, and had the sense to tuck it carefully into his own belt. "We need to get back before someone realises we're missing. Can you tie it round?"

Ander nodded and used the jacket sleeves to tie a knot around Cas' back. It was a poor excuse for a bandage, already Ander could see blood oozing out from the sides.

"How do you plan on getting down?" Ander asked. The climb would be no problem for him- General Laric had nicknamed him Spider many years ago after seeing him scale a hundred foot cliff without breaking a sweat. But even he might have struggled with only one working arm and missing an impressive amount of blood.

"I always come prepared." Cas said, and unzipped his backpack. Right arm hanging limply by his side, he used his other arm to pull out a length of rope. He secured it to the pillar separating what was the left of the windows and gave it a hard tug to test it. He offered the rope to Ander.

"After you." Another wise move Ander thought. No chance of Ander cutting the rope above him. Perhaps the 'King' wasn't as stupid as he'd first thought. He took the rope and lowered himself out of the window, keeping one eye on Cas above him, alert for any sign that he was planning on sabotaging the rope.

"Catch me if I fall," Cas said, and with one hand on the rope began climbing down.

Ander climbed down quickly and stood waiting for Cas at the base of the tower. He could see the other boy trembling with the effort, but his pace remained steady. Ander found his hand clenched around his knife handle. It wasn't too late- injured and distracted Cas would be easy to kill. The single flash of memory could have been anything. Another boy. His imagination. A dream. He dropped his hand- he needed to be certain. He would confront General Laric tonight.

"Sometime today would be nice," he called up to Cas.

"Yes, Your Majesty," Cas called back. He was only about ten feet away; he stopped climbing and slid the rest of the way down the rope, coming to a rapid stop two feet off the ground and jumping down. He blew on his hand.

"Rope burn," he complained. His voice was light and pleasant, but his face turned the colour of chalk.

"I'd put some pressure on that wound if I were you," Ander said, "If you pass out I'm not carrying you."

"I'll be fine," Cas said, but he pressed his free hand to the wound as instructed. "Come on. The guard will be back soon." He turned and started picking his way back through the ruins.

Ander allowed him to get a dozen metres ahead and then surreptitiously pulled the phone out of his boot. He typed out his message whilst walking, one eye on Cas in case the other boy turned around. WE NEED TO TALK, he sent and heaved a sigh as he vaulted over a low wall to catch up to Cas.

Chapter Six

Cas shut Ander's door. He had to lean against it to catch his breath. His shoulder hurt, and he could tell from the way Ander had stared at him that he hadn't been walking in a straight line. But he'd made it; Ander was safely back in his room and no one would be any the wiser. They'd made progress- Ander was starting to remember. He hadn't yet proclaimed his affection for his long lost brother, and the stab wound was a nuisance to say the least, but Cas was confident that his brother wouldn't be making any further attempts on his life. Now all he had to do was convince Tom and Skye of that.

He picked himself up off the wall and staggered into the walk-in closet that abutted Ander's room. When they were small, they had taken turns sleeping on the camp bed hidden amongst the clothes in the wardrobe. Since Ander had disappeared, Cas had slept in there a few times. It had let him pretend his brother was still alive. He didn't have to pretend anymore.

Tom had demanded to see him as soon as he woke up, and he would be getting suspicious if Cas left it any later. He tugged his bloodied shirt over his head and stuffed it deep into the laundry basket. He found a bandage in his first aid kit and wrapped it around the wound as tightly as he could. He pulled on a loose black T-shirt and a grey sweatshirt and examined himself in the mirror. The bandage was hidden by the bulk of his clothes, no blood was leaking through. He tucked his right hand into his front pocket, easing the pressure on his aching arm.

He looked almost normal. Pale maybe, but if Tom asked he would put that down to lack of sleep.

"Cas? Are you in here?" Tom's voice, followed by a short knock on the door.

"Yeah, come in."

Cas turned to face his mentor, mentally preparing himself for the warnings that were about to follow.

"Sleep well?"

"Couldn't sleep." Cas said. He met Tom's gaze, any sign of weakness and Tom would know he was being lied too. Tom looked away first and sighed.

"I don't know what to do, Cas." Tom sat down on a chest of drawers; shoulders slumped. His hands were clasped together in an unusually nervous gesture. Cas couldn't look at Tom's face. Anger he could handle. Gentle mocking he was used to. But helplessness was unexplored territory. He ended up staring at the scar running down the side of Tom's neck, from below his ear until it stopped just above his collarbone. Tom had that scar for as long as Cas could remember and whenever he was asked how he got it he would give a different story. It had become something of a legend around the castle. Tom continued speaking,

"When the two of you were born your father and I made a plan. As you know, the plan entailed making sure no one ever knew that twins had been born. An heir and a backup. Chances were slim that you would both survive to adulthood, but we hoped for the best. We planned that the two of you would rule together, in perfect harmony, continuing the secret. Two heads are better than one the old saying goes." Tom paused. "I'm sorry."

Cas was so surprised he looked up at Tom's face. But his godfather was staring at the floor. Apologies from Tom were as rare as a clear blue smog free sky over London.

"What for?" Cas had always known about his father's plan. At times he had resented having to keep the secret, but it had been all he'd ever known.

"For making the two of you pawns in the game."

"To rule is not a right but a responsibility. That's what Dad always taught us." He said it in the careful measured tone his father had always used for that particular phrase. For many years he had said it in that way just to imitate his father- now he was beginning to understand it.

"So you were listening…" A faint smile appeared on Tom's face and then quickly disappeared. "Regardless, now that Ander is back our plans will need to be adjusted. He has every right to the throne. But he can't rule in harmony with you- that much is obvious. He is the rebellion's puppet, exactly in the way that he accused you of being mine. The strategist in me would have him killed."

Cas stepped further away. Bile rose at the back of his throat. Tom was legendary for getting things done efficiently and effectively, but he had never been ruthless. Tom smiled and patted the space next to him. "I see that we've raised a kind king." As Cas sat down Tom ruffled his hair as if were still a small boy. He tolerated the gesture patiently. "I couldn't harm him. I couldn't do that to your father, or to you, or to the boy he was. Which leaves us with a problem. The only solution I can see is to split the kingdom into two. Those who wish to follow Ander may do so."

Split the kingdom in two? The idea was unthinkable. The country had remained united since pre-millennial times. Queen Eva, his grandmother, would do backflips in her grave.

"Or Ander will regain his memories and the rebellion will be squashed for good." Cas kept his tone optimistic- Ander had already shown signs of regaining his memories. But Tom couldn't know that yet.

"Maybe," Tom said, but Cas could tell by the small smile on his face that Tom was humouring him. "I'll arrange for a meeting of your advisors this afternoon. They will all have to be told the truth. Try and get some rest. You look like you need it. When you see Ander, make sure you have a guard with you- just in case. But maybe you're right and he will remember something." Tom winked at him as he stood and opened the door.

He left. Cas rubbed his throbbing shoulder, staring at the closed door. How long should he wait before he sought out Ander again? He needed to know if he had remembered anything else. Tom, like Skye, was an only child – they didn't understand what it meant to have a brother, let alone a twin. Ander would come around. They'd rule just as their father had imagined: in perfect harmony.

Chapter Seven

Skye heard a knock on her door and leapt up to open it. It had to be Cas. She pulled the door open, expecting him to brush past her and walk in without an invitation. He lingered in the doorway, unusually pale. Grey didn't suit him.

"Hi," he said. "Are you OK?" His hair was ruffled and sticking up on one side. She fought an urge to reach across and smooth it down.

"I'm fine." They had argued last night for the first time in years. She couldn't believe how easily he wanted to forgive his brother and how little regard he had for his own safety. But, she reminded herself, she wouldn't be angry at him. His brother had come back from the dead- it would take some getting used to.

"Good," Cas said, with that crooked half smile that never failed to get a smile back. "Come on. Let's go see if we can get Ander some memories back. Your father insisted I take a guard... and you're the best." His tone was light and airy. It didn't match the way he was standing, stiff and awkward, lurking in her doorway.

"You know I can't fight anymore." A year ago she'd been the best. Cas was physically stronger than her, but she'd beaten him every time: she was faster, more agile, more imaginative. And then she wasn't. It was getting worse and worse- now she could barely run down a corridor without becoming short of breath. Cas wanted to tell her father, he'd begged her actually, but she'd refused. *It will pass,* she'd insisted. Now she wasn't so sure.

"It won't come to that," Cas said. He'd skirted around the topic but she didn't call him up on it. "We'll take him to that millennial wax museum we used to go to. You love that place."

The Last War had spared very few of old London's public buildings, and the wax museum was one such oddity. There were no useful resources in there so it had been left untouched over the years, the wax works inside gathering dust but remaining impressively intact. King Kenneth had declared it a sight of historical importance and opened it to the public. It wasn't very popular; Skye imagined that most people found the idea of walking around looking at wax replicas of a dead society a little bit creepy.

She ought to tell him no, insist that he brought along a proper guard and that they stayed closer to the castle. But she couldn't bring herself to crush that look of excitement in his eyes.

"Fine let's go." Skye said.

"Excellent!" Cas caught her in a fleeting, one armed hug, then dragged her by the hand through the doorway. Skye sighed and allowed herself to be pulled down the corridor. This was typically Cas; exuberant, energetic and ceaselessly optimistic.

"You won't regret this," he was saying. "He's already started remembering stuff. I'm sure if we keep giving him triggers more stuff will come back. I read a book, by Dr Ndoro and she said-"

He's already remembering...? Ander had shown no sign of recollection last night. Cas had already been to see his brother this morning. Wrenching her hand out of Cas' grip, she forced him to a halt. He winced almost imperceptibly.

"What do you mean 'he's already started remembering stuff'? What did you do this morning?"

He stared at a spot near her boots when he answered.

"Nothing. I just meant," he started, pushing his hair back from his face. It was a nervous gesture he'd had since they were small, and it meant he was hiding something, or about to tell a lie. He must have changed his mind, because when he met her gaze his blue eyes were wide and sincere. "I took him to the ruins this morning. We used to play there when we were kids. He attacked me, but then he remembered something. He could have left me to die, but he didn't, Skye. He saved me."

"He attacked you?" Her mind conjured up all sorts of horrible images- Cas broken and bleeding, Cas being strangled....But he was right here in front of her, and she grabbed his shoulder to reassure herself. This time he really winced. He said nothing, even when she pulled the collar of his jumper down revealing a blood-stained bandage on his shoulder.

Skye forced herself not to scream at him. Punching him wouldn't help either. Footsteps approached from the end of the corridor- a castle maid on her morning tea round. Cas quickly pulled the collar of his hoodie back up. He smiled at Skye like they were having a normal conversation.

"We should really get going. We don't want to waste any more time."

The maid clinked past them in a puff of tea scented steam. Skye dragged Cas to the nearest room- a spare office- and forced him onto the worn leather chair.

"Skye, I really think-" She cut him off.

"Let me see." She gripped the edges of the desk behind her. She wasn't squeamish usually, but this was Cas, and there had been a lot of blood on that bandage.

"Fine. You can satisfy yourself that I'm not about to keel over and then we're going OK?" Grimacing, he pulled his sweatshirt over his head and held down the collar of his T-shirt. Biting her lip, Skye peeled back the bandage. Cas hissed in pain; his face was turned away from her, his fingers gripping the chair were white.

"How does it look?" Cas asked. He may as well have been asking about the weather.

The wound was deep, about an inch wide, just over his collarbone. Skye had been reading a lot of medical text books recently whilst trying to figure out what was wrong with her. The wound was dangerous- just a touch lower and it would have hit the subclavian artery and Cas would have bled to death. Just a touch deeper and it would have pierced his lung. It was still wet and raw looking, but at least blood wasn't pouring out.

"Did you clean it?" He shook his head. Skye's insides clenched uncomfortably. "Cas, this is bad. We need to get you to the hospital."

"Not a chance. No one can know about this" His eyes cast around the room, alighting on an unopened bottle of whiskey stashed in the bookcase. "Just pour some of that on and let's go."

"I don't think that's a-" She gave up when she saw his expression. Sometimes, talking to Cas was as effective as talking to the castle walls. His face became stone, hard and impenetrable.

Crossing the room, she grabbed the whiskey bottle, blew off the dust and unscrewed the top. Her nose burned from the smell of alcohol. She didn't want to think about how it would feel to pour it into an open wound. Before she could change her mind, she emptied the bottle onto Cas' wound.

He leapt out of the chair, clutching his shoulder and swearing under his breath. His chest rose and fell rapidly. He swayed as though he might pass out, and lowered himself back down onto the chair. Through watery eyes and gritted teeth, he smiled at her.

"You could have saved me a bit." He took a deep breath and glanced at the wound. "There's a spare bandage in my backpack." Skye bent to retrieve it from where he'd dropped it by the door and reached inside. A knife. A flashlight. Matches. When had Cas started carrying this stuff around?

She found the bandage and taped it over the wound. Cas stood and pulled his sweatshirt back on.

"See, good as new." He smiled, though his face was grey and he smelt like blood and whiskey.

"Cas- he could have killed you."

"I'm fine," he muttered. He gripped her hands tightly. She was struck suddenly by how tall he was- a handful of years ago she'd been able to look down at him, now her eyes were level with his collar bone and she had to crane her neck back to look at him. "I know you think I'm being naïve about this. I know Uncle Tom does too. But he's my brother- we were bound together when we were born. We still are. I know I can get through to him. And even if I can't- I owe it to him to try everything. He's been gone for years and the rebellion could have done anything to him. And in the meantime, I've been here, comfortable, surrounded by friends. I owe him, Skye."

"It wasn't your fault, Cas," she said.

"It could have been me," he said simply. The blood drained from her face. If Cas had been taken, what would have happened? Would she now be standing here having the same conversation with Ander instead? She nodded.

"I knew you'd understand," he said. He winked at her, slung his backpack onto his good arm and started walking again. He held his injured shoulder stiffly, supporting it with his other arm. He'd never let her take him to the hospital. She would keep a close eye on him- at the first sign the injury was causing him problems she'd drag him to a doctor kicking and screaming if she had to.

"So, what were you saying about this Dr Ndoro? You read a book on amnesia?"

"I read all the books on amnesia. Basically, the more you stimulate the mind of the sufferer- like take them to familiar places, do familiar activities- the more likely it is memories will resurface." He stopped outside Ander's bedroom door. "So just be yourself. It's important. You can't treat him with suspicion or fear or anger."

"I'll try my best". She kept the bitterness from her voice. She tried to imagine Ander as the boy he'd been, instead of the stranger who'd stabbed her best friend. When Cas opened the door it was easier than she'd expected. Ander was sprawled on the sofa, fast asleep and snoring slightly. He looked young and vulnerable. He looked like Cas, down to the way his tongue stuck out when he was asleep.

"He looks just like you," she said quietly.

"There is no way that I drool like that," Cas replied. He walked round to the back of the sofa and placed both his hands on the backrest. "Time to wake up!" He tilted the sofa over, sending sleeping boy and several cushions tumbling to the ground. There was a muffled yell and then Ander's head popped up, his expression deadly. Skye grinned at the sight of him clutching a knife in one hand with drool on his chin and cushions piled up around him.

Ander looked back at her and lowered the knife.

"Get up, it's time to go." Cas said.

"Where are we off to this time?" Ander said. The knife disappeared. He smoothed down his hair, his expression tightly controlled.

"It's a surprise," Cas said. He bent down and threw the cushions haphazardly back onto the sofa.

"I can't wait," Ander said. He stuck on a fake moustache and a blonde wig. "See? I'm all ready to go."

"You look ridiculous," Skye said. "Put your hood up- I don't want to have to look at that thing any longer."

As Ander pulled his hood up and zipped his jacket up; Cas caught her eye and smiled approvingly. Skye checked the corridor was empty and then gestured for the boys to follow her. The three of them had snuck out of the castle more times than Skye could remember when they were children- to the cemetery to tell spooky stories, to the gardens for a midnight feast. There was a disused garbage chute leading off the main corridor that led straight to the courtyard outside.

Skye examined the entrance carefully- it seemed as structurally sound as it ever had been.

"Uh- I'm not sure we're going to fit in there." Ander said, peering over her shoulder. He had a point- Skye would be able to squeeze through, but the boys were a lot bigger now.

"You'll fit. I've tried it," Cas said, throwing his backpack into the chute. He brushed past Skye to climb in first. She stared at his back. He'd snuck out? When? Where? Why hadn't he told her? Cas was keeping secrets.

He had been since before Ander had appeared. Next time they were alone, she would confront him.

Cas had to lie flat on his stomach and crawl forwards inch by inch commando style but he was making progress. Skye climbed in behind him- she was nervous about being defenceless with Ander directly behind her, but she couldn't very well let him go behind Cas.

The garbage chute was damp and slippery, numbing her hands and soaking through the knees of her jeans. Her chest tightened. She concentrated on her breathing. If Ander realised her weakness...

"Almost there," Cas called. His silhouette was outlined against a square of greyish black sky. The ash cloud was bad today- that wasn't going to do her breathing any favours. And it meant power cuts later on as the solar cells struggled.

"Man it's chilly!" Cas said, helping her out of the chute. His breath went up in a little puff of white smoke. "I'll get the bikes." He disappeared into the bushes, leaving Skye alone with Ander. She struggled to think of something to say.

"Terrible weather don't you think?" she blurted out and inwardly cringed. Ander had the decency to ignore her question.

"We were friends right?" He said. There was no emotion in his voice; he may as well have been talking about the weather. "What did you like about me?"

She stared at him. For a second she wanted to give him a flippant remark, *nothing*. Although to the untrained eye he looked disinterested, to Skye- who had known his identical twin for all her life- pushing back his hair from his forehead was a dead giveaway. He *wanted* her to answer.

A particular incident stood out in her memory; one of the rare outings where the King had taken out both boys at once. She had tagged along for the ice cream. And she'd dropped her cone. Cas had laughed. Ander had given her his.

"You were always up for a laugh, playing pranks and things. You were funny. You were kind. Kinder than Cas." She looked him up and down, trying to reconcile the laughing boy swapping his father's shampoo with glue to the serious youth in front of her. "Are you still the same guy?"

"No," he said, and turned away, and then almost so quietly Skye didn't hear him. "I don't think so."

Cas came crashing through the bushes dragging two bicycles along behind him. He handed one of them to Ander. The tyre on his own had recently been repaired- Skye could see the fresh sealant tape. Cas had definitely been sneaking out.

"Skye you're with me," he said. He shook his head at her and said to Ander, "Honestly, the girl can do a double front flip but she can't ride a bike. It's disgraceful". The lie sounded natural on his lips. Skye had been able to ride since she was three, but they both knew if she tried now she'd end up on the floor panting for breath after about 100m.

"Some of us are too busy training to waste our time on millennial hobbies," Skye replied. She didn't look at Cas; she didn't want to give herself away. He was lying to Ander for her sake.

"You can ride with me," Ander offered. "I wouldn't be so sure of his steering abilities with one arm." If he suspected anything he didn't show it.

"I warn you though, she's a lot heavier than she looks," Cas said. He gave her the crooked grin, and Skye was smiling before she had even realised what she was doing.

Ander swung a leg over the bike and sidled forwards so she could sit on the saddle. She climbed up behind him, her hands resting lightly on his shoulders to keep her balance.

"Follow me!" Cas said, mounting his own bike. In one smooth motion he was off and pedalling.

"You might want to hold on properly," Ander said, barely glancing back at her. "I don't intend to let him stay in the lead for long." He set off without further warning and Skye automatically grabbed him around the waist as they bounced across the cobblestones.

"Right onto the drawbridge," Cas called back to them. Skye caught a glimpse of his face, his teeth gleaming in the mid-morning light, before he disappeared around the bend.

Ander whipped them round onto the drawbridge, leaning so far into the turn that Skye's right knee skimmed across the wooden planks.

"Your driving needs practise!" She yelled into Ander's ear. She tightened her grip as he made another hairpin turn. The muscles in his abdomen contracted as he laughed.

"What? You want to go faster?"

"I'd rather live to see my next birthday." The wind made her eyes water. Her legs ached from trying to stay on. But she couldn't help smiling. It had been a long time since she'd had an experience this exhilarating. She couldn't go this fast herself anymore, and Cas had begun to treat her like a fragile piece of china.

They were now out in London proper and Skye zipped her jacket up over her mouth and nose to stop from breathing in the smog. The smog was bad; the air glimmered grey and the streets were empty. People had even taken their horses in. They passed a couple of electricians making repairs to solar panels, blackened respirators tied to their faces, but that was about it. London had once been a bustling place, full of people and cars and glossy red double decker buses. It was hard to imagine all these crumbling and dilapidated buildings had once been inhabited.

"We're here!" Cas called, and vaulted off his bike. Without slowing, Ander headed straight towards him.

Skye froze- she couldn't even shout a warning. Cas just stood there, watching them about to plough into him. He barely blinked as Ander swerved at the last second and came to a dead stop an inch from his shoe. Skye flung herself off the bike.

"Sorry. Did I scare you?" Ander smirked. She ignored him and strode up to Cas.

"Why didn't you move?" She poked him hard in the chest. Ander deserved a chance, but Cas leaving himself in harm's way was just careless. Skye stared at him until the smile slipped off his face.

"He was just messing around, Skye. That's what brothers do. This is a good thing."

"If we're going to do this, we need to do it carefully. If someone who tried to kill you this morning charges towards you on a moving vehicle you move out of the way. You don't go out to deserted ruins leaving them armed and without even a guard! Whether or not you want to accept it- he is a threat to you and others. So use some common sense!"

Cas nodded, and Skye brushed past him to pull open the door. He drove her insane. He was so stupid, so reckless, so brave-.

"Smart girl," She heard Ander say as he sauntered past Cas to join Skye inside. "What on Earth is this place?"

For the first time, he sounded genuinely surprised. He walked over and tapped a waxwork on the shoulder.

"This is just freaky," he muttered.

Skye moved past him to the stack of flashlights King Kenneth had provided when he'd restored the place years earlier. She blew the dust off and switched it on, checking it still worked. She clicked it off again. The upper levels had large windows that meant she could see for now.

"Come on, the good bit is downstairs." Cas said, and took the lead. Ander followed directly behind him and Skye took the rear. "This room is full of – what was the word, Skye?"

"Popstars," Skye supplied. She sighed to herself- Cas had once again left his back exposed to attack. She watched Ander carefully. He seemed unnerved; his usually smooth movements were jerky and restless. He actually jumped when they turned the corner and a huge statue of a man with an old weapon- a machine gun she thought it was called- appeared suddenly in front of them. So, the would-be- King was scared of a few wax works?

"This room is dedicated to the military," Cas was saying. Skye grabbed Ander by the shoulder, trying to startle him. It didn't work.

"Be careful," he whispered. "I could be armed." She couldn't tell if the menace in his voice was fake or genuine. Then he smiled- a crooked, Cas-like smile, and her face betrayed her by smiling back. "I like this room," Ander announced.

They had reached the throne room; full of old kings and queens. As was her habit when she came to this room, Skye scanned their faces for any resemblance to Cas. She knew it was ridiculous- he wasn't a descendent of these monarchs. That line had died out generations ago.

"And now for the best part," Cas said. He stood at the top of a dark, crooked staircase. "The dungeon." He raised his arms dramatically and slid down the bannister. His movement wasn't particularly fast or sudden, and yet Ander jumped as if he'd been shot.

"Stop messing around. You'll make him think he's actually scary," Skye said to him lightly. Then she got a proper look at his face; his pupils were dilated, almost obliterating the blue of his eyes, and his cheeks were flushed. His pulse twitched at his temple.

"Ander? Are you OK?" Skye's hand hovered next to his arm, not sure whether to touch him. He took a slow steady breathe and when he met her gaze his eyes were back to normal.

"His constant prattling is giving me a headache," he said, pushing his sweaty hair back from his forehead. He gestured to the staircase. "After you."

She hesitated. It was dark down there, he could easily pull a knife and she wouldn't see it, not until after it was plunged into her exposed back.

"I'm not going to attack you, Skye," Ander said, rubbing his temples. It was the sound of her name that did it- he said it quickly, familiarly, as if he'd said it a thousand times before. Red cheeks and dishevelled hair made him look younger, more like the boy she remembered. That boy had given her his icecream.

But he'd stabbed Cas just this morning- she couldn't forget that.

"It's not me I'm worried about," Skye said, but descended the stairs ahead of him. She switched the flashlight on, illuminating a small circle ahead of her with pale white light.

Cas was nowhere in sight. Instead she found herself face to ragged neck with a decapitated ancient thief. His head was on a pike about three feet away. She had to forcibly remind herself that it was a wax model.

"Where is he?" Ander's voice broke the silence, startling her.

"He's hiding somewhere, obviously." She spoke quickly to hide her nervous jump.

"Ugly looking things aren't they?" Ander said, and bent to examine the decapitated head. One minute he was jumping at shadows, the next he was fearless. Skye rolled her eyes.

"Come on. He can't be far."

"Oh look, a guillotine!" Ander said, and pushed past her to lean into the display. He ran a finger against the blade and looked disappointed. "It's plastic."

"Well, they're not gonna leave a real-"

A figure leapt out at them from amongst a mob of plague victims.

"Beware the zombies!" he shouted, and went to grab both their faces. Cas. Skye screamed and dodged out of the way. Ander grabbed his brother's arm and twisted him into a headlock. He let go quickly, leaving Cas laughing even as he gasped for breath and rubbed his injured shoulder.

For once, it wasn't Cas she was worried about. She took a step towards Ander. He was breathing hard, bent over with his hands on his knees.

"Are you injured?" Skye asked. Cas had barely touched him…

"Sorry, Ander. Didn't mean to scare you that much!" Cas said. He moved to grasp his brother's shoulder, but Ander shrugged him off.

"I'm fine. Just getting a migraine. We should head back."

He straightened up. He smiled at Cas, but his hands were clenched into tight fists at his sides.

"Of course. They'll be expecting us at the advisors meeting," Cas said. "There's a short cut through here." He took the flashlight from Skye and picked his way through the plague victims to a door marked fire exit.

"What's going on with you? Why are you so jumpy?" Skye muttered to Ander. They followed a few feet behind Cas, and she didn't want him to overhear.

"It's a dungeon. It's meant to be scary." His tone was calm and even, but Skye could see his gaze flickering from side to side. For a second she thought she saw the gleam of a knife in his clenched fist, but she couldn't be sure in the darkness.

"Have you remembered anything?" Skye asked casually, whilst her gaze was concentrated on his hand, held stiffly by his side. He jumped, seemingly at nothing, and his hand- empty- moved up to wipe his forehead.

"I remember being here with you and Cas. And my father, the King. He wouldn't let us come down here. So we snuck away. You and I wanted to hold hands but Cas-" He cut himself off by jumping again. They'd reached a brightly lit passageway- arched windows lines both sides- and Skye caught a glimpse of his face. He was drenched in sweat, and there was dried blood on the fake moustache quivering on his lip.

"Ander!" She reached for his hand, and hers came away wet with blood. "What the- Cas!"

Cas turned. His eyes widened.

"What's wrong with him? Is he sick?"

"I'm right here- I can hear you." Ander said. "I'm not sick. I'm just-" He hesitated and pushed his damp hair back from his face. "Claustrophobic." Skye frowned at him. That didn't make sense, he had crawled through the tunnel- a much smaller space, with no problems. "I'm feeling better already."

Cas stared at him wearing a look of mixed horror and suspicion. But the colour had returned to Ander's face, his breathing was steady and he was looking at them both with his favourite disdainful expression.

"What happened to your hand?" Cas took his brother's hand and turned it palm up. Skye saw blood oozed from a long straight cut before he snatched his hand back.

"I stumbled on the staircase and put my hand out to save myself. Must have caught something sharp."

He didn't look at Skye as he said this. He had come down the staircase silently, if he'd stumbled, she would have heard him. She said nothing; whatever the reason for the lie, she'd figure it out later when Cas wasn't around to defend him.

"Can you still ride?" Cas asked. "I'll take Skye."

Ander nodded and they retrieved the bikes. Skye got on behind Cas and wrapped her arms around him without hesitation. She leaned her cheek against his back, taking a breath in. He smelt of Cas- familiar and safe. And of whiskey. She lifted her head so she could talk into his ear.

"How's your shoulder?"

"It's ok. I still wish you'd given me the whiskey to drink instead."

That was probably the closest he'd get to admitting he was in pain.

"Don't you remember when we found that bottle of wine?" They'd been thirteen at the time. Tom had been livid when he found them; Cas with an apple balanced on his head, giggling, and Skye bragging a that she could knock it off with a throwing knife. Then Cas had vomited all over Tom's shoes and they'd been banned from seeing each other for two weeks.

"Of course I remember. I'm still never drinking wine again. Whiskey is different."

They cycled over a pothole, and the bike juddered uncomfortably. Skye tightened her grip around Cas. She was glad she couldn't see his face as she posed her next question. If he was going to lie, she didn't want to see it.

"Cas, where have you been sneaking out at night?"

He took so long to answer that Skye thought he might not have heard her.

"Nowhere important," he said finally. He'd put up the brick wall, even without seeing his face, she could tell. "Don't worry about me, Skye."

"Ok, Cas." And even though she could feel each breath he took, he'd never felt so distant.

Ander got to the castle ahead of them; he'd already stashed his bike in the bushes when Cas and Skye arrived. He looked better, but his right hand kept twitching. He clasped it with his left to still it.

"Are we taking the tunnel back in?" He asked. He directed his question at Cas, though he was looking at a spot about three feet above his head and to the left.

"It's the best way- though not if you're going to pass out," Cas said.

"I won't. But I need to go first." Ander said, and before either of them could react he pulled himself into the old garbage chute.

Skye exchanged a look with Cas and then followed Ander into the garbage chute.

"Should we get him a doctor?" Cas' voice floated towards her from the darkness of the tunnel. She could hear the hesitation and the concern in his voice.

"I don't know. One minute he seems fine, the next he looks like he's about to collapse. If he was sick I don't think he'd be able to move this fast. Maybe it's an emotional thing- like the shock of getting his memories back."

"Yeah, maybe. You'd think Dr Ndoro would have mentioned that!" Cas sounded betrayed by the Twenty First Century physician.

When Skye climbed out Ander was waiting for them, leaning nonchalantly against the wall. He didn't wait for Cas to climb out after her but started off down the corridor back towards his room. They found him a few minutes later, sat on the sofa, cradling his injured hand to his chest.

"I'll get some bandages," Cas said, and disappeared back out into the corridor. Ander tore off the fake moustache and wig and tossed them behind the sofa.

"What really happened to your hand?" Skye asked, perching on the sofa next him. He was silent for several moments, then smirked at her. "What's so funny?" He looked suddenly much better.

"You." Ander said. "You're like a love struck puppy"

"What are you talking about?" Skye replied. Her heart pounded in her chest.

"I see the way you look at Cas." Ander said slowly. "I've seen the way you look at me- just because I look like him." He pulled her close, their faces inches apart. She could have counted each of his dark eyelashes. He was an almost perfect replica of Cas, but Cas never looked at her with such dark intensity. Ander gave her a disdainful half smile. Her eyes were drawn to a tiny chip in his left upper incisor- a tiny flaw that could differentiate the brothers. "He's never going to notice." He pushed her back to arm's length.

The door opened and Cas walked in. Skye jumped.

"Wow, everyone's jumpy today," Cas said. *He's never going to notice.*

Skye stood, her chest tightening. She couldn't bear to be in a room with either of them.

"Be careful," she muttered to Cas, pushing past him and out of the room. He called after her but she ignored him, breaking into a run. It felt liberating for all of five seconds, and then her lungs refused to cooperate. She tried to take deep breaths but all that happened was she emitted a high-pitched whistle. She managed a few more steps, stumbling against the wall, and then she collapsed to the ground.

Black spots appeared in front of her eyes. Then someone was with her, sitting her up, making her lean forwards. She sucked air into her lungs- the black spots disappeared. She could make out the figure next to her: a girl, red hair, dressed in the light blue polo shirt and skirt of the castle maids. Skye couldn't get the words out to thank her.

"Skye!" Cas sprinted towards them. He must have heard her fall.

The maid hastily stepped back and curtseyed.

"Your Majesty," she muttered, lowering her eyes. She was lost from view as Skye found herself cradled in Cas' arms.

"Don't speak a word of this to anyone." She heard Cas say. His voice was harsh.

"Yes, Your Majesty," the maid said. Her skirt rustled as she curtseyed again.

"Let's get you to your room," Cas said, a soothing murmur close to Skye's ear. She didn't trust herself to speak, but she managed a nod and rested her head against his chest. She could hear the steady thumping of his heart. She closed her eyes and concentrated on her breathing- one breath for every two of his heart beats- and fell into an exhausted sleep.

The maid watched them disappear down the corridor. She smiled to herself, then pulled out a pen and scrap of paper. *I've found our target. The Kingmaker's daughter.* She left the note in the third plant pot on the left. It would find its way to headquarters by the morning. The maid picked up her duster, humming to herself as she worked.

Chapter Eight

Cas nudged the door open with his good shoulder. He tried not to jostle Skye, but cringed as the door emitted a rusty screech and she stirred. He glared at the door as it crept shut behind him. He placed Skye on the bed; she mumbled incoherently but didn't wake. Cas threw a tartan quilt over her and then sunk to the floor beside her bed. The wooden floor was freezing, but he was too exhausted to move.

Skye's breathing slowed, becoming more regular, gentle. The whistling noise faded and then disappeared. Asleep, he could pretend she wasn't sick. That she was the same Skye she had always been. He hated lying to her- but if she found out the truth behind his night time trips she would try and stop him.

Cas sighed to himself. Clutching his sore shoulder, he forced himself to his feet. She was safe for now; listening to her breath wasn't going to cure her. He snuck out of the room and headed back up the corridor to Ander's room. What was he even going to say to the advisors? *I have a secret, identical twin. It didn't seem worth mentioning since I thought he was dead for years. But hey, surprise!*

He knocked on Ander's door and entered.

"Ander?"

"Where's your body guard?" Ander asked. He lay on the sofa with his feet propped up, a book in his hands- *A Brief history of the Last War.* He didn't look up.

"She's taking a shower," Cas said quickly. He didn't want Ander to dwell on the subject. He trusted his brother with his own life, but not with Skye's. "Come to the King's advisor meeting. Showing will be much easier than telling in this situation." He couldn't wait to see their faces.

Ander bolted upright so fast the book fell to the ground, landing cover up. Cas raised his eyebrows- the meeting wasn't *that* exciting. Usually it was downright boring.

"Not today," Ander said. He seemed to be making an effort to steady his breathing, his head bent forward. He tugged at the bandage around his cut hand, twisting it so tightly his fingers turned white. "I don't feel well. A bunch of advisors arguing will only make my migraine worse."

"But-"

Ander looked at him and Cas swallowed his protest. He looked terrible- his eyes were red rimmed and sweat had broken out on his forehead. Blood trickled out of his right nostril and he wiped it away in annoyance. It stained back of his hand, bright red and alarming.

"Before you ask, I don't need a doctor. I just need to get some sleep." Ander said. "Please." Please? Ander never said please.

"Ok. I'll be back to check on you later." Cas forced the words out, he had no choice but to agree. His insides churned. At this rate both his brother and his best friend would end up in the hospital... and he was powerless. He left the room, shutting the door behind himself as quietly as he could.

Could migraines give you nosebleeds? He didn't think so. His first impulse was to ask Skye, but he didn't want to burden her, not now when her own condition was deteriorating. He had to deal with this himself. His shoulders slumped at the thought. Maybe Dr Ndoro would be able to shed some light on the problem. Or the Tommies- he needed to talk to Grant again anyway.

Lost in his thoughts he walked into the Advisors Hall without looking and collided with Ben Varcoe. The tall advisor was pacing up and down at the head of the long table and gesticulating wildly. He stopped to throw Cas an exasperated look.

"Sorry," Cas muttered. His hand went automatically to his injured shoulder, jostled by the impact. He dropped it quickly when he remembered he was supposed to be keeping the wound secret. All but two of the seats around the grand oak table were occupied, and none of the occupants looked impressed.

"Thank you for joining us, Your Majesty." The deep voice was laced with sarcasm and came from the figure sitting furthest from the door. Shafiq Faruqi was Cas's least favourite advisor. He smiled his thin lipped smile and gestured for both Cas and Ben to take a seat.

"Ben was just telling us how unhappy the people are that you didn't kill the challenger. They want to know what happened to him and that he's been suitably punished. The rebellion needs to know that this kind of behaviour will not be tolerated." Shafiq enjoyed telling Cas how annoyed the people were with him. How disappointed. How his father would have handled it so much better.

Cas remained standing and took great pleasure in seeing Shafiq's eyebrow twitch in annoyance. Tom, sat on Shafiq's left, gave him a small nod. Cas waited for Ben to finish scraping his chair across the tiles and then glanced at each advisor in turn. Five in total; Tom would support him unconditionally, Shafiq and Ben generally disagreed with most things he said, Orla was kind hearted and a big believer in family loyalty- he was pretty sure she would be on his side. Lucida was the wild card, at seventy-eight she was the oldest of the advisors and had surprised him before.

The room was quiet, and to his annoyance, they all looked towards Shafiq and Tom for further instructions. Time to show them who was really king around here. He took a step back and vaulted onto the table. The wood wobbled but held his weight. The advisors had to crane their necks up to look at him. Good.

"The challenger will not be punished," Cas stated.

"But Your Majesty the rebellion will-" Ben's voice had taken on a nasal, pleading quality.

"I cannot punish him. Any act against him would be high treason."

Shafiq laughed, displaying the large gap between his two front teeth.

"Do you even know what treason is, boy?" Cas smiled pleasantly back. The word *boy* grated across his skin. Luckily, he had perfected the art of looking amicable whilst wanting to punch someone's teeth out long ago.

"Treason: any act or planned act that would harm the king or his heir." Cas met Shafiq's beady brown eyes and took great pleasure in telling him the biggest secret of the kingdom. "The challenger is my brother, Ander, the boy who should have been king."

Shafiq's bushy eyebrows retracted all the way up to his thinning hairline. Cas climbed off the table and took his seat. He leaned back and crossed his legs in front of him. It would be taking things a little too far to rest his boots on the table, though he was tempted. The advisors were glancing in turn at each other, at Cas and at Tom.

"Are you sure he's not lying? It could all be a ploy by the rebellion. We all knew the old King and Queen- they only had one son. We would have known if you had an elder brother" Orla found her voice first. She had been raised in the far West of the kingdom, and her r's rolled nervously off her tongue.

"I never said I had an elder brother." He was enjoying this far too much. He didn't dare look at his godfather, he was sure Tom wouldn't approve of this behaviour. At this point he didn't care.

"I don't see how-"

"Ander and I are identical twins- conjoined in fact. The unusual circumstance of our birth meant that we were born at exactly the same moment. There can be no doubt about his identity. My father planned that we would one day rule together. For a long time we thought Ander was dead- but he's returned now. And he has every right to the throne that I do."

"We? You knew about this." Shafiq said, his eyes narrowed at Tom. Cas met Tom's gaze. His expression was impossible to read. After a moment, Tom's eyes flicked to Shafiq.

"Yes I knew. He's telling the truth." Tom stood. "As Cas said, King Kenneth intended that the two brothers would rule in harmony. However, given Ander has spent so much time under the influence of the rebellion, and as evidenced by his recent attack on the King, I don't think it's possible. I feel our only choice is to split the kingdom in two. Those who wish to follow Ander may do so."

"I'm sure I can convince him. He just needs some time to regain his memories." Cas sat forward in his chair, his fingers gripping the table tightly. This wasn't fun anymore.

"With all due respect, Your Majesty, he tried to kill you and has shown little to no remorse." Your Majesty? Tom never called him that. Cas glared at his godfather.

"We should have him executed. The people don't need to know who he is. They will be happy knowing the challenger is dead," Ben said. Shafiq nodded in agreement.

"We will not execute him!" Cas said. He couldn't help the tremor that punctuated the end of his sentence. "He is a rightful heir to the throne. He's my brother!"

"Yes but even royalty must obey the law and he has committed grave crimes by working with the rebellion." Shafiq said. His long fingers were steepled in front of him. "I agree. If we kill the boy the problem is resolved quickly and painlessly."

Painlessly?! Half out of his chair, Cas opened his mouth to protest, but Tom gestured at him to stay seated.

"We will not harm the boy. He was kidnapped by the rebellion as a child; any betrayal is no fault of his own. And he is Kenneth's son. We owe him our protection for his father's sake. He is family," Tom said.

Orla, Lucida and even Ben nodded in agreement. Cas felt a flash of pride towards his father- Kenneth had been a well loved and respected king. Shafiq's mouth twisted.

"Well, we know what you're like with family," he said. The colour drained from Tom's face. He opened his mouth as if to speak, then closed it again. He left the room without another word.

Cas stared after his retreating back in shock. Tom had never left him like that before. He glanced around at the advisors and didn't like the understanding looks on their faces. Tom didn't have any family aside from Skye. What could Shafiq have meant? He schooled his face into an emotionless mask, it would not do to let the advisors know he knew less than they did.

"I will begin drawing up plans to see how the kingdom will be split," Ben said. Even his weedy voice was a pleasant interruption in the silence. "It seems we really do have very little choice."

"Very well." Cas was pleased to see they all turned to watch him. "You have two weeks. At that point we will announce to the people that Ander exists. If I have convinced him by then to join us in the fight against the rebellion then we will rule side by side. If not, we will split the kingdom as you suggest."

Cas vowed to himself that it wouldn't come to that.

Chapter Nine

Ander wiped the back of his hand across his face and grimaced as it came away streaked with blood. Something was seriously wrong with him. Every time Cas walked into a room Ander was struck by an overwhelming urge to grab whatever was closest and strike him or stab him or throttle him. As soon as he tried to push the thought away, the headache started. A pounding, throbbing agony that made his ears ring so intensely he could barely hear his own thoughts. He'd find himself clutching a weapon and the pain would ease, just enough for him to come to his senses, and then build all over again. Earlier when he'd grabbed Cas in a headlock, the pain had disappeared.

Like Pavlov's dogs, his body was conditioning him to attack his brother. But how?

He pulled out his phone and stared at General Laric's reply to the message he'd sent earlier. *Dusk. Tonight. Down in the crypt.* He hadn't expected her to reply to him so soon, and certainly not that she'd come to the castle herself. Outside the window the sky was pink tinged and the castle grounds had been thrown into shadow. He stood and silently left the room.

Before arriving at the castle he'd memorised several maps and floor plans, and he confidently made his way through the castle's twisting passageways. He heard voices coming towards him and doubled back ten paces to slip into what had been labelled on the map as 'store room- D floor'. He slid the door shut as two figures rounded the corner. One was gesticulating loudly to the other about the rising cost of bread. Ander waited until they were out of earshot before slipping back into the corridor. He stayed close to the walls as he travelled through the castle. *Imagine you are a shadow,* his instructor had once told him, *constantly moving, rarely noticed....*

Ander reached the heavy iron doors that barred the entrance to the staircase leading into the crypt. They would scrape across the ground as they opened, alerting anyone nearby to his presence, but there was no other way to get down. He heaved the door open and slipped through, leaving it ajar- he didn't fancy becoming entombed in the underground crypt. The gap in the door let in enough light to see that the steps leading down were uneven and crumbling. The last half a dozen steps and the crypt beyond were shrouded in darkness and all he could make out were the blurred shapes of large stone plaques and monuments.

A rusty gas lamp hung off a hook on the wall and a red and blue box of matches rested on a small shelf just beneath it. Reluctantly, Ander lit the lamp and picked it up. He would have preferred the steady light of his phone- the flickering of the real flame made the shadows jump out at him unnervingly- but General Laric would never approve of the waste of power.

He picked his way down the steps, the air growing steadily colder until his breath was misting in front of him and his arms were covered in goose bumps. The air was stale with the heavy scent of dirt and dust.

"Ander," a voice said out of the gloom, and Ander jumped. He hadn't expected her to be here first. He hadn't expected her to make it here at all. How had she gotten in? How would she get out? Likely the same way she could still sneak up on him when no one else could.

General Laric stepped out from behind an ebony tombstone and strode towards him. She embraced him- a rare gesture of affection- and then stepped back. Ander stood to attention as she watched him, her green eyes scanning him from head to toe in one glance. She was tall enough to look him in the eyes. As usual, her brown hair was smooth and immaculate, her uniform pressed and neat. It made him feel messy. He was glad he'd taken the ridiculous fake moustache off.

"Why is the imposter still alive Ander?" The General demanded. "It's not like you to be sloppy." She had never been one for small talk. Ander swallowed hard, now that she was here, the closest thing he had to a mother, his doubts seemed unreasonable, ridiculous even. The memory of the dark haired boy flashed through his mind. '*Ander!*' the boy screamed and reached for his hand. Ander couldn't ignore that.

"Well that's the thing General, it seems he's not really an imposter at all." Ander said. He wanted to sound cocky and confident, but if he could hear the slight tremor in his voice he was sure that she could too. She stared at him, and though he couldn't make out her features he could imagine the exact expressionless look in her green eyes. "I remember him," he said, and bit his tongue to prevent himself from rambling more excuses. He tasted blood.

General Laric paced in a slow circle around him. He had the oddest feeling he was a mouse and she was a prowling cat preparing to swat at him. Her hands were clasped behind her back, and there was a feline grace about her posture.

"I had hoped I wouldn't have to tell you this Ander," she said. "Cas is indeed your brother." She paused as Ander digested the news. He hadn't fully believed it until now. He had a brother! "He betrayed you, Ander. He abandoned you. He stole your crown."

"He thought I was dead." Ander said. "He's offered me half the kingdom. We could take it for the rebellion. Cas has been fair."

"No! He can't be allowed to live." General Laric spat out. A stray strand of hair fell out of her perfect bun. Ander stared at it as he spoke.

"I can't kill my brother." He spoke firmly. General Laric was not someone who was easily disobeyed.

"You can, Ander, and you shall. *We are but helpless pieces of the game he plays*." This was one of the General's favourite sayings, a quote from a pre-millennial poem. The whole stanza was pasted on her office wall in impressive calligraphy. "We each have our destiny. Eventually, you will see sense. But until you do.... I have a back-up plan." She looked at him fondly, patted his cheek. "My perfect little soldier."

"What back up plan?" Ander asked. The cut on his hand burned. He'd made it intentionally, anything to distract him from the terrible headache earlier; the headache that had disappeared as soon as he thought about hurting his brother.

"The millennials were a cruel and creative selection of human beings, especially towards the end of the Last War. Weapons of mass destruction weren't good enough anymore. They wanted something more personal. Amongst their successes was project 2022rx. Essentially it's a microchip inserted into the base of the skull and it can be programmed to encourage certain behaviours." Ander stared at her. His scalp tingled and he became aware of each individual hair follicle on his head and the small patch of scar tissue where hair was missing. "Yours for example is programmed to cause pain every time you are with Cas and not thinking about killing him. I turned it on as soon as I heard about your wasted opportunity."

Ander could think of nothing to say. She was the closest thing to a mother he had ever known. And she had used him- trained him and reared him as one might train a bouncing puppy into a vicious guard dog.

"We are but helpless pieces of the game," she said. She stared at him and he wondered if the chip let her read his mind. "Be grateful, Ander. Don't forget, I'm making you into a King. You have your orders."

She strode briskly away, and Ander did not call after her or even look to see where she went. He traced the scar just above his hair line, surgically precise. *You cut your head open in the attack on the castle,* General Laric had said. *We had to stitch it.* She had been planning this for years. His fingers probed around half expecting to find a tell-tale lump of a hidden chip under his skin. He found nothing.

Ander was struck by an urge to grab the knife hidden in his boot and dig it into his scalp to rip out whatever was hidden in his brain. But no, he needed help. He had to avoid Cas. Tom would lock him up, or worse, kill him, if he found out Ander was a threat to Cas. Which left… Skye.

Chapter Ten

Skye woke up; someone was knocking on her door. She dragged the pillow over her head to try and block it out. The noise grew louder and more insistent.

"Skye! Let me in, Skye." Cas. "I need to talk to you."

Skye forced herself to roll out of bed and drag the door open. Her chest ached with even that small amount of exertion. She flopped back onto her bed without looking at Cas.

"How was the meeting?" she asked him. He came in and perched on the edge of her chest of drawers. It creaked under his weight.

"I didn't go." Skye rolled over to face him, and then sat up. "Ander," she said, covering her surprise. "What did you want to talk to me about then?" He looked at her, his blue eyes wide.

"You have to keep my brother away from me," he said. *My brother.* She'd had never heard him say it like that before- possessively, protectively.

"Why? I thought you weren't going to kill him now."

"I'm not. I mean, I don't want to." Ander said. He rubbed the back of his head and turned away from her. Skye could see the outline of an old scar; red and inflamed as if he'd been picking at it. "General Laric did something to me, Skye. She's put a chip in my brain. If I'm with Cas, and I don't attack him, it makes me sick. My head hurts, my nose starts bleeding, my ears ring until I can think about nothing but hurting my brother. I can't be sure I'll be able to control myself."

"That's ridiculous. She can't have put something in your brain. You would have died!" Skye said. It was impossible. That kind of technology no longer existed.

"The rebellion have a ton of millennial technology. Look," Ander said, and pulled a device out from his boot. He flipped the cover over to reveal a small screen and a dozen buttons, labelled with numbers and letters.

"The rebellion has working mobile phones?" She had never seen one in real life before, only in old photos and in the movies they played once a month at the castle cinema.

"Yes, several of them. They hacked into the satellites still in orbit." Skye swallowed back a surge of fear. The rebellion were better equipped than they had ever imagined. She made a note to tell her father as soon as she could, but forced herself to concentrate on the issue at hand.

"How do you know she put a chip in your head?"

"She told me." He stood and paced to the other side of the room. There was anger in his voice, but Skye sensed it wasn't directed at her. He sighed and turned to face her again. "I saw General Laric today; she met me down in the crypts. I told her I had started remembering things, that I knew Cas was my brother. I told her I couldn't kill him."

His voice shook and his hands curled into tight fists by his side. "And she told me she could make me."

Skye didn't know what to say. The boy in front of her looked wretched and lost, nothing like the slick, intense soldier who'd pulled her close and mocked her hours previously.

"It can't make you do anything. You haven't attacked Cas since it was activated, have you?"

"It was close," he admitted, "very close." He sounded sincere. If this was some sort of ruse to trick her it was a ridiculously elaborate one.

"OK, so as far as is possible we should try and keep the two of you separate until we can think of a way to turn this thing off. We can start in the library, there's a pretty decent section on millennial tech."

The castle library was a rarity in London, one of the largest collections of printed books that remained intact. Around twenty years ago King Kenneth had started a search and rescue operation for all books- teams of soldiers had gone into the city, searching every nook and cranny for books that were still legible. Kenneth had made copies of each and sent them to several sites across the country, each site equipped with their own printing press so new works could also be printed. But all the originals remained in the castle.

"The library? That's your solution?" Ander smirked at her. It lit up his face, but simultaneously made her fingers itch to slap the disdainful expression away.

"Do you have a better one? Perhaps we should ask your buddy General Laric?"

"We've had a bit of a disagreement." His tone stayed light but the smile had become plastic on his face. He turned away from her.

She stood up and placed a hand on his shoulder. She shouldn't have brought up Laric. How would she have felt if her father had tried to turn *her* into a monster?

"She betrayed me, Skye," Ander said. "And I still feel like I'm disappointing her." The dark intensity was back in his gaze. His eyes were blue, like Cas', but Ander's contained specks of dark grey, the colour of a storm at dusk.

"I disappoint Dad all the time." Skye said, "He hasn't put a chip in my head."

"As far as you know." The corners of his mouth turned upwards.

"The point is, we're not little kids anymore. We can't make all our decisions to please Mummy and Daddy. You've just got to make sure you're not disappointing yourself."

"You should write one of those self-help books the millennials were so fond of. A teenager's guide: what to do when your parent wants you to be a murderer?" She slapped his arm.

"Don't mock me when I'm trying to help you with your soul searching!" She was pleased he had snapped out of his melancholy, and surprised at how easy it was to talk to him. "Let's go."

Pulling her door open, Skye stepped through and into the corridor. No one was in sight and she beckoned Ander to follow her.

"What should we tell Cas?" she asked as they walked side by side down the corridor.

"The truth. It might make him a little more cautious." Ander frowned. "I had so many opportunities to kill him it was getting slightly ridiculous…."

"Cas is never cautious." Her best friend's blatant disregard for safety was a constant source of anxiety for her, but she had to admit it was also part of his charm. No one wanted a coward on the throne.

Ander was silent for a moment. His next question caught her off guard.

"Can you really not ride a bike?" Ander's tone was light when he asked, but Skye could sense his underlying meaning. *Are you lying to me too?*

"I couldn't have gotten more than a hundred feet." The truth, but not all of it. Ander looked at her carefully and she hoped he couldn't see the dark circles under her eyes from a breathless, sleepless night, or the way her chest was rising and falling more rapidly than was normal for a teenager walking at a slow pace.

"I'll have to teach you." Ander said.

They reached the library. As Skye had expected, it was deserted, no one ever came in here. A square-faced librarian sat at a small reception desk in one corner. Her skin was crumpled and thin as though it was made of tracing paper, and her eyes were eclipsed by thick glasses. She had very poor hearing, Skye knew, and didn't look up from her cataloguing when they entered.

"I can feel mould growing on my skin already," Ander whispered. Skye glared at him but the librarian remained oblivious. She led him around the corner, to the section marked 'Millennial technologies'. She pulled a book off the shelf and was appalled to feel something soft and furry along the spine. It wasn't mould- just really really old paper, fraying and disintegrating at the seams.

"Start reading." Skye shoved the book into Ander's arms.

"Warfare through the 21st century." Ander read off the golden lettering of the book title. Skye picked up another book- *Weapons of the Millennials*- and started reading.

Chapter Eleven

It was almost dark when Cas dropped out of the garbage chute.

The advisor's meeting had left him unsettled. They had discussed murdering his brother far too easily, and though he'd worked hard not to let it show, their casual ruthlessness had rattled him. He'd left the meeting torn in several directions. He'd wanted to find Tom and demand the truth. He'd wanted to find Ander and see if he'd regained more of his memory. And he'd wanted to find Skye, to make sure she'd recovered from earlier.

He'd done none of those things. Cas dragged his bicycle out of the bushes, pulled on a pair of black gloves and vaulted on. A harsh wind hit his face and his cheeks were instantly numb. The smog was so thick this evening there was very little moonlight to see by, but Cas had made this journey so many times now it didn't bother him. He'd memorised each of the eleven potholes on his route and avoided them automatically.

Once he'd crossed the castle bridge he stopped. Out of his backpack he pulled a wind up torch and attached it to his handlebars. As he wound the mechanism he turned to look at the castle behind him. Even with three of the four towers crumpled it cut an impressive silhouette across the sky. Once upon a time, Cas knew, the castle had been a dwarf in the skyline, overshadowed by insurmountable towers of steel and glass. They were long gone, leaving the North tower a lonely giant in the smoke.

He mounted his bike again and set off. He pedalled hard, pushing his muscles until his thighs burned and he was no longer shivering. The streets were empty. It was far too dangerous for respectable citizens to be out on the streets of London at night. He barely slowed as he crossed under a large red and blue sign and onto a set of stairs. *Go fast. Take chances,* he muttered to himself as he hurtled down the stairs. *Have fun.* His father had said this to him many years ago when he first learnt to ride a bike.

He emerged into a wide underground tunnel. The tunnels crisscrossed like spaghetti underneath the whole city. Cas knew them like the back of his hand- he knew which ones had collapsed, which were blocked by the carcasses of old trains, and which were controlled by gangs and black market sellers.

Cas headed to one of the latter now. Tommie's gang ran the area around what had once been Waterloo underground station. Their gangs specialisation was medicine. They ran their operation out of a millennial hospital, pilfering what equipment and resources they had found there, and with varying amounts of success, using the labs to replicate more. They were expensive, and they were dangerous, but they were also doing things that the castle doctors could barely dream of. And though Cas knew his duty as King meant he should be arresting them, he couldn't help but admire some of the things they'd achieved. Rumour had it they had machine's that could breathe for you, and they could take the kidneys of a dead man and put them into another person.

This was what Grant had meant by his 'official' office; his gang headquarters.

"I need to see Grant," Cas said, as he slid off his bike and approached the guard. The guard was stocky, blonde and young looking. Cas hadn't seen him before.

"He's busy. Get lost." A badge on his red and white jacket named his as Dave. There was a fresh Tommie's tattoo on the right hand side of his neck- a white cross dripping blood. The same symbol was painted onto the door behind him.

"I'm not used to repeating myself." Cas was too jittery to be patient or to offer a bribe. He suspected that Grant had picked this new guard based on his physical presence rather than any true fighting skill. This Dave guy was massive, but his nose was perfectly straight, his knuckles unscarred, his stance too narrow. Cas was willing to bet he'd never been in a fight in his life.

"Neither am I. Now get lost." When Cas didn't move, Dave gave him a shove and chuckled to himself as Cas stumbled backwards a couple of steps.

"Look Dave, I don't want to embarrass you with your new boss." Dave shook his head and took a step towards Cas, a stupid little grin on his face. "I guess you leave me with no choice." Cas ducked under the lazy punch Dave threw at him and grabbed the big guy around the neck. He applied firm pressure to his windpipe, and Dave was forced to bend over backwards or suffocate. In this position, Cas could lead him wherever he pleased. For added insult, he flicked out a knife hidden beneath his shirt sleeve and nicked the inflamed skin across the tattoo.

Dave yelped and clutched at his neck as Cas released him and shoved him away. To Dave's credit, he got up quickly and put a hand to his front pocket. Cas realised two things at once; the door was locked and the key was in Dave's front pocket.

"I don't want to hurt you. Chuck me the key," Cas said. He held out his hand, palm up.

"I can't disappoint the boss," Dave said. He seemed to have realised he was out matched, but he pulled a baton off his belt and squared up to Cas. There was a thin line of fuzz on his upper lip and chin, and Cas realised this kid was probably even younger than he was. His insides squirmed unpleasantly and he hesitated. What kind of kingdom was he ruling if kids were risking their lives and inking their skin to protect gang leaders behind locked doors? The fight against the rebellion took so much of their time and resources little thought had been given to the plight of people like this in years.

The door behind him burst open and a fist smashed into his jaw before he could react. He was slammed and then pinned against the wall. Sparks flooded his vision but he could make out the slick blonde hair and bespeckled green eyes. Grant.

"Oh, it's you." Grant relinquished his grip on Cas' shirt front and stepped back. "You need to start making appointments. And don't rough up my guards." Cas straightened up and winced, clutching his shoulder. His jaw throbbed.

"Go clean yourself up." Grant ordered his guard. Dave closed his open mouth and shuffled away. "Come on in," Grant said to Cas and led the way through the open door.

Cas entered a large office, all polished wood and leather sofas. It smelt like the briefcases Shafiq liked to flounce around. There was a desk in the centre of the room, and Grant gestured at him to sit on the high back chair facing it. He tried to lean back, but it was uncomfortable and he ended up perched on the edge.

"Have you found him yet?" Cas got straight to the point. Talking was painful. He prodded all his teeth with his tongue to make sure they were still there.

Grant walked round to the corner of the room, opened the mini-freezer door and bent to retrieve a blue ice pack. He chucked it at Cas, who caught it with his good arm and pressed it to his jaw. A blissful numbness followed in its wake. Grant, like many of Tommie's gang, had once been a medic. It seemed that old habits die hard. He pulled down Cas' collar and peered at the wound.

"That should have been stitched." He walked round to the other side of the desk and sat, leaning back in his reclinable desk chair. Like everything else in the office, the chair looked brand new. Cas wondered if Grant was manufacturing furniture himself. Grant interlaced his fingers and placed them behind his head.

"Well, have you found him?"

"Money first. Then we'll talk."

Cas sighed and reached into his pocket. He pulled out a large wad of banknotes and threw it onto the desk. Grant didn't care who he was- he had never even asked. As long as he could pay, Grant would continue to supply him with information. Grant stretched across the table and tucked the money into his shirt pocket.

"He's right here under our noses." Grant laughed. "He works here." He stood and gave Cas a careful look. "I'll take you to him now. But like I said before, I don't see how he's going to help you."

Cas dropped the ice pack onto his chair and followed Grant out of a second door. Finally, he might get some answers. They were in a long corridor with plastic floor tiles, and his boots squeaked as he walked. The sound echoed eerily. The ceiling was lined with millennial-style strip lights, filling the space with an unnatural white glow. Very few buildings had the privilege of electrical lighting; they must be in the bowels of the old hospital itself.

They reached a set of double doors which Grant pulled open and held as Cas walked through.

"He works on the eighth floor. Elevator's out of order I'm afraid."

Cas began climbing the narrow staircase. There were four flights between each floor and by the time they reached the faded blue door with the large plastic 'eight' glued onto it, Cas was clutching his shoulder and out of breath.

"I hope you're not squeamish," Grant said, and opened the door. Cas stepped into a warzone. Beds lined the walls on either side, and they were all occupied. There was a cacophony of noise; one man knocked over a chair as he hastened to get away from two nurses who were trying to pin him down; another woman was screaming, a third was crying. Several telephones were ringing at once and a high pitched alarm was bleeping intermittently. Cas fought his gag reflex and tried to breathe through his mouth- the stench of rotten meat was overwhelming. As he followed Grant down the ward his foot encountered something sticky and he didn't dare look down to see what bodily fluid he'd stepped in.

"Dr Bonnington around?" Grant stopped the first staff member he saw. She was a slender young woman with slanted eyes and a sleek curtain of black hair framing her face. She is very pretty, Cas thought, but couldn't help noticing the stain that looked suspiciously like fresh vomit down her shirt front and over her stethoscope.

"He's with bed two. Now if you don't mind-" The doctor pulled herself out of Grant's grasp and hurried away. Cas sincerely hoped she was going to get herself cleaned up.

Bed two was at the far end and the curtains were drawn, but Grant stepped through and Cas had no choice but to follow him. A young man lay unconscious in the bed. It was probably for the best, because the man leaning over him, Dr Bonnington, Cas guessed, had his index finger stuck through a hole in the side of his chest. Cas held onto the drip stand as the room started to sway around him. He took deep breaths, counting them out to himself. The floor was spattered with blood, and even parts of the ceiling. He closed his eyes.

"This young man needs a word with you Dr Bonnington." He heard Grant say. He wanted to tell him not to disturb the doctor in the middle of whatever he was doing. He opened his eyes, saw the doctor shoving a thick plastic tube into the man's chest, and lost the ability to speak.

"I'm a bit busy." Bonnington said without looking up.

"This can't wait." Grant cleared his throat. Bonnington looked up, glanced at the Tommie's tattoo on Grant's neck and rolled his eyes.

"Wait in my office. I'll be there in two minutes."

"Come on, kid. Before you pass out." Grant grasped Cas firmly by the elbow and led him out. The doctor's office was neat and simple. Cas let himself be led to a battered plastic chair and sank down. He put his head in his hands and didn't look up until the world stopped spinning. He'd been in fights before. He'd seen nasty injuries, even death. But nothing had prepared him for so much misery in such a small enclosed space.

"Is it always like this?"

Grant had found a glass somewhere and filled it with a dark purple liquid. Wine, Cas guessed. He took a sip and watched Cas with what looked like pity in his eyes.

"*Semper idem.* Always the same." He leaned against the desk, his legs crossed in front of him. "You get used to it." He scratched idly at the tattoo on his neck.

Cas nodded automatically. His insides were churning. He couldn't imagine ever getting used to this.

"Please make yourselves at home," Dr Bonnington muttered as he entered the room. He stripped off his blood stained gloves and threw them into the bin. His hair was cut short and thinning, the remaining brown strands were interspersed liberally with white. There were laughter lines around his eyes and mouth, and despite everything, Cas got the impression this was a man who smiled often. He did so now as he looked Cas up and down.

"Well, this is a surprise. What can I do for you, Your Majesty?"

Chapter Twelve

Grant spat out his wine.

"I refuse to believe I've had the King under my nose for months and I didn't realise." He leaned in to peer at Cas' face. "I knew you looked familiar!" Cas shrugged. Grant looked bitterly disappointed. "I should have charged you more…"

"Don't breathe a word of this to anyone and I'll pay you double what I already have," Cas said. Grant may have been a criminal but so far he'd always been true to his word. "You can leave us now."

Grant raised his eyebrows ever so slightly. He downed the rest of his wine.

"Triple." Cas nodded in acceptance and Grant grinned. He winked and turned to leave. "And get some ice on that face. I don't want my postage stamps to end up looking bruised," he called over his shoulder and shut the door behind himself.

"How did you know who I was?" Cas asked. His face wasn't actually on any postage stamps, though his father had set up a rudimental postal service. He'd made few public appearances- it was considered too dangerous. Very few members of the public would be able to recognise their King by sight.

"I never forget my patients." The doctor nodded at Cas' chest. Cas looked down at himself, his top few shirt buttons had come undone- probably when Grant had grabbed him earlier- and the edge of his scar was visible. "So what can I do for you?"

Cas slowly did up his shirt buttons. It was kind of intimidating, sitting before the man who'd saved his life before he was even born. Cas had read about conjoined twins. He'd read about how rare they were and how difficult they were to separate, even in the days when electricity was unlimited and equipment was abundant. Dr Bonnington therefore had to be considered one of the best doctors in the country- he had delivered not one, but two twins safely and separated them in the midst of a war. And that was why Cas had sought him out. He needed the best.

"My friend, Skye, she's sick."

"Skye? The Kingmaker's daughter?" Cas gave him a blank look. "Tom Candler's daughter?"

"Yes." He filed away the term 'Kingmaker'. It struck him as unpleasant. He explained Skye's symptoms as Bonnington listened, a thoughtful look on his face. "From what I've read, it sounds most similar to something called asthma. But I've met other people with asthma and it didn't start so suddenly or get worse so fast. It's something else."

"I agree. It doesn't sound typically like asthma." Bonnigton shrugged. "I wish I could help. But this isn't my area of expertise. I'm a surgeon- I cut and stitch. I'll ask around. Grant will send you a message if I find anything."

Cas felt disappointment snake round his body, sink into his bones and weigh him down. He'd been so sure this doctor would know the answer.

"I take it the Kingmaker doesn't know about his daughter's condition?" There it was again, that phrase which sent an odd shudder of annoyance through him. Cas shook his head. "You should tell him. He'd want to help." Bonnington moved to the door.

"Wait. You must have known Tom right? Does he have any other family?"

The doctor's finger's tightened on the door handle.

"No." His face was a blank mask. "Good luck, Your Majesty" The door shut behind him. Cas was left alone in the office with more questions than he'd started with.

Cas made the journey back to the castle fast- he slowed for nothing. When he stowed his bike in the bushes his clothes were damp with sweat and his hair was plastered to his forehead. He pushed himself into the garbage chute, his fingers slippery on the metal. He had very little choice but to tell Tom about Skye now. And he could demand honesty in return. Why would he be called the Kingmaker? Why did he walk out of the meeting today? And what had really happened to Skye's mother?

Tom refused to talk about her, even to Skye. It had been Kenneth who'd sat down with the twins and Skye and told the three of them that their mothers were dead. They'd been about four and Kenneth had comforted them with stories of angels and fluffy white clouds. When they were a little older, he'd taken the twins to Celine's gravestone. There was no grave for Skye's mother. No one had ever told them why. *You're too young to understand,* was the response they'd whenever they'd asked.

Cas climbed out of the garbage chute and brushed himself down. He was filthy and exhausted- he couldn't be seen like this. He headed to his room for a fresh change of clothes, and ducked into an alcove when he heard voices coming towards him.

"We need to tell Cas what we've found." Skye.

"I guess if it would help convince him he needs to stay away from me." And Ander.

"Shouldn't take much convincing. You're not that pleasant to be around." She was joking with him. Cas felt an odd pang- jealousy? He ignored it and stepped out from behind the alcove.

They were walking side by side. Ander was carrying a stack of books in his arms. They stopped when they saw him. Ander stiffened and flinched, and Skye pushed him behind herself in an oddly protective gesture.

"Cas! What happened to you? Where have you been?"

"I went for a bike ride."

"And what? Your bike punched you in the face?" Cas could see the hurt in her eyes. He almost flinched, he hated lying to Skye. "Never mind. I need to talk to you. *Alone.*"

"I trust Ander. The three of us can talk together," Cas said. He wanted to tell them both about what had happened at the meeting. Ander was still stood behind Skye, shoulders hunched, staring resolutely at the ground.

"Ander, wait for me in my room." Skye ordered.

"Listen to her," Ander hissed through gritted teeth. His face was the colour of smog-stained snow. He walked away.

"What are you doing?" Cas demanded. It wasn't like Skye to start giving orders. He was surprised by how irritated it made him.

"We shouldn't have this conversation in the corridor."

Cas crossed his arms and leaned against the wall. She was right, but he was too annoyed to care. Skye exhaled loudly, it made her nostrils flare.

"Ander will try to kill you again." She continued before Cas could protest. "He doesn't want to. But General Laric has put an electronic device in his head that's capable of influencing his actions."

"That's ridiculous." He pulled away from the wall, pacing up and down the width of the corridor. Ander's behaviour had been odd; he'd seemed to become more unwell the more time he spent with Cas, he'd lingered on the headlock just a little too long back at the wax work museum. "Can we get it out?" Dr Bonnington's words came back to him. *I cut and stitch.* Surely this would be in his realm of expertise.

"I don't know. In the meantime, you need to stay away from each other." Skye looked up at him, and he could see his own face reflected in her green eyes. He saw himself nod. "Now are you going to tell me where you've been?" Her fingers brushed against his bruised jaw. He couldn't lie to her any longer.

"I went to see a doctor. My doctor. The one who separated Ander and I when we were born. I figured he must be good, but even he doesn't know what's happened to you." Cas didn't sugar coat it. They needed help. "You have to tell Uncle Tom."

Her fingers stayed warm against his cheek but her gaze dropped from his.

"I think we've all got more important things to worry about right now."

"But-"

"Just drop it, Cas." She walked away, leaving him alone in the corridor.

Chapter Thirteen

Ander wiped his face clean and then tossed the damp cloth onto Skye's floor. He stared at it for a second; it looked horribly out of place in an otherwise meticulously neat room. Skye's spare boots and shoes, of which there were several pairs, were lined up against the wall in order of colour, from dark to light. There wasn't even a single stray hair trapped in the comb carefully positioned by her bedside mirror. Ander sighed, picked up the cloth and tossed it into the laundry basket instead.

He picked up one of the library books from where he'd placed them on Skye's desk and sat on the bed with it open on his lap. *Diagnosis in neurosurgery consists of three crucial steps: an extensive history, full physical examination and subsequent advanced imaging and expert interpretation. In patients who...* His attention drifted. The text was tiny, the paragraphs long and half the words might as well have been in a foreign language. This wasn't going to get him any closer to a solution.

He'd have to go back. General Laric had done this to him and he suspected only she had the resources to reverse it. The thought filled him with dread and an odd longing that he tried to suppress. But perhaps if they met again, face to face, she'd have an explanation. Some way to justify everything she'd done to him.

There was a knock at the door. Ander jumped and simultaneously reached for the knife in his boot. As the doorknob turned he leapt off the bed and dropped into a crouch. Behind the bed was quite possibly the worst hiding place he'd ever contemplated, but he'd been caught off guard. Why hadn't he even thought to lock the door?

"Skye?" The voice was instantly familiar- Tom.

"She's not here." Ander said, and stood, sheathing the knife. Tom lingered by the open door. His eyes were red rimmed as if he hadn't slept and his hair was sticking up in odd clumps. The sight of him made Ander's insides clench with hatred; just General Laric influence or an actual triggered physical reaction from the microchip? Ander pondered this as Tom stared at him for a moment, clearly trying to work out which twin he was speaking to.

"Ander," he said finally. "I need to have a chat with you." He came into the room and sat back on an old armchair. Ander remained standing; despite everything he could not bring himself to trust this man. He waited for Tom to speak.

"The advisory council decided that you will take over half the kingdom. It was the fairest thing to do." Ander said nothing. He had no particular desire for the throne. Tom stood. He placed his arm around Ander's shoulders in a seemingly fatherly gesture, but his grip was too tight. Tight enough to hurt.

"I can't let that happen," Tom continued. His tone hadn't changed in the slightest, but for the first time Ander felt a shiver of fear as well as dislike. Rumour had it that the scar on Tom's neck was the result of a wolf's bite; years ago on a solitary journey to the wild highlands of the north. The story stated that to save himself Tom had bitten through the wolf's neck and ripped its throat out. Ander reminded himself he'd never believed it.

"General Laric can never have any influence over the throne. Not even half."

"I don't follow her orders anymore." Ander said. Tom was taller than him, and Ander had to look up to meet his gaze. He was momentarily jolted by how similar Tom's eyes looked to Skye's.

"Don't you?" The two words were laced with meaning. Tom knew. How could he possibly know? Had General Laric used this microchip brain washing before? "I need you to leave the castle. And make sure Cas won't try and come after you." Ander pulled out of Tom's grasp and they stood face to face.

"How am I supposed to do that even if I wanted to? I stabbed your *King* this morning and he still treats me like some returning messiah." Ander spat out the words like a curse. Tom didn't even blink. Didn't he care that Cas had been stabbed? That he was constantly putting himself in danger? Hatred blossomed in the pit of Ander's stomach, and this time he was sure it was from him.

"Think of something," Tom said. "I'm sure you're a smart boy." He patted the top of Ander's head and left, pulling the door gently shut behind himself. Ander stared at the closed door, his hands balled into fists by his sides. How could he trust anyone anymore? Judging by that conversation, Tom wanted to keep the kingdom for himself as much as General Laric wanted to take it. And Skye… Skye was his daughter. Did she know what her father was really like? Or was she like Cas, duped into believing he was the King's loyal champion?

He took a slow steady breath and uncurled his fists. He had to talk to Cas. He couldn't let his brother be betrayed in the same way he had.

He took one step towards the door, then Skye walked in.

"Ander? You look like you've seen a ghost."

"Where's my brother?" Ander demanded.

"I thought we agreed-"

"I know but this is urgent. I can control myself." *I hope.*

Skye stared at him a moment longer, a small crease between her eyebrows.

"He's just outside. I'll grab him." She disappeared. Ander sat down at the far end of the room and tucked his hands underneath him. He heard Skye call Cas' name down the corridor. They both appeared in the doorway a moment later. He caught a glimpse of Cas' concerned face, then quickly cast his eyes downwards. It was easier if he didn't look at him. His head started to ache.

"Tom was just in here. He told me about the advisor's meeting. And then he told me to get lost. Sorry Skye, I know he's your father, but I don't think we can trust him. He's just like Laric; he wants the power for himself." Ander spoke quickly. They wouldn't like hearing this.

"Don't be ridiculous," Cas said. Ander didn't look at him, but he could almost hear the hesitant half smile. Poor Cas, naïve, trusting Cas. Tom's betrayal would break him.

"He knows about the chip and he wants me gone."

"How could he possibly know about the chip?" Cas. He sounded angry now. Ander could feel blood trickling down his upper lip from another nose bleed. His hands trembled underneath him. He looked at Skye. She had turned a very pale shade of green, one shaking hand covering her mouth.

"I'm being honest with you," Ander said. "Ask Tom yourselves. He wants me gone."

"Maybe you misinterpreted what he was trying to say. If he knew about the chip then he must have been worried about Cas." Skye said.

"He was very clear." Without deciding to, Ander stood up. The ringing in his ears was back.

"Tom would never betray me. He practically raised me."

"Yeah, well look where thinking like that got me!" Ander couldn't tell whether he'd shouted that or not. The ringing was so *loud.* Cas was moving closer, Skye's hand was on the back of his shirt, trying to pull him back. Her mouth was moving, but Ander couldn't hear a thing. His head was about to explode. Cas' face loomed in front of him, dark bruises standing out starkly against his pale skin. Ander's right hand formed a fist. Then everything went red.

Chapter Fourteen

Never had he wanted to kill his brother more than he did in this instant.

Cas blocked Ander's wild punch towards his jaw. He grabbed his brother around the neck and threw him over his hip. Ander hit the stone floor with a sickening thud. He rolled back to his feet and shook his head as if to clear his thoughts.

Cas used the opportunity to slam his elbow into Ander's nose. A satisfying gush of bright red blood poured out. How dare he accuse Tom of betraying him? It couldn't be true. If it was… Cas didn't want to think about it. Not after what had happened at the meeting today. He kicked his brother in the stomach, sending him backwards into the wall. Skye was shouting at him, he ignored her. He raised his fist, prepared to slam it into Ander's eye socket, but met brick wall instead. His lungs collapsed in on themselves as Ander's foot connected with his chest.

Ander's hands covered his ears as if to block out some terrible noise. Cas didn't care. He raised his fist again, ready to knock his brother out, but instead found his legs taken out from under him. *Skye.*

"Get out of my way," he snarled at her, climbing back to his feet.

Ander pulled out a knife. Skye kicked it out of his clenched fist, and threw him to the floor. Cas went to move towards him as he climbed unsteadily to his feet. Skye caught Cas in a head lock and forced him back, simultaneously blocking a wild punch from Ander with her free arm.

"Control," She took a sharp breath before continuing, "Yourselves." Sweat dripped down her face; her nostrils flared rapidly with the effort of breathing. *Damn.* Immediately ashamed, Cas nodded and she released him. She leaned against him and he could hear the wheezy, whistling sound she made when she was at her worst.

"How long has she been like this?" Ander was watching from the other side of the room, sprawled on the floor. There was a very odd expression on his face.

"A few months. It's getting worse." Cas said without thinking. Skye threw him a horrified look. Ander scooted closer.

"I'm under control. For the moment," he said wearily, and reached into his boot. He pulled out a round blue cylinder with a small button on the top. "I want to try something." He knelt in front of Skye and held the blue object out to her. "Take a couple of breaths through this." She hesitated for a moment, then leaned forwards and did as he asked.

The whistling noise quietened and then stopped and Cas could feel the rise and fall of Skye's chest was steadier against his side.

"I feel so much better," she said, and gazed at Ander with something like awe. Again, Cas felt that weird pang of jealousy. "What is that?"

"It's called an inhaler."

"How did you know what to do? Do you know what's wrong with Skye?" Cas asked. If Ander could fix Skye, Cas vowed to himself, then he would forgive him instantly for what he'd said about Tom.

Ander nodded.

"It's a rare genetic disorder called alpha 1 antitrypsin deficiency. It basically turns young people's lungs into the lungs of someone who's smoked for sixty years. The inhaler helps but it's not a cure."

"How do you know all this?" Skye asked, and sat up straight. Cas saw Ander hesitate before answering.

"It's very rare, as I said, but genetic. Passed down from father to son. Or mother to daughter. I know someone else with it. She told me her family was the only family that she knew of in the kingdom to still have this condition. I carry the inhaler around with me all the time. In case she needed it."

Cas felt Skye take his hand. Her fingers were freezing and he squeezed them tightly.

"Who was it?" Cas asked. From the look on Ander's face he was sure he wouldn't like the answer.

"General Laric." Ander hesitated again. "What happened to your mother, Skye?"

Chapter Fifteen

"My mother is dead." Skye felt light-headed; the room wobbled around her. Cas' fingers tightened over hers. Did he remember? She'd only asked once, and they'd been very young. They'd stood beside Celine's grave, King Kenneth with an uncharacteristically grim expression. She'd felt so small when she'd asked him: *Why is there no grave for my mother?* He'd tucked her overgrown fringe behind her ear, his hand pausing on the back of her head. *You're too young to understand.* That her mother wasn't dead at all but a traitor? Skye felt an odd mixture of hope and revulsion.

First Ander had accused her father of being a traitor, and now he was implying her mother was General Laric.

"If, and this is a big if, she's Skye's mother, then she's also Tom's wife. Is it possible they have been working together?" Cas asked the question in a monotone. His face was smooth and expressionless, but it looked so fragile that she was afraid if she touched his cheek he would shatter into a thousand fragments.

"I don't think so. She hates him. More than anyone I've ever seen." Ander said. He pushed himself back, leaning against the wall. He brushed a hand through his hair, making it stand up in all directions.

Skye's mind whirred. Her mother. Her father. General Laric. Traitors. Secret passages.

"The crypts," she said out loud. Both boys turned towards her. "Ander met General Laric in the crypts. Da-Tom must have told her about the secret passage. No one else could have." She couldn't bring herself to say 'Dad'. Cas turned away from her, his fingers disappeared from around hers. She gave Ander an explanation in response to his blank look.

"There's a passage that runs from the crypts all the way out of the city- a secret escape route. Only the King and a selected advisor knows about it. Kenneth told Tom. Tom showed Cas on his 16th birthday. And Cas showed me."

"And Tom must have told Laric." Cas muttered. He stood and punched the wall- hard. His knuckles came away bloody.

"Cas-" She reached for his hand, but he didn't notice, his forehead pressed against the stone wall. She could only see the side of his face, sharp and jagged in profile, as still as stone. "He might have told her years ago. Before the rebellion even," Skye said. She wasn't sure she believed the words coming out of her own mouth, but she had to say something. Anything to get rid of that filthy look on Cas' face.

He whirled to face her.

"What about you? Were you in on it too?" Skye stepped back from him. Her mouth hung open. Her entire body went numb and she couldn't think of a single thing to say. She wanted to take him by the shoulders and rattle some sense back into his brain. She wanted to punch him. She wanted to kiss his snarling lips and never let go.

"Don't be an idiot." Ander. She had almost forgotten he was in the room. "She would never betray you. She's-" *in love with you.* Skye knew that's how he wanted to finish the sentence. *I've seen the way you look at him. I've seen the way you look at me, just because I look like him.* "-the most loyal person I know." Ander glanced at her quickly and Skye let out the breath she'd been holding.

Cas rubbed at his face, erasing the jagged edges, turning back into the boy she knew.

"I know. I'm sorry, Skye. I just lost it for a second," Cas said. He leaned in and kissed her on the cheek. His face was damp with tears. "I think I need to go talk to him. Alone."

He straightened up, wiped his eyes and took a deep breath. He walked to the door stiffly, as if held back by invisible chains. Skye wondered if she should call after him, insist on talking to Tom together. But she wasn't ready to face her father yet, and she didn't think Cas could wait. She let him leave.

"Sorry Skye." Ander said. He was still sat on the floor, leaning against the wall. "Believe it or not, I know how you feel." Wincing, he stood up. "That was a hell of a kick by the way."

"My father taught me." Skye said automatically. She wasn't sure she should voice her next thought out loud, but Ander's open expression compelled her. "If it's true and my father is a traitor… I'd still love him you know. I don't think I could stop."

Ander clasped her shoulder.

"Like I said, I know how you feel." He walked out, leaving her alone with her thoughts.

She stared at the closed door long after he'd left. Then she went and lay on her bed. She closed her eyes and tried to conjure any memories of her mother. A fuzzy face appeared, ducking down to kiss her forehead. Try as she might the face never came into focus.

There was a knock at the door. Could Cas be back already? She opened it with some trepidation, but it was just a castle maid. Her light blue polo shirt was freshly pressed and she was surrounded by the scent of apple disinfectant. She was carrying a bucket with a mop precariously balanced inside. As the maid bent to courtesy the mop fell, banging lightly against Skye's arm.

"Terribly sorry. May I come in, Miss?"

"Could you come back later?" Skye rubbed her arm. The mop hadn't hit her hard enough to bruise, but her hand was going oddly numb.

"Are you alright, Miss?" The maid pushed past her and into the room, closing the door behind her.

"I'm-" *fine,* Skye tried to say but all that came out was a groan. The tingling had spread all over her body, and the maid draped Skye's arm over her shoulders to keep her upright. She glanced down, saw a single spot of blood where the mop had struck her arm. The edges of her vision turned black. Poison. *You got poisoned by a maid with a mop?* Ander's mocking voice echoed around her head as she faded into unconsciousness.

Chapter Sixteen

Walking as fast as he could, Cas had no idea where he was going. He wanted to find Tom, but at the same time he was terrified of seeing him. The part of him that was boy rather than King was protesting furiously- Tom would never betray him.

Power corrupts all men, another part of his brain reasoned. Tom had taught him that himself. Voices rushed around and argued in his head until he raised his fist and knocked on the heavy wooden door of Tom's bedroom. His knuckles smarted. He'd half turned to walk away when the door opened.

He didn't know what he'd expected. That Tom had suddenly grown little red devil horns on either side of his head? Tom looked tired but otherwise unaltered. Still boyishly handsome, Skye's eyes, and a patient fatherly smile. He hadn't bothered to comb his hair.

Cas walked in without being invited, and Tom made no objection. He knew this room as well as he knew his own; as a baby he'd crawled over the thick Persian rug, slightly older, he'd bounced on the large four-poster bed. At six, he'd still been small enough to hide in the biggest drawer of the oak desk. Older still, he'd spent hours sat at the desk completing his schoolwork where Tom could keep a watchful eye on him.

He sat on top of that desk now, swinging his legs so that they struck the back of the wooden chair. Tom hated that habit.

"You left the meeting abruptly today." Cas kept his voice light. His heart pounded in his chest. He felt sick.

"You were better off without me in there." Tom watched him from across the room, leaning against the wall with his arms crossed.

"What did Shafiq mean- we know what you're like with family?" He stopped swinging his legs and allowed a heavy silence to replace the thumping of his boots against the wood.

"I have no idea," Tom said. He didn't look away. He smiled like it didn't matter.

"Don't lie to me." Cas slid off the desk and onto his feet. His hands were shaking; he balled them into fists. Tom stopped smiling.

"Why not? You lie to me all the time. Sneaking out of the castle, dragging Skye with you. Ander nearly killed you this morning. And those bruises on your face? Were those him too?" The last time Tom had yelled at him Cas had been thirteen and he had broken another boy's arm during a maths lesson.

He fought the urge to yell back.

"I'm your King. I don't have to answer to you. You'd do well to remember that." His voice came out cold. Good.

"King or not, you're still only seventeen years old and you're my responsibility. I promised your father I would keep you safe!"

"My father?!" He felt like spitting. "How dare you bring him up. If he knew what you'd done… I trusted you for all these years, and all you wanted was my power. 'The Kingmaker!' I get it now!" Cas was breathing hard; all the pent up rage and frustration of the past few hours burst out. "What about Ander? What about keeping him safe?"

"General Laric can't be allowed to have any influence over the ruling of this kingdom. Not even half." Tom's voice had calmed, but he looked tensed as if for a fight.

"But you can just keep happily using me as your puppet king?" Cas snarled. He couldn't help it- he raised his fist and threw all his weight behind a blow aimed at Tom's face. It struck him in the mouth and his lip split open.

"Feel better?" Tom asked calmly. He dabbed at his mouth with his sleeve and winced. "At least I taught you something right."

Cas had nothing else to say. Angry as he was, his insides squirmed with guilt. He was no closer to the truth than he had when he'd first walked into the room. He needed answers. Perhaps a different line of questioning would catch Tom off guard.

"What happened to Skye's mother?"

"What?" Tom's eyes flickered and a small crease appeared between his eyebrows. Finally, a reaction. Cas was on the right track.

"What happened to Skye's mother?" Tom frowned at him, opened his mouth to answer. Before he could, the door burst opened and a harassed looking messenger stumbled into the room. Her name was Julia, Cas remembered, though all the other castle servants called her Fringe on account of the thick curtain of dark brown hair constantly falling over her eyes.

"Your Highness, Sir." She said breathlessly, bowing twice in quick succession. "Sorry to- uh- disturb you." Fringe shifted nervously as she caught sight of Tom's bloody face, but pressed on. "Skye has been kidnapped."

Cas felt an odd falling sensation as his heart summersaulted. Maybe he'd misheard.

"Skye's been what?" He heard himself say the words. His voice sounded colder and calmer than he'd expected.

"She's been kidnapped, Your Majesty. We've received a ransom note." Fringe held out a trembling hand. A single sheet of paper was clenched in her sweaty grip. Cas took it and turned it over. Tom moved to stand beside him, one pale hand gripped the top of the sheet so they could both see.

WE HAVE THE KINGMAKER'S DAUGHTER. AWAIT FURTHER INSTRUCTIONS.

"Where was this found?" Tom asked, his voice crisp. Cold radiated off him as though he were an ice furnace.

"In her bedroom, Sir. A maid went in for the evening dust and tidy. She was gone, no sign of struggle, and this note was on the bed."

"Thank you, Julia. You may go." She curtseyed hastily and scuttled away. Cas stared at the note. It seemed to be mocking him.

"How did this happen?" Tom asked. He sank onto the bed. His face had gone slack and grey like putty, his cut lip a shocking scarlet. "She's the best fighter in the castle. And what, she didn't even put up a fight?"

"Skye is sick. She has been for months now." He crumpled the note in his hand. He wanted to rip it to pieces.

"Sick?" Tom croaked out the word. Cas felt almost sorry for him.

"You were right. You're not the only one around here who's been keeping secrets." Cas stared at his godfather. Whatever else he might have done, Tom loved Skye, Cas was sure of that. They would have to work together to get her back. "Do you think it's the rebellion?"

"It's possible. But it's not really Laric's' style."

"You would know," Cas muttered. He stared at the note again. If not the rebellion, then who?

"We need to question the maid. And search Skye's room." Tom said. "And you better let Ander know." He either hadn't heard Cas' previous comment or was pretending he hadn't. He was a good liar, he always had been.

"Right." Cas said, and moved to the door. He turned to look at Tom. Conflicting emotions battled inside him and he wasn't sure what was going to come out of his mouth until he spoke. "We need to finish this conversation. After Skye is safely home."

Tom nodded, and Cas left. He shut the door behind himself.

Chapter Seventeen

Skye felt cold. Face down against a hard smooth surface, the bare skin of her hands and right cheek were numb. She could smell lemons- a fresh citrusy smell like disinfectant. There were flecks of something sticky on her chin. She opened her eyes and saw a rectangular, brilliantly white room.

A young woman was staring at her.

"You're not going to vomit again are you?" the stranger asked. "The drugs really should have worn off by now."

Skye swallowed. There was a horrible acidic aftertaste in her mouth, her tongue rasped against the roof of her mouth. She peeled her face of the ground and pushed herself up to a seated position. Her head pounded. She glared blearily at the stranger.

"Who are you?" Her throat was so dry she wouldn't have recognised her own voice. She took the cup of water the girl offered and rinsed her mouth out, then spat it out onto the shiny floor. The stranger stared at the glob of spit in disgust. It was only a few centimetres away from the toe of her very shiny left boot.

"My name is Adira. I, and I hope I'm getting the phrase right here, am holding you for ransom."

Adira looked no older than eighteen or nineteen. Her skin was a uniform golden brown- no visible gang tattoos. She was petite to the point of being delicate. Her hair, of which there was plenty, hung down past her shoulders in inky black waterfalls. She looked like a fairytale Princess- not a kidnapper.

"What do you want?" Skye asked. Her mouth was still dry, she gulped down more water. Neither her hands nor her feet were bound. Even sick, she was certain she could overpower Adira easily and make it to door on the other side of the room. But she had no way of knowing if it was locked or sealed, and no way of anticipating what kind of security was waiting for her on the other side.

"I want your friend, the king." Adira knelt down and Skye could see own bedraggled appearance reflected in Adira's bright hazel eyes. "If he agrees to our demands, we will give you back to him."

"What demands?"

"We want him to abdicate the throne."

"Changed your minds about killing him have you?" Skye's heart was racing, drumming incessantly against the front of her chest. She had been kidnapped by the rebellion. General Laric had to be here. She might finally get a chance to meet her mother.

"Killing him?" Adira stood up and stepped back, her eyes narrowed. "Oh, I see. You think we're the rebellion?" She laughed, a sound as light as a tinkling bell. "Come on. I want to show you who we are."

Adira walked to the door and it swung open. Skye followed her. She couldn't figure out a reason for Adira pretending not to be the rebellion, but she didn't know of any other group with the resources or the power to plan such an elaborate blackmail.

Adira led her down a bright, white corridor. Skye couldn't see any other doors or windows. It was impossible to tell what time it was, but judging by the way her stomach was growling it had to be at least midday.

The corridor ended at a dark grey concrete staircase, a welcome contrast to the startling white. Adira started climbing and Skye hesitated before following, her hand wrapped around the bannister. There was rust and peeling paint under her fingers.

"It's only one flight." Adira said. "You can take it slowly." *She knew.* Skye concentrated on the steady rhythm of her feet and timed her breathing to each metallic clank her boots made when they struck the next stair.

At the top, Adira pulled open an old wooden door.

"This is who we are," she said, gesturing to the room ahead. Skye stepped through and was instantly struck by the smell –fried bacon and eggs. She swallowed a mouthful of saliva as she looked around. It was nothing like what she'd been expecting. It was a large room with high ceilings and dozens of arched windows. A rarely seen mid-afternoon sun streamed in, reflecting off the rows of kitchen surfaces, hobs and long dining tables. The room was packed - every one of the hundred or so benches were occupied, another dozen people were perched on the edges of tables.

Skye tried to pick up on something, anything, that marked them as belonging to the same organisation, but she couldn't. She could hear the high pitched cry of a new born; several toddlers were running between and under tables, older children sat in loud clusters, a group of middle aged men clutched large mugs, two elderly women sat across from each other playing a game of chess. Some, like Adira, were dressed in military style loose trousers and black T-shirts. Others were in jeans or long skirts.

"Who are all these people?" There was nothing overtly threatening about these people, and yet Skye felt a vague thrill of unease. It was something about their eyes, the tense set to their jaws. Underneath the smiles and games there was a universal sense of purpose.

"They're just ordinary people. They get free food and shelter here as long as they help out." Adira approached a kitchen counter and picked up a plate. She handed another one to Skye. "I doubt you see it from your pretty little castle on the hill, but there are a lot of people going hungry out here."

"There are programs in place to help the poor," Skye said. A man ladled food onto her plate and she followed Adira to a table. They squeezed on to a wooden bench. Steam rose from her plate, warming her cheeks. It smelt amazing; she stuffed as much as she could into her mouth. She glanced around, assessing the entry and exit points. But there were far too many people in here to attempt any kind of escape.

"A single loaf of bread a week isn't really enough for a family of five," Adira said. She ate like a princess as well, cutting each bite into a perfect square with equal amounts of bacon and egg before nibbling it delicately.

"The King would do more if he could. Once the rebellion is defeated, there will be more money to spare." It was what her father had always said in response to such people. Her father, the traitor. The words felt sour in her mouth. She lost her appetite.

"You really are the Kingmaker's daughter, aren't you?" Adira said. The look on her face was half pity, half disgust. Pushing her plate away, she leapt up on to the table. "You'll enjoy this," Adira bent down to whisper to Skye, and then ran towards the middle of the table. Skye watched her open-mouthed. The others at her table were cheering; they'd expected this. "Ladies and gentleman," Adira announced at the top of her voice. "I present to you your King!" For one heart stopping moment Skye thought Cas was here. But no- that would be ridiculous.

Adira lifted her arms towards the ceiling and a huge banner unfurled. Skye stared at the larger than life copy of Cas' face. It was an old picture, Cas was perhaps thirteen or fourteen years old; his cheeks soft and smooth with the roundness of childhood. The crown sat on top of his mop of dark hair, and he was wearing that crooked grin that Skye adored. She expected the crowd to leap to their feet, to cheer and clap as the crowds had done the day Cas had fought Ander in the stadium.

The skinny boy sat to Skye's left handed her a battered lime green plastic bucket. It was full to the brim with raw animal intestines- pig, Skye thought, given the bacon they'd just eaten.

"Pass it here if you're going to be squeamish." The grey haired woman on Skye's right grabbed the bucket and plunged her meaty fist inside. With a war-like cry, she threw the handful of entrails at the banner. It hit Cas' right nostril and dribbled down in a slimey, blood-stained mess. More handfuls of raw meat came from other directions and soon the fake Cas was covered in slime, still smiling his crooked grin.

Skye fought the urge to gag. These people, some of them, were just having fun, letting off steam. Others, they had this look on their faces, a calm intensity. They hated Cas.

Adira jumped down from the table. Drops of blood had landed in her perfect hair, but she didn't seem to care. She bent down close to Skye's ear; surrounded by the scent of rancid meat.

"Long live the King," she whispered, her breath hot against Skye's face. The smile on her face was fake- the pretty patterns on a poisonous snake. "Guards!"

Two men appeared and grabbed Skye from behind by the arms, dragging her to her feet.

"Take her back to the dungeon." Adira ordered. Skye didn't bother to struggle. She walked silently in between the guards until they reached her cell. The two guards shoved her in unceremoniously. The door shut, and Skye had nothing to look at but white walls and the image of Cas' meat soaked face pasted on to the backs of her eyelids.

Chapter Eighteen

"It makes more sense if I go alone," Ander said for what felt like the twelfth time. He leant against the wall of Cas' study. Tom sat at the large oak desk, and Cas paced up and down the other side of the room. The ransom note was face up on the desk, glaring up at the three of them. Like the first, it was written in block capitals in elegant penmanship.

DEAR KING CASSANDER,

THE KINGMAKER'S DAUGHTER IS BEING HELD AT NOTTINGHAM CASTLE. WE WILL EXCHANGE HER SAFETY FOR YOUR IMMIDIATE ABDICATION. WE EXPECT THE ANNOUNCEMENT TO BE MADE BEFORE SUNDOWN ON SUNDAY.

YOURS TRULY,

ADIRA

(A REPRESENTITIVE OF THE COMMONERS)

"I'm going." Cas said. His whole profile was taunt and sharp. Ander was convinced that if he touched his brother he would get cut. In some ways, Skye's kidnapping was helpful, Cas was so distraught that the microchip in Ander's head seemed to be satisfied. They had now been in the same room for several minutes and neither had punched the other.

"You can't leave Tom to rule," Ander said. Whatever words had been exchanged between Cas and Tom earlier, something had changed. Before, Tom had always looked at his surrogate son fondly, like an owner might look at a prized horse. Now, Tom looked at Cas like his horse had turned rabid and might bite.

"He's right, I should be the one to go," Tom said. He ignored the thinly veiled threat in Ander's words. "She's my daughter."

"I'm not arguing about this any further." Cas said. "Ander and I are going, end of story." Ander nodded at his brother. He had his misgivings about accompanying Cas, mostly because he wasn't sure he could stop himself hurting him if the chip started acting up. But he also refused to be left behind. The idea of Skye being held somewhere, threatened and possibly tortured…worms crawled along the inside of every bone in his body.

He crossed the room and stood close to Cas. He spoke in a voice low enough that Tom wouldn't be able to make it out.

"Are you sure this isn't the rebellion? If Tom and Laric are working together, then this is the perfect opportunity. Both of us gone, they could have god knows how many soldiers waiting for us." It was odd, being precisely at eye level with someone else. Ander could see his brother's pupils dilate by the tiniest fraction.

"I don't think he would do that to Skye," Cas whispered back.

"If he could do it to you, then he could probably do it to her too," Ander said. For a second, Ander knew that he and his brother had exactly the same repulsive thought. *What if Skye was in on it?* But Skye was far too loyal for that.

"Either way, we have to get Skye out. Even if it's a trap, she's more important to me than the crown," Cas said. That wasn't what the King was supposed to say.

"I'm not what you think I am," Tom said. He was still sat at the table, his head resting in his hands. Maybe he'd been able to hear them after all. "Bring Skye back safely. Don't get killed. I'll have your kingdom waiting for you. Both of you." He stood, straightened out his shirt front and left.

Cas watched him leave with a look of almost longing on his face, as if he wanted more than anything to believe in his godfather's innocence. But he said nothing, and a moment later turned to Ander.

"Get ready. There's somewhere we need to stop first."

"I'm ready," Ander said. His mobile phone and knives were hidden in his boots. He was wearing comfortable trousers, a T-shirt and a warm jumper. He needed nothing else.

"Good," Cas led the way out of the room, across the corridor and into an old bathroom. He stood staring at the cracked mirror above the sink.

"If you need to pee before we leave I can wait outside for a minute," Ander said. For now, he was under control. But he was acutely aware that the longer he spent with Cas the more likely it was he would attack him. And now there was no one to break them apart.

"Shhh, I'm trying to remember-" Cas dug his finger into the crack in the mirror. A shard of glass broke off, clattering into the sink. "This better be worth it," Cas muttered. He picked up the glass and sliced it across his palm. He pressed his bleeding hand flat against the mirror's surface. Nothing happened.

"Yep, totally worth it." Ander commented. "Was something supposed to happen?"

"I must just be-" Cas moved his hand an inch to the right. "In the wrong spot," Cas turned back to Ander and grinned. The mirror pane swung forward, revealing a metre by metre crawl space. From what Ander could see, it sloped downwards like a slide.

"This is another emergency escape route, for the King only. Tom told me about it and told me to only use it in a dire emergency. He said there would be transportation and a route out."

"Transportation?" Ander followed his brother's lead, climbing onto the sink first and then boosting himself up into the opening.

"I don't know exactly what kind. This escape route hasn't been used for decades. It gets reprogrammed with the new monarch's DNA as soon as the old one dies. Oh, it gets really steep here!"

Skin squealed against metal, and then Cas shot forwards into the darkness. *Why on earth do I allow him to lead me into these ridiculous situations?* Ander stretched his hand forwards; he could see nothing but he could feel the gradient of the slope go from gentle to near vertical. He wished he wasn't going head first. Then he pushed himself forwards.

His heart moved in his chest, dropping about a foot towards his feet as he plummeted down the chute. Wind whistled in his ears, and then a thump- Cas landing. Ander fell on top of him a second later. He rolled off and onto a soft surface.

"I think you broke my ribs," Cas wheezed, pressing a hand to his chest as he rolled to his feet.

"Don't be dramatic," Ander said. A strip of electric lights had come on as soon as they'd hit the ground, flooding the room in a soft white glow. They had landed on a giant cushion type thing, put there precisely for that purpose Ander suspected. Aside from the cushion, the room was bare stone and dirt. There was a passage on one side; it stretched as far as Ander could see. And there, in the centre of the room was an object that had Cas foaming at the mouth.

"I have always wanted to try one of these!" Cas said and ran a hand along its handle bars.

It was a motorbike, shiny, sleek and painted all black.

"Does it still work?" Ander asked. He wasn't sure he liked the idea of sitting on something so old and so flammable. The keys dangled from the ignition; Cas twisted them almost reverently. He vaulted onto the bike and squeezed the gas. The engine roared to life, smoke venting out of its exhaust.

"Get on," Cas said. Ander climbed on behind him. He really didn't want to. This was worse than a horse.

"Do you know how to operate this thing?"

Cas didn't answer. A moment later they shot out into the passageway, kicking up a cloud of dust. It was much faster than a bicycle. Particles caught in the air current smashed into Ander's face, his eyes watered from the bite of the wind; could Cas even see where they were going? But his brother was fully in his element.

"I'm keeping this thing!" Cas yelled, and leaned hard into a tight corner. Water dripped from the ceiling: they were probably passing under the moat. The ground started to slope upwards and Ander could see daylight.

The air became crisp and cold as they left the tunnel behind and emerged into a residential street. It was deserted, but Ander could see faces pressed against living room windows, attracted by the noise of the engine. It wasn't a noise many people would have heard before.

"People are staring." Ander yelled.

"Don't worry, we'll be out of sight in a second."

Ander frowned. Where would they go to be out of sight? Ahead of them was a long staircase leading to the pre-millennial underground tunnels. Surely Cas wasn't considering steering them down there? They had been banned from public use for decades.

"This is a really bad idea." Ander said. He tightened his grip around his brother as the staircase loomed closer.

"Go fast. Take chances." Cas whispered the words like a mantra. "Have fun!" They hit the first step and immediately Ander felt his bones rattling inside his body, his teeth chattering together. He would have sworn his eyeballs were bouncing up and down.

They reached flat ground again and Cas drove the bike through the tunnels, making turn after turn without hesitation. Ander was impressed; Cas wasn't the closeted little king General Laric had made him out to be.

Cas pulled hard on the breaks and they skidded to a dramatic stop, tyres squealing across the ground. The brothers dismounted. A young man stood before them, guarding a door. His eyes widened when he saw Cas, and then almost popped out of his head when he saw Ander.

"Dave. You remember me?" Cas asked. Dave put a hand to the tattoo on his neck and nodded. His gaze flickered repeatedly between the two brothers. "I need to get to the hospital. I trust there won't be any problems."

Dave shook his head, fumbled in his front pocket for the key and opened the door. Ander followed his brother into an empty office. They walked through and out of a back door. Cas seemed to know exactly where they were going- down a corridor floored with squeaky tiles, and then up a staircase.

"You've surprised me, Cas." Ander said, panting slightly as they jogged up the stairs. Cas grinned at him, and Ander's head began to hurt. He needed a distraction, quickly. Cas stopped on the 8th floor and pulled open the door.

"Try not to breathe in," Cas said, He looked grey as he rushed down the ward, barely glancing from side to side. Ander followed a few paces behind. He paused, mesmerised by the sight of a young boy sat stoically with a bone jutting out of the lower half of his leg.

"Ander! Come on!" Cas grabbed his arm and jolted him forwards. "Dr Bonnington is in his office."

Ander wondered whether he should try to pull the boy's leg straight. He must have been in agony, and it didn't seem that hard to do. But Cas was now rushing towards a man yelling at the end of the ward. Dr Bonnington, Ander guessed.

"Ring him again, Laura! We needed those drugs yesterday!"

A harassed looking secretary, easily identifiable by the grey and white chequered shirt she was wearing, nodded and rushed away. Her shoes clunked across the floor.

"Cas," Dr Bonnington said. "And… Ander." He smiled, though his eyes widened. "Come in, you two shouldn't be seen together." He ushered them into his office. The boys sat down. Dr Bonnington leant against his desk, fingers tapping on the wood behind him.

"I thought you were dead," he said to Ander. "I'm glad I was wrong." He turned his attention to Cas. "I'm afraid I haven't found anything out about your friend yet."

"That's not why we're here," Cas explained. Ander couldn't look at him; if he did his headache would worsen. He stared at a photograph on the wall. Dr Bonnington was in the centre, receiving what looked like a diploma from a young King Kenneth. The crowd watching in the background was even more interesting. Tom was there, and right next to him, a young and pretty General Laric. He had been so sure that Laric hated Tom…

"Ander! Show him where the chip is!" Cas said. Ander had missed a large chunk of what Cas had said. He turned around and showed Dr Bonnington the back of his head, pushing his hair to one side. The doctor came up behind him and felt around the edges of the scar.

"It would be risky to try and remove. And it would take several hours. But I reckon with an x-ray beforehand, to check the size and position we might just be able to pull it off."

"Several hours?!" Ander and his brother spoke at exactly the same time.

"We don't have several hours," Ander explained. "Skye has been kidnapped and we need to find her."

"Kidnapped? Well, that is bold," Dr Bonnington said. He returned to drumming his fingers against the desk, deep creases on his forehead. "There may be a way we could diminish the effects." Bonnington strode to the cupboard in the corner of the office. He unlocked it using the key dangling from his lanyard and pulled out a white and blue cardboard box. "These are strong sedatives. Use them sparingly- no more than two tablets an hour." He handed the box to Ander. "They should calm you down enough to maintain control. They will make you drowsy so be careful."

"Thank you," Ander said. He stuffed the box into his jacket pocket. His head pounded, but he was in control. He wouldn't take the tablets unless he had to.

"Good luck in your search." Dr Bonnington said. He stared at them, a wistful look passing over his face. "It's quite something seeing you both together. Your father would have been very proud."

"Thank you," Cas said. "For everything."

"Yes, thank-" The door burst open and cut Ander off midsentence. A blonde, bespeckled man entered. His glasses were broken and lopsided and there were fresh scratches across his left cheek.

"Grant! What happened to you?!" Cas exclaimed.

"You need to leave. Now," the man named Grant said. "The rebellion are here."

Then Ander heard her. The voice was unmistakable, even through a thick wooden door and from metres away.

"Find me the King. I don't want him harmed!" General Laric.

Chapter Nineteen

"How did she find us?" Cas said. "Tom didn't know where we were going!" Had they been followed? Maybe it wasn't just Tom. Maybe there were more traitors. He shoved the thought out of his head-they needed to get of here.

"Dozens of people saw us on that bloody motorcycle," Ander replied. He crossed to the window and peered out. "I think I could climb down."

Cas joined him. They were impossibly high- far higher than the tower in the ruins. The brick walls were rough and uneven, providing hand and footholds, but they were tiny. An animal the size of a peanut prowled on the ground, probably a cat. Cas felt dizzy just looking at it.

"It's impossible! We have a better chance of fighting our way out." Cas said, pulling away from the window.

"They don't call me Spider because I can spin webs." Ander replied. He unlatched the window and it creaked open. His hands left marks against the wooden frame; his skin melting the thin layer of frozen dust. "Dr Bonnington can disguise you as a patient. I'll climb down and the rebellion will chase after me. They won't be expecting the motorbike. I'll be able to outrun them. I'll meet you in one hour at the waxwork museum."

There was no time to argue. Cas nodded and turned to Bonnington. Ander disappeared out of the window. Cas braced himself for a scream, a whoosh of air and a sudden final thud, but for now it seemed Ander was holding on.

"Come on," Bonnington said and rushed him out of the office. Dave and Laura the ward clerk were bracing against the door to the staircase. Yells and thuds came from the other side. Grant ran ahead and found an empty trolley. He pushed it in between two occupied ones with a squeal of rubber against the tiled floors. A nurse leapt out of the way, clutching her trampled foot, and a drip stand clattered to the ground.

"Get on," Grant ordered. Cas climbed up and pulled the thin blanket over his legs. Bonnington grabbed a roll of bandages and wrapped them around his forehead, whilst Grant quickly and expertly tied a sling around his arm. Bonnington righted the drip stand, grabbed a bag of fluids and hung it up. He shoved the end of the tubing under the blanket.

"Hold this," Grant said, and shoved a cardboard bowl into Cas' free arm. "If anyone starts taking a proper look at you, pretend to gag. No one wants to get close to someone vomiting."

Cas nodded. Gagging wouldn't be a problem- the smell coming from the man next to him was vile. The man's left foot was cracked and blackened; literally rotting away. It was probably lucky he was unconscious.

The door burst open. Laura was immediately grabbed and shoved to the floor. Dave was flung into the wall, hit his head and crumpled to the ground.

General Laric walked in, a lioness flanked by her guards. Cas knew her instantly; her eyes were exactly the same shape as Skye's, she had the same slight point to the tip of her nose. She prowled down the ward, unaffected by the sights or the smells. Cas closed his eyes and let his head go floppy and his tongue hang out slightly. Drool dripped onto his cheek but he ignored the uncomfortable warmth- it would make his disguise more believable.

"Where is he, Bonnington?" General Laric's voice was silky smooth.

"He escaped through the window." Cas heard Bonnington reply. He sounded unapologetic. "You'd better hurry. He seemed rather agile to me."

Cas let his eyes open a crack. He saw General Laric smile.

"What a good little spider he is," she said. Her voice changed, became sharp and clawing. "If I find out you're lying to me…" she said.

Cas gasped and turned it into a cough. General Laric looked over and he pretended to retch, holding the vomit bowl close to his face. His heart pounded and he didn't dare look up to see if she'd turned away.

"Guards!" She ordered. "We have a spider to catch. Move out."

Boots thumped across the floor. Cas held his breath, his eyes tightly shut, the vomit bowl losing its shape in his tight grip. His throat hurt from pretending to retch.

"They're gone," Grant said. Cas opened his eyes and scooted off the trolley. Grant disappeared into the office.

Cas slipped out of the fake sling, tugged the bandage off his head and tossed both onto trolley.

Bonnington took down the bag of fluid and carefully placed it back on a shelf.

"Did Ander make it down?" Cas asked Grant as he came back onto the ward. Cas wanted to run to the window and check for himself but he was scared of what he might find.

"He made it," Grant said. "That's some skill." He looked as though he wanted to offer Ander a job.

"Thank you for your help. Both of you." Cas said. He shook hands with them both and hurried down the ward before either of them could speak. He kept his head down; if the patients were staring at him, or worse had recognised him, he'd rather not know.

He raced down the stairs two at a time. It was too slow. He glanced over the bannister. The next landing was about two metres directly below him. He flung himself over and landed in a crouch. A wave of pain shot though his ankles and knees, but he was uninjured. He grinned to himself and did it again.

Blood rushed to his muscles as he leapt from landing to landing. He was breathing hard but he felt invigorated. The nervous anticipation before each jump, the thrill of the drop, the heady relief of landing; it cleared his mind, allowed him to think.

He reached ground level and without stopping began to run. He had several miles to cover, and Skye was counting on him. He was ridiculously grateful now for the hours he'd spent roaming these underground tunnels on his bike; he knew them like he knew his own reflection. He wound up his torch and held it in front of him, chasing the patch of light. It was warm underground and he turned his face eagerly to the random gusts of wind that breezed past him from time to time.

Cas slowed down, the path ahead was obstructed. He wiped his face with his sleeve as he approached the rubble blocking his path. It hadn't been there a few weeks ago; this was a fresh collapse, spirals of dust rising in pretty little columns. Going around would take far too long. But there were gaps in the rubble, parts he could squeeze through or climb over.

"Take chances...." He muttered to himself, and stepped onto a mound of crumpled bricks. He crawled forwards on his stomach. There was a draft of icy air from above him. He looked up, almost expecting to see sky above him, but all he saw was stone and dust, melting together into darkness. The rubble shifted under him and a couple of bricks fell about a metre to his left.

Cas held his arm over his mouth and nose, half blinded by the stream of dust. He forced himself forwards. There was a grating noise from above him. Oh crap. A segment of ceiling the size of a horse came tumbling down. Something struck his temple and he pitched forwards. Rubble shifted all around him and the ground moved, or he did, or both- he couldn't tell. The pretty spirals of dust turned into tornadoes. He stared as one barrelled into him.

Chapter Twenty

Ander couldn't believe he was still alive. For all his bravado to his brother, he'd given himself a fifty-fifty chance of getting down unscathed. As he'd felt the gusts of freezing cold wind he'd reduced his chances to forty per cent. Then he'd stopped thinking and directed all his energy into his fingertips and the soles of his feet, feeling every slight crevice in the bricks, every nook and cranny that would keep him alive.

He'd made it. His fingers were rubbed raw and his muscles were trembled from exhaustion but he was back on solid ground. He resisted an urge to kiss the wall; he didn't have any time to waste. He jogged around to the other side of the building and down the underground stairs. The motorbike was still there.

Ander climbed on and twisted the handlebar. The engine roared to life with a cloud of black smoke and the bike jerked forwards. He picked up speed, heading towards the stairs- upwards this time. What was it Cas liked to say? Go fast…Take chances…*Don't die.* Ander hurtled up the stairs, knuckles white on the handlebars.

He'd made a mistake. General Laric's' soldiers had been swarming around the main entrance of the hospital tower. Now, alerted by the noise of the engine, they veered towards him, like hungry soldiers to a buffet bar. He was outnumbered two dozen to one and they weren't all on foot as he'd hoped. Several were on horseback and they lined up in perfect formation, blocking his way forwards. They were armed with bows and arrows; General Laric's favourite weapon.

Ander recognised their leader: a whisper of a man who looked as if the slightest breeze would knock him off his horse. No one, not even General Laric, knew his true name. He was known only as Umbra- the shadow. Despite his insignificant appearance Ander knew he was deadly; he'd slit your throat in a room full of people and no one would realise until you dropped down dead in a pool of blood.

"That was an impressive climb," Umbra said as Ander brought the bike to a halt. He could accelerate towards their line, the horses would likely buck and scatter. It wouldn't stop their arrows though.

"I had excellent training" Ander said. Maybe Umbra didn't know that Ander had decided not to kill his brother. Maybe Umbra thought Ander was still Laric's' puppet. "General Laric's has instructed me to ride out into the city to find the imposter. He's been communicating with one of the doctors in the hospital."

Umbra laughed. The sound dissipated like a wisp of smoke.

"Don't try and trick me boy. You know better than that." He turned to his soldiers. "Capture him. *Alive*."

Ander revved his engine back to life at the same time the riders spurred their horses towards him. He swivelled the bike around and raced back towards the stairs. The tunnel was his only option. His could lose the soldiers underground and then surface to re-orientate himself; he didn't know the tunnels well enough to find his way to the waxworks underground.

Arrows whistled past his head and he ducked down, almost flush with the handle bars. The sound of galloping hooves was drowned out by his bike clunking down the stairs. Another arrow struck the back wheel and the whole bike shuddered for several moments as Ander clung on for dear life.

He reached the bottom of the stairs and gained speed. Ander hoped the horses wouldn't follow him down the stairs, but it was Umbra so he should have known better. He could see his old instructor in his side mirror, ghostly red in the dim lighting from the bike, an arrow notched and ready. The shadow never missed.

Ander swore and swerved to one side. He wasn't fast enough; the arrow buried itself in his thigh. The bike skidded out of control, the wheels screeching against the stone floor. He managed to right himself and blinked sweat out of his eyes. His leg was on fire. He struggled to think straight.

He glanced in the mirror. Umbra and two other riders were still behind him. About a hundred metres ahead of him the tunnel split three ways. And there was an emergency escape hatch on the roof; a big manhole with two metal handles to hold on to. If he timed it right…

Now.

He switched off the bike's lights, plunging the tunnel into darkness. A horse whinnied. Ander gritted his teeth and stood, balanced precariously on the bike's seat. His injured leg shook, but he got enough of a jump to grab the handles for the manhole. He pulled himself up and hung silently, the metal cool against his hands. The bike continued without him and the horses followed the noise of its engine down the middle path. With any luck their next step would be to assume he'd fallen to the ground and check the other tunnels.

He made himself count to ten in the pitch black, his arms aching with the strain of holding himself up. His trouser leg was warm and sticky. He shoved open the manhole and hauled himself out into the middle of an empty road. He replaced the manhole cover; the metal was so cold it made his hands numb. Abandoned millennial age shops lined both sides of the street. He had to take shelter whilst he figured out where exactly he was. He was lucky; looting had been minimal in this area. A few of the shops even had all their windows intact.

He dragged himself to the closest one- London's top gift emporium. The wooden door had stiffened with age and he had to barrel into it with his shoulder to force it open. An eerily cheerful bell rang above his head. At least it was a bit warmer inside. He collapsed against a shelf of folded T-shirts. For the first time, he dared to look down at his leg. The arrow was thin and metallic, buried about half way into the muscles of his thigh. Blood oozed out around it. It would make the bleeding worse if he pulled it out, but he wasn't about to get to a hospital any time soon. He had to risk it.

He twisted round to grab one of the faded T-shirts off the shelf behind him and shook the dust out; it would make do as a bandage. He gripped the end of the arrow and braced himself. This would to hurt. Skye's face popped into his head; *don't be a wimp,* she said. He yanked the arrow out. His whole leg went numb, and then began to throb intensely. He bit his lip to stop himself screaming.

He tied the T-shirt around the wound, and when that quickly became saturated, tied a second one over the first. He staggered to his feet, using the shelves to hoist himself up. Every step was excruciating, but he could walk. He approached the counter; there was a laminated map pasted down to the surface. A helpful arrow pointed to where he was. He found the waxwork museum, luckily only a few streets away.

Ander stared at the map until he had memorised it. He really regretted losing the bike. He sighed and grabbed an umbrella from a bucket. It would make a good crutch. He left the shop and limped towards the waxwork museum.

Chapter Twenty-one

Cas blinked grit out of his eyes. It took a few moments before he could see again; the rocks and debris surrounding him were blurred and watery. He winced and put a hand to his temple; his hair was matted and sticky. His wind-up torch was still running; he couldn't have been unconscious for too long. His thoughts were muddy and slow, trickling through his mind like treacle.

Cas had to get out. The next brick to hit his head might kill him. Or the tunnel could collapse completely. He couldn't move forwards; his left arm was buried under a pile of debris. He braced himself and tried to tug his arm free, but all that happened was spikes of pain up his shoulder and into his neck as his muscles and ligaments were stretched. Cas reached over with his other hand, throwing bits of brick and tiles to one side. He worked as quickly as he dared- any movement could cause further avalanches.

There was a creaking noise from above him. He swore to himself and pulled on his arm as hard as he could, almost dislocating it from its socket. It scraped free and he dived forwards; just in time. An entire roof segment came down, showering Cas in tiny pellets of stone as he pressed forwards.

He flexed his left hand experimentally; his forearm was sticky with blood but everything seemed to be working. As he jogged he added the collapsed tunnel to the underground map he'd created in his head. He'd have to adjust several of his regular routes.

Cas reached the right set of stairs and climbed them three at a time. He reached the crisp outdoor air and took a deep breath. The smog felt wonderful in comparison to the near suffocating dustiness of the tunnel.

A woman gasped nearby.

Startled, Cas ducked his head.

"Are you alright, son?" A male voice asked. Cas darted his gaze upwards without lifting his face. The couple were in their sixties, well dressed and clearly wealthy. Very wealthy judging by the roundness of the man's belly and the perfect painted nails on the woman's hands. If they were wealthy they may have been to court. And if they'd been to court they could recognize him….

Cas nodded and brushed past them. He didn't dare speak or look back. *Please let them think I'm some homeless kid….* He let out a sigh of relief as he heard their footsteps moving away and the woman's prim voice fading into the distance, "I just don't understand why the King allows children to live like that! Poor boy looked as …." Cas ignored the uncomfortable feeling in his throat that her words brought and crossed the street to get to the waxworks museum.

He sat on the wooden bench just inside the entrance. There was no sign of Ander yet. He drummed his fingers against his knee. The woman's words echoed in his head. *I just don't understand why the King allows children to live like that.* It was an accusation. What did she expect him to do? What could he do?

Cas wasn't sure how long he'd sat there, but he jumped when the door swung open.

"Ander!"

His brother limped inside, clutching a polka dot covered umbrella of all things. His left leg was wrapped in a blood soaked T-shirt and beads of sweat appeared on his forehead with every step.

"I have bad news," Ander said. He collapsed on to the bench at the same time as Cas leapt to his feet. Cas crouched by his side and peeked under the T-shirt around Ander's thigh. He was greeted by an ugly puncture wound. Weeks ago, Cas had been sat in Grant's office when a man had dragged himself through the doorway, bleeding heavily from a knife wound in his side. Grant had chucked Cas a bandage and told him to stop the bleeding. As soon as Cas approached, the man had screamed, tears carving salty tracks across the dirt on his face. Cas had hesitated, and then Grant had looked him in the eyes. *Screaming means he's still alive. Press down until your arms ache, and he might survive to thank you later.* Cas had done so, ignoring the man's screams and the weak attempts to push him away. A lifetime later a medical crew had arrived and rushed him away. Cas had never asked Grant if the man had lived or died.

Ander's wound was less serious, but still oozing blood. Cas pressed firmly against it, ignoring Ander's hiss of pain. "I lost the motorbike," Ander said through gritted teeth.

What? How were they supposed to get to Skye now? Cas had a sudden urge to stamp on his brother's injured leg.

"Keep the pressure on it," Cas said, His voice came out angrier than he intended. "I need to find you a real bandage." Ander winced; Cas wasn't sure if it was from the pain in his leg or the tone of Cas' voice. He moved away, searching the entrance hall for the tell-tale green of a first aid box; many of these old buildings had them. It's not Ander's fault, he told himself. He located the box and picked it up from behind a desk with trembling hands. They were lucky no one had looted it already.

"I'm sorry," Ander said. The words sounded odd on his lips, Cas doubted he had uttered more than a handful of apologies in the last five years. Cas inspected the wound again; it had stopped bleeding. He wrapped a fresh bandage around it.

"It's not your fault," Cas muttered. He sat by Ander on the bench; his head heavy in his hands. His fingers stank of blood and engine oil. "I knew she was sick. I should have been protecting her."

"Cas, do you love her?" Cas looked up at his brother in surprise. What a stupid question, of course he loved her! Ander was looking at him in earnest; his face white, a slight crinkle in his forehead. Cas realised what he was really asking 'Are you *in love* with her?' Skye was his best friend, closer even than a sibling; he'd do anything for her. She was beautiful; he hadn't failed to notice that. And those odd pangs of jealousy he'd been feeling…

"I- I don't know," he said honestly.

"Well, we better find her so you can find out," Ander stood, staggering slightly. "General Laric has a stable nearby. A couple of guards are all that stand between us and a heroic gallop to Nottingham."

Ander led the way outside. The couple were long gone and the street was deserted. The weak afternoon sun had faded as quickly as it had appeared and London had returned to its layers of grey upon grey. Rain fell like sharp blades of ice against Cas' skin.

"I wish you'd kept the umbrella."

"A bit of rain never hurt anyone." Ander said, but he was shivering in his now sodden sweatshirt.

"What happened anyway?" Cas asked. He wanted to give Ander his waterproof jacket, but he knew his brother well enough to know that Ander would never accept it.

"Laric's' soldiers chased me into the tunnels on horseback, armed with bows and arrows. I had to use the bike as a distraction to get away." Ander stepped into a large puddle- water splashed up both their legs. That wasn't like him at all. Cas wondered if he'd be able to convince his brother to stay behind. "What happened to you?" Ander asked.

"Tunnel collapsed." Cas said. "Look Ander, maybe-"

Ander shot him a look that he was sure froze the streams of rain on his face.

"Fine," Cas said. "Just walk faster. You're slowing us down." At least moving would keep him warm.

"Wait," Ander said, and grabbed Cas' shoulder. His hand was like a block of ice; cold spread through Cas' shoulder despite the clothing protecting his skin. Ander pointed to a small terraced house across the street. The windows were blacked out. "It's that building. The horses are in the basement. There's one guard on the ground floor and one in the basement. They'll be armed."

"Follow my lead," Cas said, and led his brother across the street. He threw Ander's arm across his shoulder and hammered his fist on the peeling baby blue door. He plastered a smile on his face as he heard heavy footsteps approach. The door swung open and he found himself with a loaded bow and arrow inches from his chest. He ignored it.

"Hey man, can we use your bathroom?" He kept his gaze unsteady and his voice slurred. "My brother is like really bursting."

"Cause it's RAINING." Ander chimed in. He hiccoughed.

"Get lost kid," The man at the door said. He was tall and slim and everything about him was immaculate; from the equally sized knots in his boots to the parting of his smooth hair. "Pee in the street like everyone else."

"Hey, is that an arrow?" Cas waffled on. He swayed as he spoke. "Or is it two arrows? I'm seeing double. Ha, but I bet you're seeing double too?" He giggled as if this were a running joke. The man moved to close the door, and Cas tilted forwards, his hand over his mouth. *No one wants to get close to someone vomiting.* Especially not someone so neat. "I don't feel so good."

As the man stepped back, Ander burst forwards. He knocked the man to the ground and grabbed his bow by both ends, pulling it hard against the man's neck as they grappled on the ground. The man tried to yell but all that came out was an odd croak. His eyes bulged in his reddening face before he passed out. Ander shoved the man off himself.

Cas gave his brother a hand up.

"Good acting," Ander said. Balancing awkwardly on his good leg he bent to retrieve the bow and quiver of arrows.

"You know how to use that thing?" Cas asked as they picked their way across the room to a set of rickety stairs. He had suggested trying to learn once, and Tom had laughed at him.

Ander lifted one eyebrow and held the bow to his shoulder, an arrow notched and ready. He certainly looked as though he knew how to use it. Cas caught the earthy scent of hay as they descended the stairs. They were definitely in the right place. He went to pull open the door at the bottom of the stairs but Ander pulled him back and went first.

A grin broke out on Ander's face as he peeked around the door. Cas followed his gaze. Laric obviously wasn't too worried about her horses. There was a second guard posted, but this one was fast asleep, slumped against the wall and with one arm in a sling. His bow rested just out of reach beyond his booted feet.

The twins crept past him and to the stable beyond. This was one of those odd London buildings where one side was higher than the other, so although they'd descended a set of stairs they were now level with the ground again. Three horses were nibbling on bundles of hay. Cas pulled two saddles off the wall and threw them onto the closest two; one chestnut brown and the other dappled grey. He found a pile of bridles dumped in one corner and selected two at random.

"Thanks," Ander said, and vaulted onto the grey one with a grunt of pain. Cas settled himself onto the chestnut horse and led it towards the paddock outside. A short fence was all that separated them from the street.

"Watch this," Ander said and aimed his bow towards the sleeping guard. Cas felt a thrill of fear- was he going to kill him? Was he angry the guard had abandoned his duties, some lingering loyalty to the rebellion? Ander loosed his arrow and Cas gasped as it headed straight for the guards head.

Chapter Twenty-two

The arrow struck the wall and stuck there a centimetre above the guard, ruffling his hair as it passed. The sleeping guard didn't stir. Dang, Ander thought. He could usually get a lot closer.

"You missed." Cas said. His voice was thick with relief. Ander felt something heavy, almost like disappointment. Cas thought Ander would kill a sleeping man.

"I never miss." Ander hooked the bow over his shoulder leaving both his hands free to grip the reigns. His knuckles turned white and he forced himself to loosen his grip. He'd never liked horses. He glanced up at the sky. He couldn't see the sun itself, but he judged its position from the lighter grey of the sky. They had to head North, out of the city and onto the old middle road. He kicked his horse into a gallop, Cas following suit beside him.

Ander could see rain pelting into him, but for better or worse he was already too cold and too numb too feel it. The only part of him that felt anything was his leg; sharp spikes of pain every time the horse's hooves hit the ground. Ander shifted in his saddle, trying to get more comfortable. The bow dragged on his shoulder and he regretted picking it up. This was going to be a very long journey.

London flashed past, broad streets turned into narrow alley ways and back into broad streets. Big patches of dead grass and even bigger patches of black concrete. So much space. It had all once been full Ander knew; with cars and buildings and signs and animals. And people. There must have been so many people.

It was all empty now.

Cas took the lead. He may not have known how to shoot an arrow, but he rode well. From the chip, Ander felt nothing. He wondered if it was clever enough to know that if he tried to confront Cas now he wouldn't last a second.

Ander considered his brother. He had hated him for a time, but he had never before been scared of him. Today, when he'd told him he'd lost the motorcycle… Cas had turned into ice, sharp and frozen. Ander had thought his brother was too loving, too kind, too soft. He'd been wrong.

Skye's face flashed into his head again. *Cas is never cautious.* Her eyes glowed when she talked about Cas. General Laric's' eyes, though in Skye's softer face, with her dimpled smile, they were far more beautiful. Ander shoved that thought out of his head. Cas had feelings for her.

"Ander!"

"What?" Ander said. Cas' horse stopped in front of him. They had reached the middle road; by far the widest road Ander had ever seen. They were surrounded by fields on either side, flat and sleek with rainwater. Cas was staring at Ander, his hair dripping rainwater so fast the black looked almost grey. Cas' eyes, a touch brighter blue than his own, seemed out of place here in the bleakness.

"You slowed down," Cas said. "You looked like you were about to fall off."

"I'm fine. Let's go," Ander said. The bow was no longer on his shoulder- it had fallen off and he hadn't noticed. He pushed himself straighter, surprised by how slumped he'd been. He was struck by a wave of dizziness and fell forwards again. His horse moved restlessly, kicking at the ground with a forefoot.

"I wish you would have agreed to stay behind," Cas muttered as he dismounted from his horse.

"What are you doing?" Ander asked. His head swam as he tried to focus on his brother moving in the rain. Cas was fiddling with the buckles on the grey horse's saddle, and abruptly Ander was pulled about a foot backwards. He blinked- there was rain water in his eyes, blurring his vision.

"You can't ride in your state." Ander couldn't tell if Cas was angry or concerned or both. Cas climbed up and sat in front of Ander's saddle, holding the reigns for both horses. He kicked the horse and they started moving. The chestnut horse galloped beside them, riderless, it moved in a blur.

Ander slumped forwards against his brother. Cas was like a furnace against his numb skin; it was so hot he wanted to pull away. But he didn't have the energy. His ear was pressed against the centre of Cas' back, and even louder than the horse's hooves and the driving rain, he could hear the pounding of his brother's heart. It beat perfectly in time with his own and for the first time in many years the echo of two hearts vibrated thorough his veins.

If two hearts beat together was it any wonder really that they would fall in love with the same girl?

When Ander woke up darkness had fallen and Cas was pulling him off the horse, his hands on Ander's shoulders. Ander dangled across the horse's back for a few moments, staring blearily at rivulets of water staining the tarmac, the horse's saddle digging into his stomach, until Cas grabbed him under both armpits and dragged him to the ground. It had stopped raining, though Ander's clothes and hair were still damp.

"What's happening?" Ander asked. His mouth was full of fur. He sat up, leaning on his hands. The dizziness seemed to be at bay.

"We need to swap horses." Cas had his back to him, adjusting the saddle on the chestnut horse. His shoulders were hunched as if collapsing under invisible weights. Ander tried to stand, but his leg had stiffened up and refused to support his weight. Cas turned sharply.

"Just wait. I'll help you."

Ander dropped back down to the ground. It was freezing, he couldn't help shivering.

"How far are we?" His teeth chattered violently and his words came out in sharp bursts.

"About half way." Cas crouched next to Ander and pressed the back of his hand to Ander's forehead. Checking his temperature. No one had ever done that before- the few times he'd been ill as a child General Laric ordered him to bed and refused to see him until all his symptoms were gone.

"I don't think you've got a fever," Cas said. He checked the wound, seemed satisfied and pulled Ander's arm over his already burdened shoulders. His voice was a monotone; his face shrouded in shadows.

Ander knew what he should say. He hated himself for saying it, but it could make all the difference for Skye, and for Cas.

"Look, you should go ahead without me. You were right, I'm slowing you down." The words burned his mouth as he spoke them. He forced himself to look at his brother and not stare at his boots. Cas' lips pressed together into a thin line. His chest rose and fell quickly several times before he answered.

"I wish I could leave you behind, Ander. You should have stayed in London. But you insisted on dragging yourself out here." Cas shifted. Cas' arm was the only thing keeping him upright- would Cas let him fall? He clearly wanted too. "But what, you expect me to leave you now? Injured, bleeding, can't even stand- in the middle of nowhere?"

He hadn't thought Cas would say no. Guilt cramped in his chest. He felt a surge of affection for his soft-hearted brother.

"Let's just get moving then," Ander said, "Help me up, would you?" Cas nodded. He vaulted up onto the horse first and then held out his hand to pull Ander up. Cas kicked the horse into a canter, and the noise triggered a memory in Ander's mind.

Skye was well acquainted with her white pony and had already ridden him around the paddock three times. She fed him shiny red apples out of her small hands.

Cas was even better. Even after only six weeks of lessons he and his pony were symbiotically linked; they moved as though they were one creature. He rode effortlessly, his cheeks flushed, a gap toothed grin wide on his face.

And Ander... He perched pressed against the fence, as far as he could get from his pony. It was the smallest pony of the three, but it was still massive, lumbering around chomping stray strands of hay. He couldn't feed it apples; what if it bit him with those large, dirty teeth? And he couldn't ride it; what if he fell off its hulking back?

Tom knelt down in front of him. Ander clutched at the fence, imprinting the pattern of the grain on his palms.

"Ander," Tom said, "Why don't you just sit on the pony? I'll be leading it the whole time. I won't let you fall." Ander opened his mouth to speak but Tom pre-empted him, "I won't let him bite you either."

Ander shook his head. Tom sighed, rubbed a hand through his hair. He stood straight, becoming impossibly tall.

"Ander!" Cas yelled. His pony trotted over. Ander wanted to run away, but Tom's hand was heavy on his shoulder, holding him in place. "Come sit behind me. I'll teach you to ride!"

"That's a good idea," Tom said. "How about it Ander?"

Ander thought about it for a second. The horse was connected to Cas, and Cas was connected to Ander. So surely, if they rode together, Ander wouldn't fall? He nodded, and before he could change his mind Tom had lifted him up and sat him behind his brother.

"Take it nice and slow Cas," Tom instructed. But Cas had already spurred his pony and it shot forwards as fast as its little legs would take it. Ander screamed, his hands trembling as he held onto to his brother for dear life.

"Have fun, Ander" Cas yelled. And with the sun warming his face, and the wind blowing through his hair Ander smiled for the first time that morning.

There was nothing fun about it now. The grey of the sky had turned into charcoal, lit only by a pale moon sliver.

"Ander, are you awake?" Cas was half facing him when he spoke.

"Yes, I think I can ride now." His leg still hurt, but the dizziness had abated and he could sit up straight without shivering.

"We're almost there," Cas replied. They had left the middle road behind. This one was narrower, curvier. A millennial power station stood out against the horizon. Such an odd shape, like giant salt and pepper shakers clumped together haphazardly. Cas pulled the horse to a stop and dismounted. He led the second horse to the metal barrier running parallel to the road and tied it there.

"What are you doing?" Ander asked. Cas looked exhausted. His hair was a bird's nest of damp black strands, glistening white and silver where it caught the moonlight.

"I was actually thinking that we're less likely to be spotted if we turn up on one horse," Cas explained. He heaved a breath before leaping back up.

Ander had no idea what kind of security they were about to come up against. Skye's kidnapper's had already proved themselves resourceful and clever. They followed the main road into the centre of the town. A small castle stood on a hill; and whilst the rest of the town was deserted, people swarmed around the castle like flies. Ander couldn't make out individual faces. The figures ranged from small enough to be young children to the bulky forms of grown men. Many of them were armed: the moonlight glinted off their right shoulders as if reflecting off a quiver of silver arrows. If the twins tried to enter they would be spotted for sure. Perhaps some sort of disguise would work?

Cas stiffened in front of him and twisted around to face Ander. There were bags under his eyes, staining his skin like bruises. Cas gripped Ander's shoulders.

"Ander, I'm really sorry about this," he said.

"About wh-" The rest of Ander's sentence turned into a yelp as Cas shoved him off the horse. He landed sprawled in a bush and pain spiked through his leg. "Dammit! Cas!"

His brother rode away without looking back.

Chapter Twenty-three

Water dripped from the ceiling. The steady sound was driving Skye insane. Hours had passed since Adira had taken her down to the dining hall, and since then no one had been in or out of her cell. Skye had combed every inch of the walls, even scratched at the white paint with her fingernails, and all she'd found was solid stone. A dungeon straight from a fairy tale. Except for the door; that was magnetically sealed and could only be opened from the outside.

Skye rested close to the door. As soon as it opened, she would leap on whoever came through, knock them out and make her escape. Until then, she'd conserve her energy. She just hoped Cas wouldn't do anything stupid in the meantime, like actually abdicate his throne.

Heavy footsteps approached the door. Skye jumped to her feet. If only she had a weapon…Her fingers flexed and extended involuntarily. She stared at the tiny gap between the door and the wall, not daring to blink. As soon as the door opened she had to move. There would be no second chances.

The door opened and Skye leapt. Her arm was around the guard's neck before he'd even passed through the doorway. But the guard was quick too, grabbing the knife off his belt. Skye felt its sharp point against her abdomen.

"Let my brother go," Adira was directly behind her guard. "I'd rather not have to repaint in here."

Skye removed her arms from around guard's throat, and he stepped back, sheathing the knife. Skye had left angry red marks on his neck. It wasn't often she encountered someone as fast as she was; but this guy, Adira's brother, would have given her a run for her money even before she'd gotten sick. Adira had her guards well trained.

"Seth is the Captain of my Guard," Adira said, while Seth stared at a spot somewhere to the left of Skye's head. Like his sister, he was dark haired and slim, only a couple of inches taller than Skye. The expression in his brown eyes was unreadable. Skye had a moment of panic- was he here to torture her? Did Adira need some information about Cas? Or the castle? "He's got something to show us."

Us?

Adira walked out of the cell. Was Skye supposed to follow? She glanced at the captain of the guard; she didn't want him getting near her with that knife again. "After you," Seth said. "Adira doesn't like to be kept waiting."

Skye moved into the corridor. Seth followed her and pulled the door shut. "Go on," Adira said, "Keep walking until you reach the stairs." She dropped back so that both she and Seth were walking behind Skye.

At any moment Skye half expected a knife in her spinal cord. She didn't have a chance of over powering both of them. Where were they going? Surely, if she was going to be tortured it would be in the cell? Or were they about to defile more pictures of Cas? The thought filled her with almost as much dread as the knife.

"You didn't warn me she'd be that fast," Seth said behind her.

"I'm sorry. I thought you'd be able to handle one sick girl." Adira didn't sound sorry.

"Now I have a sore throat. Next time, you can go in first."

"What kind of guard lets their leader go in first?"

"The smart kind," Seth said. "Are you sure you want her to see this?"

Adira murmured a reply but Skye couldn't hear it. She reached a staircase; there were flights going both up and down.

"Go on up, Skye." Adira ordered. Skye hesitated. Could she run? The knife jabbed into her lower back. She started climbing. Out of the corner of her eye she saw it was Adira holding the knife. Seth had disappeared.

The stairs were crumbling in places and Skye had to concentrate hard not to trip on the cracks. Her chest began to tighten. The higher she climbed the colder it got. Cold air always made her breathing worse.

"We're almost at the top," Adira said. She'd put the knife down and grasped Skye by the elbow, half dragging her up the final few steps. Skye leaned against the parapet at the top, catching her breath against the cold wind. She could see for miles: rows of ruined houses, fields of dead grass and the millennial road disappearing over the horizon.

A single rider was coming up the road- distant enough that she couldn't make out his features, but Skye recognised him regardless. The sweep of dark hair, the set of his shoulder's, the way he moved as if symbiotically linked to his horse. She almost thought she saw the flash of his blue eyes when he lifted his face up, looking towards them.

Cas.

A group of guards had gathered at the castle entrance; Seth at their head. Cas must have seen them, but he neither slowed nor tried to hide himself. What are you doing, Cas? Skye didn't want to watch what happened next, and yet she couldn't tear her eyes away.

Cas pulled his horse to a stop, just feet away from where Seth stood waiting. Cas walked forwards with his hands in the air. Even from here, Skye could see his left sleeve was ripped and covered in dried blood.

"I have come alone," Cas said. His voice carried upwards surprisingly well. "I'm here to trade myself for my friend Skye. Let her go, and you may keep me prisoner in her place."

A vice tightened around Skye's chest. She wanted to kill him herself, the idiot. She watched as Seth grabbed Cas roughly and secured his hands behind his back.

"Come on," Adira said. Her eyes glittered and her face was flushed. "I'll even let you say goodbye to your boyfriend." She dragged Skye by the hand and down the steps. Bits of stone crumbled away as they rushed down, and Skye couldn't help imagining her heart doing the same, crumbling away at the thought of Cas being held captive by this dangerous girl.

At the base of the tower Adira threw the door open, dragging Skye with her. Guards leapt out of their way and Cas was there in front of her; stood calmly beside Seth who had a hand grasped around the collar of his jacket.

"Let's let the lovebirds say goodbye shall we?" Adira said. She released Skye and pushed her towards Cas. "After all they may never see each other again."

Seth nodded to another of his guards. The guard lifted a bow and arrow and took aim at Cas, and only then did Seth release his jacket and allow him to step forwards. Seth clicked his fingers and all the guards retreated. It was almost as if Skye and Cas were alone.

She stared at him. He seemed to have aged ten years overnight; the lines of his face familiar but more haggard. She wanted to kiss him, right then and there. But she didn't dare, not in front of all these people. Not in front of Adira. She threw her arms around him instead.

"You're such an idiot," she whispered into his ear, and felt him laugh.

"I'd do anything for you Skye," His breath was warm against her ear. "Listen, Ander is here, a little further up the road. He's injured, you have to help get him back to the castle. And help him be a good King."

Skye pulled away from him, staring up at his face. Cas' eyes were her favourite shade of blue; like the oceans in old pictures, before the smog. She knew what he wanted:

he intended Ander to take over as if nothing had happened. She had no choice. If Ander was injured, and she didn't help him get home, Cas would never forgive her. She had to leave him here.

"I love you," she whispered. She didn't even know what she meant by it.

Cas just smiled. That crooked, half smile that never failed to get a smile back. Except this once. Seth grabbed the back of Cas's jacket again.

"Take his horse," Seth said. "If we see you here again, we'll kill you both."

Skye took the reins of Cas' horse. She leapt up. If she looked at Cas, she'd never be able to leave. Eyes fixed on the horizon, she rode away.

Chapter Twenty-four

Ander missed the polka dot umbrella. Trudging uphill to try and follow Cas when every step was agony was indeterminably slow. Dawn had finally arrived, but the ground was still wet and icey and Ander suspected parts of his hair had frozen solid. Stupid Cas. Reckless, idiot, stupid-

Ander broke off his mental tirade. A rider was racing down the road towards him. He ducked behind the bushes and peered through a small gap in the branches. He held his breath. The rider was small, female, brown haired. *Skye.* He exhaled in relief and limped out onto the road so she would see him.

"Ander!" Skye yelled, and pulled on her reigns so hard the horse reared up. She brought it back under control and leapt down, throwing herself into Ander, almost knocking him over. She'd been crying, he registered, before she buried her face against his shoulder. "Ander, she's got him. And they hate him there. They really despise him." Her voice hitched in the middle. He hugged her tightly- at least she was safe.

"I'll get him out," Ander said. Cas may have thought he was being noble, sacrificing himself for Skye, but Ander wasn't about to lose the brother he'd only just regained.

Skye pulled away from him, leaving a wet patch on his sweatshirt. She sniffed and then composed herself, staring him straight in the eyes.

"We can't," Skye said, "He needs us to go back to the castle and show those commoners they can't win."

"They could kill him," Ander said. He wanted to shake her by the shoulders and make her see sense. He would send Skye back to castle on the spare horse. She could bring help, but in the meantime, Ander would go after Cas himself.

"Ander you can barely stand. If you go in there like that, they'll probably just kill you both. I can't deal with that. Not after everything." She grasped his arm. "I'd have to go after you, and then I'd end up dead too."

"But-" She was right, Ander knew that. This was why Cas had pushed him off that horse. They would come back when he was healed, with an army. Skye had been held there, she could give information on the layout, the number of guards, who they were actually dealing with. "Fine. There's a second horse tied a little further ahead. You ride for now."

Skye glanced at his bandaged leg, but nodded and climbed back onto her horse. She had won the argument but Ander sensed nothing but misery from her. She kept glancing backwards, even once the castle was out of sight. Ander limped beside her. He felt like there was an anchor attached to his legs, trying to pull him back towards Nottingham.

"Who are they?" he asked. He looked up at her, her face partially hidden by early morning shadows. The little girl on the white pony popped into his head, happily sharing apples with her new steed.

"They called themselves The Commoners. They want to take the throne."

"Great... Maybe Laric and these 'commoners' could wipe each other out and leave us in peace." They reached the second horse and Ander climbed up. The horses were tired, they trotted along and Ander didn't think they'd make it to a canter.

The grey road before them seemed endless. Skye reached over and took his hand. Warmth spread up his arm and through his chest, settling around his sternum. He couldn't help looking over at Skye. Her face stood out sharply against the grey world, the vibrant green of her eyes and the redness of her lips.

"I know Cas," Skye said. "Probably even better than you do. He'll be fine." She squeezed Ander's hand. She glanced back in the direction of the castle one more time.

"He shouldn't have given himself up. He's too reckless!" It felt good to let the anger out. It felt better than guilt. Deep down, he knew he probably would have done the same.

"He will come back," Skye said again. She looked at him the way she sometimes looked at Cas- a half adoring, half 'you're an idiot' look. Was she looking at him that way because he looked like Cas? Or because he was Ander? He tore his gaze away, and Skye's hand fell from his.

His leg throbbed painfully- riding was almost worse than walking. At some point, the wound had reopened and bled- his trouser leg was wet. He'd drank the entire bottle of water Cas had left with the horse but he was still thirsty and lightheaded. He didn't want to panic Skye, but equally he didn't want to pass out unexpectedly like yesterday and leave her to fend for both of them.

"Skye, I think-"

"Yeah I hear it too." Hear what? Skye's voice was taut, her face tense. She pulled her horse to a stop; it pawed the ground nervously. All the hairs on the back of Ander's neck stood up. The next second something struck him, hard, and he flew off the horse. The back of his head hit the ground and he saw sparks. He blinked rapidly, trying to clear his vision, trying to get rid of the heaviness crushing his chest.

A low growl vibrated through his skeleton. A blast of hot rancid breath hit his face. Yellow eyes glared down at him. Ander blinked again, but it was still there. A wolf. A real wolf, sat on his chest with its teeth inches from his throat.

"What a catch! Two young ones." A male voice growled.

Ander held perfectly still, avoided looking the wolf directly in the eyes.

"Get this half breed dog off me!" Skye's voice snarled somewhere nearby. She was alive, and similarly pinned. What on earth had just happened?

Rumours of trained wolves had been circulating amongst the rebellion for years. Laric had even tried to purchase some for herself, but she had never found one. These creatures were imprinted onto their handlers, followed their commands obediently, and only their commands. They had been used very effectively at the end of the Last War, and then destroyed according to official sources. But every child had heard the stories of wild wolf attacks, far up in the North.

"The boy doesn't look so good." Another voice said. This one was female.

"I'm sure he'll be good for kidneys at least," the first voice said, the man. Kidneys? Ander didn't like what that sentence implied. "Beta, release and guard." Ander heard movement nearby, a wolf's paws on tarmac.

"Alpha, release and guard." The woman spoke the same command. The wolf sat on Ander's chest leapt off. It paced in a tight circle around him. Ander struggled up onto his elbows. The wolf, Alpha, growled but came no closer. It's nostrils flared- Ander wondered if it could smell the blood on him.

"Ander?" Skye called out. She sat on the ground a couple of metres, a streak of blood ran down her face. A second, smaller wolf paced around her- Beta.

"Keep still Skye, it won't attack unless they tell it too." Ander called back. They'd been captured. By wolves. He had to think straight. He concentrated on the wolves' controllers.

They were both dressed head to toe in animal fur-Ander guessed it was wolf pelt. The woman stood closest to him- she was in charge of Alpha. Her face and hair were dirty. Ander caught the scent of damp animal and blood, from her and not the wolf. A badly drawn tattoo stood out on her withered left cheek- a skull with a pink heart for a mouth.

The man had the same tattoo, his was on his right cheek. His left was marred with a knotted scar like a burn. He was lean to the point of looking malnourished. He'd grown out his fingernails to sharp points, Ander noticed, they were yellow and dirt stained.

The tattoos marked them as part of a gang, which one Ander couldn't remember. He knew many of them roamed the outskirts of London, they were part of the reason people rarely ventured out of the city. The gangs could be helpful; Laric regularly employed members of the Apples- who specialised in millennial tech, and the Tommie's- who were medics, like Grant.

"What do you want with us?" Skye demanded. The man bent down next to her and tied her hands behind her back. Ander could see her chest rising and falling rapidly, hear a slight wheeze. He had to get her out of this. Cas had rescued her and Ander had taken her straight to another set of kidnappers.

"Don't you know who we are little girl?" The man growled at her, pointing to his tattoo. "We're the ORT! Organ Retrieval Team!" His teeth were black.

The woman glared at him.

"Quit showing off, you idiot." She approached Ander, inspected the blood on his leg like a farmer weighing up her livestock. She prodded his thigh with a leather boot. The pain made him dizzy; he swayed.

"The boy is half dead." The woman said, somewhere above his head. He was flat on the ground again. His eyes were closed. Seeing he was injured, the woman hadn't tied his hands. This was a stroke of luck- if he could stay conscious. Skye called his name; he didn't answer. *Sorry Skye.* "Get the cart, I'll watch them both," the woman ordered. She snapped a command to her wolf.

"Alpha, stop. Guard the girl." Ander heard the wolf pad away from him and towards Skye.

"Beta, with me." The man barked. He and his wolf marched away; Ander heard boots and paws squelch in a puddle. This was his opportunity. There was a dagger tucked into his belt- he just needed the woman close enough to use it.

Ander had seen a man die once. A soldier old enough to be his grandfather- the older man had fallen during a training run clutching his chest. Ander had watched his breaths speed up, gasp and then stop. Then he had become still.

Ander stopped breathing. He willed his body to be still. He heard the woman notice; an annoyed little huff.

"Maybe more than half dead," she muttered. Cold fingers pressed against his neck. His eyes snapped open and he leapt up, dragged the woman down, his blade pressed against her throat.

"Call your wolf off," he hissed into her ear. The sudden movement struck him with nausea, but he clenched the dagger tightly and stayed on his feet. Where were the horses? This would be a whole lot easier if he didn't have to run. The chestnut was nowhere in sight- it must have bolted. The grey had found a patch of weeds and was nibbling at it experimentally.

"Alpha, attack," The woman said. There was poison in her voice. The wolf didn't hesitate. It leapt at Skye, it's fangs bared. She tried to twist out of its way, awkwardly, with her hands tied, and then was lost from view in a whirlwind of grey fur.

Ander's heart froze. He shoved the woman to the ground and threw the dagger. The wolf howled and staggered backwards. Skye shoved it away, staggered to her feet. She was cut, bleeding, Ander couldn't tell how badly before he grabbed her arm and ran. He threw her and then himself onto the horse, clinging to its neck as it bolted in alarm.

Ander allowed the horse to gallop as far as it could- he needed as much distance between them and the ORT as possible. Only when the horse was panting and dripping with sweat did he pull on the reigns to bring it under control. Skye trembled against him. Her arms were still tied, she was clinging on to the horse with only her legs.

"Ander they-" Skye started. "They wanted-"

"Yeah I know," Ander replied. Organ retrieval team. They harvested and sold human organs. To test medical therapies. To test weapons. For other purposes Ander didn't want to think about.

He glanced behind them. The road was empty. He pulled the horse to a stop.

"We'll rest here a minute," Ander said. He hopped down from the horse, grasping the saddle for support. Skye slid down beside him. He pulled the spare dagger from inside his boot and cut the rope binding her hands. She turned to face him, rubbing her wrists.

"The wolf, where did it get you?" Ander asked. He tried to look her over, but black smears obstructed his vision. He clutched harder onto the horses saddle, but felt himself slipping towards the ground anyway. Skye caught him, surprisingly strong, and lowered him onto the tarmac.

"Ander, have you been bleeding like this the whole time?" She knelt beside him, peeling back the sodden bandage on his leg. Her voice was steady like a rock.

"Not the whole time." He winced as she took his hand and pressed it against the wound.

"Keep pressure on it," she said, "You're worse than Cas." She retrieved Cas' backpack from where it hung on the horses saddle. She rummaged inside and found fresh bandages and a water bottle. She pressed the bottle into his free hand. He swallowed half in one gulp and tried to hand it back to her. "Finish it." She looked so fierce that he didn't dare argue.

"Ow!" She moved his hand and pressed new bandage against the wound much harder than he had been. She lifted his leg up, wrapping the bandage around so tightly his foot went numb. But she had made the bleeding stop. The black spots in his vision disappeared. He pushed himself up onto his elbows.

"What about you?"

"Its claws scratched my arms. That's all. I'm ok." Skye said. Ander could see three long shallow marks near both her shoulders through the ripped fabric of her T-shirt. "Pretty lucky considering I was attacked by a wolf."

"Cas is never going to believe this," Ander said. He hauled himself to his feet. Cas was waiting for them.

Chapter twenty-five

Cas followed the dark haired girl, Adira, through a decorative portcullis and into the castle. Her guard's knife was poking into his back. Had he done the right thing? Ander would be furious. Skye was devastated. Skye. Her words echoed in his head. *I love you.* As a friend? As a brother? He hadn't said anything back. *Do you love her?* Ander's question haunted him. He shrugged the thoughts away. It didn't matter. He might never see her again.

"Sit," Adira said. They had entered a bare, damp room. A solitary wooden chair sat in the centre. Cas could see mould eating away at all four legs, and it creaked under his weight when he sat. His hands were jerked behind him and fastened together using rough material, old fashioned rope he thought. The guard, Seth, moved to Adira's side and the two of them stood watching him.

They looked remarkably similar, dark hair, hazel eyes, the same slight dimple at the bottom of their chins. They had to be related- siblings. Seth was still holding his knife, tossing it from hand to hand as though it was a ball and he was bored. Cas ignored him. Adira was the one in charge; that was obvious. He addressed himself to her.

"So now you have me. What exactly do you propose to do?"

"Well that's simple, little King," Adira had a voice like honey, smooth and sweet. "We have two choices. We could wait until you are declared missing, and then take the throne. Aside from that violent criminal heading up the so called rebellion there's no other real opposition."

Cas scoffed. Adira took the knife from Seth and pressed it against the front of Cas' throat. Cas pulled his head back; uselessly- he was tied too tightly to get anywhere. He didn't dare swallow and saliva pooled in his mouth. Would it be worth making spitting at her his final act alive?

"The second choice is I kill you. Then we stick your head on a pike like the good old days and send it down to London. Would make things just a tad faster."

"Adira." Seth said. He held out his hand. Adira stepped back and gave Seth the knife. Cas breathed a sigh of relief. As good as his head would look on a pike he much preferred it where it was. She'd cut him, blood trickled down his neck and onto his T-shirt, he couldn't tell how badly.

"You're lucky my so called captain of the guard is softer hearted than I am."

"Oh yes, lucky me," Cas muttered. He was losing feeling in his fingers and he didn't know if it was due to blood loss or the ropes being too tight. He hoped the latter.

"You don't think you're lucky, little King?" Cas looked up at her. Skye would tell him to stop being so sarcastic. She'd want him to grovel, to plead, to try and win Adira over. Whatever it took to ensure his survival. Cas couldn't bring himself to do that.

"I'm tied up and bleeding, and some psycho warrior princess wants to steal my throne. So no, I don't consider myself lucky right now."

"You really have no idea, do you?" Adira drummed her fingers against her chin. "Cut him free and get him a cloak."

Seth sighed.

"Tie him up, cut him loose... can't make her mind..." Seth muttered under his breath as he bent to cut the rope around Cas' wrists. As soon as his hands were free Cas leapt to his feet and swung his booted foot towards Seth's head. Cas ended up on the floor, the back of his head throbbing and lights flashing in his vision.

"Why do they always underestimate me?" Seth was saying, somewhere above Cas' head. His face appeared in Cas' field of vision. Why did annoying people always have such perfect teeth? Cas resisted the urge to punch them out. He suspected he would be unsuccessful.

"On your feet, Your Majesty," Seth ordered. Cas ignored the hand he held out and clambered to his feet unaided. The room swam for a moment and then stilled. He hoped his neck had stopped bleeding.

"Put this on." Adira handed him a black cloak with a hood. He shrugged it on, it was long enough to trail on the floor behind him and when he pulled the hood up it fell to below his eyebrows. He imagined it would be very difficult to have a good look at his face, no one would recognise him.

"Where are you taking me?" He asked, following Adira down the corridor. She walked quickly and didn't bother looking back at him. Seth was behind him and he was sure the knife would be within easy reach.

"I'm showing you why you're so lucky," Adira said. They were soon outside; the wind sent Cas' cloak billowing around him. Nottingham was even more deserted than London; the further they got from the castle the less evidence that anyone lived there at all. The streets were narrow and hilly, Adira kept up her formidable speed both uphill and downhill. His calves started to ache.

"We call this road 'Ice End'" Adira said. Cas followed her down an overgrown path, showing brambles out of his way. Seth was still close behind him, and Cas caught a look of distinct distaste on his face. A bridge loomed above them, and Cas squinted in the sudden darkness. There was a shape up ahead, huddled against the old bricks of the bridge. It was a man, laying on his back. All that covered his skinny frame was a frayed blue blanket. Cas ought to have been able to see the man's chest rise and fall as he breathed. He couldn't. The man was dead.

Cas closed his eyes for a moment. He felt like he was spinning, and he must have swayed because Seth grabbed him by the elbow to steady him.

"He froze to death," Adira said, "In case you were wondering." She pulled out a notebook from her jacket and scribbled something on the page.

Tucking it back into her pocket, she continued past the dead man.

"Wait, we're just going to leave him here?" Cas protested. He wasn't sure he'd be able to walk if Seth hadn't been pushing him in the right direction.

"I don't have space for them all," Adira said. Something twisted in his gut. *I hope Ander does a better job ruling than I have…*

They found several more bodies along the tunnel. Each time, Adira paused and made a little note in her book. She was tucking it back into her pocket when Cas heard a faint mewling coming from the next bundle of clothing. He thought a cat must have climbed under the old blankets for warmth. Instead, when Seth reached forwards and pulled the woollen blanket away two girls blinked up at them.

Wide eyed and stick thin, they looked no more than eight years old. They clung together tightly.

"We're going to take you some place safe and warm. You'll get good food too." Adira said. She gestured at Seth and he picked both girls up with one arm. They said nothing but shuddered into an exhausted sleep.

"Let's head back," Seth said, "They're freezing." He rocked the girls up and down on his shoulder.

"Take them," Adira said, "I have one more place to take our little King." The two of them looked at each other for a moment. Then Seth nodded and hurried away.

"Don't even think about it little King," Adira said. A knife glinted in her hand- she made sure he could see it. Even so, she was well over a head shorter than him and at least 20kg lighter. Once her back was turned he would strike. "Don't make me cut that pretty neck of yours again." She gestured with the knife for him to walk in front of her.

Cas hesitated. Could he make a run for it? He bolted to the right. Branches and leaves whipped past him. He had no idea where he was going. Close behind him, Adira's boots cracked on the ice. The noise stopped, something whistled through the air and struck his hand, and he ended up backed up against a thick tree trunk. His hand throbbed. Adira had thrown her knife, it had gone straight through his palm and into the tree. He was pinned in place.

"Next time, it goes through your neck." She smiled at him, showing teeth.

Cas nodded. If he opened his mouth he would scream. Adira walked forwards. She really was very small, he could see the top of her scalp, the thin parting of her black hair. She yanked the knife out of his hand. He bit his lip hard and let out a string of curse words in his head. He cradled his bleeding hand to his chest. Adira continued walking as if nothing had happened.

They reached a narrow staircase set into the side of an old building. The sandstone steps leading down were well worn. Cas walked down, Adira close behind him- their footsteps echoed more and more as they descended deeper underground. They reached an enormous cavern, the air was mildly warmer than outside but damp. Dust flickered in the wavering light of gas lamps. Houses lined the edges, houses in the loosest sense of the word, they consisted of four tin walls and a bit of cardboard for a roof. Smoke rose from makeshift chimneys- Cas could see small ventilation shafts leading to the surface.

"This is where Seth and I grew up," Adira said. "There are hundreds of interconnected underground caverns beneath the city."

"Its very homely" Cas muttered. Several paces ahead, two men were fighting. Cas thought it was a drunken brawl, a ring of spectators surrounded them, cheering and hissing at intervals. When one man beat the other, he was awarded a slice of bread as a prize. Even as the beaten man was dragged away, two more stepped in to take his place. These two were teenagers, gangly and long limbed.

"What is this?"

"The winner gets bread to feed his family. The looser starves. Simple." Adira said. "Survival of the fittest."

"You used to do this? Knock people out for a bit of bread?"

"I won my first fight when I was eight."

"Where were you parents?"

"Dead. They starved trying to feed me and Seth," Adira said. Her breath rose in front of her in short angry puffs of mist. "Do you see now, little King, why you are lucky? You had a roof over your head. All the food you wanted. Servants and parents to dote on you. I was an orphan and fighting for my life!"

Cas stared back at her. Heat rose to his face, but he kept his voice calm.

"So was I," Cas said. "My mother died giving birth to me. My father was murdered when I was 10. My best friend is dying and there's nothing I can do about it. And there have been more threats to my life than I can count." Cas turned away before he could say anymore. He'd come so close to mentioning Ander... that would have ruined his plan.

Adira's hand came down on his shoulder. Her expression was impossible to read. Was she trying to comfort him? No, she used it to steer him back up the steps, towards the bridge. When she spoke, her voice was a degree warmer.

"I guess I forget sometimes how young you really are," she said. "You're just a boy. You should never have had so much responsibility thrown on your shoulders."

She paused. They were stood in a copse of trees. A strong wind had picked up, blowing the smog away, and for only the second time in his life Cas could see the moon in the midmorning sky.

Adira stared at him. Her eyes were hazel, but the left one contained a tiny patch of blue.

"Maybe you could help me Cassander," Adira said. His heart skipped a beat when she said his name. She took his uninjured hand in her own, small and delicate. "I don't want to steal your power. I don't want your throne. I don't think anyone should have that kind of power and responsibility."

"But someone has to rule," Cas said. Her hand was soft over his, but the words coming out of her mouth were blasphemous.

"I want to bring back democracy. Let the people vote for who they want to rule them. A council not an individual."

Cas let out a laugh.

"You're crazy!" Adira snatched her hand away, her eyes blazing. "We got rid of democracy for a reason. The public didn't know what was best for them. The council didn't do what was best for them. No one could ever really decide anything. But with a king! Everyone is united and loyal to the king. Or Queen." His great grandmother, Queen Eva, had brought back the monarchy and made it what it was today.

Adira looked up at him. There was pity in her eyes.

"Everyone is united and loyal are they?" She smiled, the slow sad smile of someone comforting the ignorant. She didn't know what she was talking about. Just because a few rebels had decided to flaunt authority…

Cas crossed his arms. He said nothing.

"Come on little King," she said. She started walking. "You need some time in a cell to think."

Chapter Twenty-six

"Skye. We're back."

Half asleep in the saddle, Skye lifted her head at the sound of Ander's voice. London stretched out in front of her; old and empty. The North tower loomed over the river, the water was inky black in the growing darkness. Skye had seen a mermaid in there once, or thought she had. Cas had laughed at her for weeks.

She stretched out her shoulders, sore from where the wolfs claws had dug in. She was in desperate need of a shower and a new shirt. She looked Ander over- he was less pale now that the wound had stopped bleeding.

"Remember you're the King now," she said to Ander. "Sit up straight."

Ander looked back at her with a frown. The glazed look of someone about to pass out had disappeared, thank goodness.

"Cas never sits straight."

"I know, but I always remind him." Ander smiled back at her, but as they approached the enormous iron gates at the castle entrance it faded from his face.

"I don't think I can do this. Just pretend to be Cas when he's imprisoned and that crazy girl could do anything to him." Skye longed to reach over and smooth the crease away from between his eyebrows.

"The people need a King, Ander. This is what Cas needs you to do. And then we will get him back. You know the plan."

Ander would take the role of King. He'd walk-limp-into the castle and tell everyone he'd been attacked by rebels and they had a secret base in Nottingham. He would call an emergency council meeting. The army would be ordered to Nottingham. They'd rescue Cas. Then they'd all concentrate on dealing with Laric and the rebellion. And her father…

Ander nodded. She watched him steel himself and sit up straighter. The guards at the gate allowed them to pass without comment. The courtyard was awash with people when they entered. Mutters reached Skye's ears. *The King is back with Skye. The King is injured. What happened? Are we in danger?*

Tom stood at the far end, ready to greet them. Her father, the traitor. He smiled at the crowd but Skye could see the tension in his face. When she reached him and climbed down from the horse, he frowned at the cuts on her arms and then pulled her into a tight hug.

"Where's Cas?" He muttered into her ear. The concern in his voice sounded genuine, but he had always been a good liar.

"He gave himself up for me," she whispered back. She wondered if she was imaging the tremor in his arms. He pulled away from her as Ander clambered down after her.

"Your Majesty!" Tom caught Ander by the elbow when he staggered, his injured leg buckling under him. "Get the doctor down here." Tom ordered and a guard scuttled away.

"I'm fine. We need to assemble the council. Immediately. There's a threat to the kingdom that must be dealt with!" Ander's words carried across the courtyard and anxious muttering followed.

"What are you doing?" Tom growled quietly. His mouth barely moved.

"Exactly what you always wanted." Ander said. "I'm taking over from Cas without anyone being any the wiser." He pulled his arm out of Tom's grasp and limped into the castle.

Skye followed him, but not before she'd seen the train of emotions flash across her father's face. Confusion. Fear. Regret. Anger.

"After the council meeting, we need to talk." She said to her father as he fell into step next to her.

"You too, huh?" His voice was heavy. Skye had never thought of her father as old before, but he looked it now. His scar stood out starkly against the paleness of his face. She remembered being very small, falling asleep running her fingers across the bumps and ridges winding up his neck. She'd felt safe then. She'd never even wondered why he would never tell her how he'd ended up scarred, the mystery was part of his charm. Now she wondered if she was better off not knowing.

"You knew your lies would catch you eventually." She looked at him, the face as familiar to her as her own. She didn't know him at all. "How could you do this to them?"

"I did this for them," Tom said. He jerked his head back towards the crowd. "To keep them safe from Laric and her violent rebellion."

"You can stop pretending, Dad. I know you're working with her." Skye spat out. "I know who she is."

Colour flushed his cheeks.

"You do?"

"We're not children anymore. We figured it out."

There was much more she wanted to say to her father, but it would have to wait. They reached the Advisor's Hall and Ander beckoned her to sit beside him. She left her father by the door and took the seat on Ander's left. He took her hand as council member's filed in and took their seats. Her father was the only one to remain standing, leaning against the back wall, a shadow across his face.

"Thank you for assembling so quickly," Ander said. Skye could tell none of the council members had any clue that he wasn't Cas; Shafiq looked disinterested as usual, Ben flustered, and Orla and Lucida concerned. "First things first. I'm not Cas, I'm Ander. Pleased to meet you all."

Skye suppressed a smile. There weren't many people blunter than Cas, but Ander had surpassed him.

"But-" Ben began.

"You look just like him," Lucida finished. They stared at him as if they'd each been slapped in the face by a wet fish.

"Well, Ander's a bit better looking." Skye broke the silence. Dirty looks were thrown in her direction. But Ander smiled. A funny feeling bubbled in the pit of her stomach. What was she doing? Cas was missing. She shouldn't be smiling. But she was, and Ander seemed encouraged by it.

"Your king has been kidnapped." Ander said. "He is being held by a group identifying themselves as The Commoners. They want him off the throne. They wanted him to abdicate, but now we suspect they will wait until he is missing for so long his rule is declared over."

"How dare they?!" Ben muttered. His face was blotchy with patches of red. "He is the rightful King!" He looked at Ander. "I mean he's half of the rightful King. I don't even know anymore."

Ander sighed and muttered to Skye under his breath. "No wonder nothing ever gets done around here...what a load of dramatic pricks."

She choked back a laugh. Lucida glared at her.

"For the time being, Ander will assume Cas' place. The Commoners will have no idea what is going on. As they ponder whether or not they've captured an imposter, we will send our army to retrieve Cas." Skye said. She was surprised they all watched her in silence and waited for her to finish speaking.

"How are we supposed to trust him?" Shafiq said. "He's working for the rebellion."

"We don't have a choice." Tom said. He remained leaning against the back wall, his arms crossed. "He's the best distraction we have. And therefore the best chance of getting Cas back."

"This is all getting very out of hand." Orla muttered. She gathered up the paperwork in front of her, snapping the wad of loose sheets together on the table. "Ander should address the soldiers immediately. I will arrange for them to gather in the courtyard." She was the council's military advisor.

"I suppose we must make sure as many members of the public hear Ander's address as possible." Shafiq said. "That way word of the King's safety is more likely to reach these Commoners." Shafiq was talking sense. It really was all getting out of hand.

Orla nodded and left the room.

"There is also another matter to discuss." Ander continued. A cold feeling dripped through Skye's chest. They hadn't discussed this, but she knew what he would say.

"We have evidence that Tom has been working with Laric." Ander's statement was met with nervous silence. No one looked surprised. Shafiq and Lucida exchanged furtive glances. Had everyone known about Tom and Laric?

Her father said nothing. He remained standing at the back of the room, eyes hooded, like a ghost.

"This will be investigated further." Ander said, "However, given that the army will be away we can't risk that he will communicate with the rebellion again. I suggest we put him in the dungeons for now."

The cold feeling spread through Skye's body. She couldn't feel her fingers. Ander wanted to put her father in prison. The worst part was she agreed with him.

Tom spoke. His voice crept through the room, the soft familiarity of it winding into Skye's head. But he wasn't talking to her.

"You all know I could never work with Laric. Not after everything she's done."

What had she done? What was her father hiding from her?

"He has more reason than most to hate her," Ben said.

It was Lucida who disagreed. Her eyes were watery with age, but she spoke with a clear voice.

"Can we ever really hate the people we once loved?"

Skye looked at Ander. He was looking back at her. There was an apology in his dark blue eyes. *If it's true and my father is a traitor… I'd still love him you know. I don't think I could stop.*

"I should be going after Cas," Tom objected. He stood up straight, peeling himself off the wall. "He needs me."

"Not anymore Dad." Skye said, and his face crumpled. The advisors said nothing else.

Ander stood and opened the door. He summoned two guards. They both looked surprised, horrified and more than a little intimidated when they were asked to escort Tom to the dungeons. Tom went without further objection. He didn't look at either of them.

"Time to make this announcement," Ander said. "You all know what you should be doing." Ander gestured at the council members to exit the room ahead of him, and looked down his nose at each of them as they passed him. He had the arrogant King act down to a tee.

"Let's go," he said. She walked close beside him, ready to support him if his leg gave away. He must have been in pain but he was hiding it well. "Sorry Skye, I didn't mean to spring that on you. With your father."

"He didn't exactly leave us with a choice. I understand." She ran her hand along the brick wall next to her as they walked, lifting her fingers only when she came to the cracks where one brick changed to the next. The repetition helped steady her breathing.

"How am I doing?" Ander asked. "At being King?" At that moment he looked more like the boy Skye had once known than the almost man he was.

"Like you were born for it," she replied. He was still smiling when they reached the balcony overlooking the courtyard. It looked like the entirety of the castle's occupants had squashed themselves in, along with half of London. The crowd purred like a lion about to roar.

"Stand next to me, Skye," Ander said. He spoke so quietly she had to watch his mouth move to figure out his exact words. His lips were red, like a splash of blood across his face. They stepped forward together and the crowd fell instantly silent. Skye placed her left hand next to Ander's right on the bannister, her little finger touching his. A shock ran up her arm, and she looked to Ander, but he didn't seem to have noticed.

"I have news to share with you all," Ander said, his voice echoing over the crowd. He stood up straight, his eyes hard. The boy from moments ago was gone and a king stood in his place. From the ground, backlit by a single golden lantern, he must have cut an impressive figure. "I have been attacked by a group identifying themselves as 'the Commoners'. They have made their home in Nottingham Castle. We must go there and defeat them for good!"

A soldier in the crowd below knelt on the ground, her knife held out as if for an offering. In twos and threes more of the crowd joined in, until they were all kneeling, a sea of bent figures. Ander's mouth widened in surprise, she could see the tiny chip in his tooth.

"Thank you for your support," Skye said when Ander didn't speak. "Please follow the emergency war plans we have all rehearsed."

The crowd dispersed with purpose. Every man, woman and child who lived in the castle had a role to play and knew it well; her father had insisted they practice for this scenario often.

"Come on, Ander." Skye took his hand and led him off the balcony. "You need to get some rest."

"There's no time for rest, Skye." Ander's limp was more pronounced than ever, and he winced with every step. "Cas is captive, there's been a traitor on the council for nearly twenty years, and who knows what Laric has planned next..." He sighed and released her hand to rub at his eyes. "You're right- I can barely think straight I'm so tired."

"I'm always right." Skye said. They stepped into Cas' room. It seemed a lifetime ago that she'd first taken the helmet off Ander's head, right here on that very sofa. Then, she'd been amazed at how similar Ander had looked to Cas. Now she was amazed how easily she could tell them apart. Ander looked at her differently, like he wanted to look all the way through her and see what she was made off. Cas looked at her like he already knew.

Ander's eyes were completely different, the specks of grey colouring the blue made him look older. Even the crooked grin was ever so slightly different, a little less arrogant, a little more shy.

"Skye?" She blinked- she'd been staring at him. Heat rushed to her cheeks and she reached up to smooth her hair to hide her face.

"What?"

"I said, can you help me with this?" Ander sat on the sofa and gestured at the blood stained bandage around his leg.

"Sure." She went into the bathroom and grabbed the first aid box. She caught sight of herself in the mirror. She was a dirt streaked, blood stained mess, and her face was bright red. What was wrong with her? This was Ander, not Cas. So why couldn't she stop staring at him? She forced herself back into the room, and then to sit beside him on the sofa.

"Thanks, Skye." She loved the way he said her name. She started wrapping the bandage around his leg so she wouldn't have to look at his face. *It's just because he looks like Cas. Obviously you're going to think he's -* "Skye, I'm scared." She lost her train of thought.

Ander had said that to her just once before, whispered on a staircase in the dark, the very first time her father had taken them to Celine's grave down in the crypt. Cas had stomped off ahead of them, even at eight years old too proud to let anyone know he was scared. Skye had held Ander's hand until they were safely back in the castle courtyard.

She took his hand now, and looked up into his face. Her breath caught in her chest. He was staring back at her as if she were the only light in the pitch black of the night. His face was close to hers, closer than it ought to be; she could count his eyelashes and the see the faint shadow of stubble across his cheeks.

"I'm scared too," she murmured, and she had no idea if he heard because her face was much much too close to his. Her mouth brushed his lips, and when he didn't pull away she kissed him. His mouth fit perfectly across hers, softer than she'd expected.

He was breathing hard when they pulled apart, his lips redder than ever.

"I'm sorry," he said. His cheeks were flushed, the red made his eyes bluer. "I shouldn't have done that. Cas is my brother and I know he has feelings for you."

"He does?" Skye couldn't help the hopeful tone of her voice. *But you just kissed Ander!* An angry voice said in her head. Ander's face crumpled in on itself a little at her words; as if someone had taken a perfect red rose and crushed it in a closed fist.

Ander nodded. He moved away, and something in her chest snapped in half. Cas was her best friend, her most trusted advisor, she'd been in love with him since she was fourteen. She could remember the exact moment she'd realised, her birthday, when he'd kissed her on the cheek for the first time and it had left her heart pounding uncontrollably.

Ander was her story book prince. The lost hero who needed saving. Who always knew the right thing to say. Who admitted when he was scared. Who looked at her like she was the only person on the planet worth seeing.

She loved them both, and she couldn't have either. Her lips tingling, Skye left the room.

Chapter Twenty-seven

Cas stared at his hand; if he held it up to the light he could almost see through it to the other side. It was fascinating and revolting in equal measure. Staring at his hand kept him from worrying about other things; like what Adira was going to do to him. Or what Ander and Skye would have to face at the castle.

His cell was a whitewashed room with only one door. He hadn't tried to open it, he knew it would be useless. Adira was far too cunning to do something as stupid as leave a door unlocked. So he had sat across from it for several hours, watching. Waiting for the moment when Adira heard that the king was back in London, alive and well and on the throne.

The door opened and he braced himself. Adira's anger wouldn't be pretty. She stepped in and smiled at him, her chocolate cake and sugar smile. He was amazed her teeth hadn't rotted away with all the sweetness coming out of her mouth.

"Come on little King," she said, "I want to introduce you to your people."

Cas pushed himself up to his feet. So the news hadn't reached her yet… He felt a moment of relief, and then a surge of fear. Had something happened to Skye and Ander to delay them? He didn't know exactly how long he'd been trapped in here. It would have taken them a while to get back, injured and on tired horses….

He followed her down the corridor, empty aside from the two of them. For a moment, he was tempted to try to overpower her. She was alone after all, and much smaller than him. A painful twinge from his hand and the glint of a blade at her belt stopped him.

"I'll be nice and let you eat before the introductions," Adira said. She had led him to a massive kitchen and handed him a plate of food: thin bread and pale yellow cheese. Cas took it and sat down at a crowded table she chose. He was ravenous and ate the meal in three bites. The skinny boy next to him looked at him with his eyebrows raised. On his other side, Adira took a few delicate bites and then passed the rest over to the boy.

She grinned, and seemed to simmer with energy as she stood and leapt onto the table. No one seemed shocked at this behaviour. In fact they looked up at her expectantly, as if waiting for some prize to be announced.

"Ladies and gentleman, boys and girls," Adira began. Her voice carried well, people even in the farthest corners of the large room were watching her. "I present to you your king! Your Majesty, if you could join me up here please."

Cas hesitated. What if he refused? In his peripheral vision, he could see Seth, standing at one end of the hall. More guards were posted at varying intervals, young men and women with sharp eyes and pressed lips, hands resting on blade hilts. Well, if he was about to die, at least he'd have an audience.

He vaulted up onto the table and stood up straight. *Skye will be pleased,* he thought. She hated slouching.

The crowd was silent for a moment as they stared at him, and then began muttering to each other. Snatches of conversation drifted towards him.

So that's him then, the mighty King…

Arrogant looking fellow isn't he?

He's just a boy…

Adira stared at him, one side of her mouth quirked up in an expectant grin. He had to say something.

"Hello, ladies and gentleman. I am King Cassander. I would really like to help you all but I'm being held here against my will. I will greatly reward anyone who helps me." Cas said. His voice sounded horribly small in the large space. He'd never felt more isolated. The people looked up at him. Not with love. Not with admiration. Certainly not with respect. They started to laugh.

"Oh dear, little boy king." Adira hissed next to him. "Maybe your people aren't as loyal and united as you thought." She raised her voice. "You all know what to do!" Battered plastic buckets had appeared along the tables. Cas couldn't see inside them, but the smell of cheese and bread had been replaced by the sourness of old meat.

Adira moved away from him. She took a bucket from the skinny boy and dipped her hand inside. Entrails dripped from her closed fist, and she lifted her arm to throw it.

It could be worse, Cas thought, *it could be a knife.* He stood as straight as he could and met her brown eyed gaze. He wasn't a coward, and he wasn't ashamed.

She launched her handful. It splattered against his chest and at the same time there was an angry noise like thunder pealing through the sky. His ears rang. Had she tricked him? Thrown something else? The table shuddered, and he almost lost his balance as it tilted to one side. He glanced across and saw Adira looked as surprised as he felt.

The room filled with smoke. The chortles of laughter had disappeared. The crowd was screaming, panicked. People ran out of the hall. The far wall had disappeared, in its place stood a pile of rubble and streams of smoke. Over the wreckage, soldiers appeared. Soldiers in the green uniform of the rebellion.

He recognised none of them. Until he saw her, prowling over the rubble at the head of her army.

Laric.

Cas leapt off the table. He had to get out of there.

"I'll kill you before I let your friends rescue you, little King." Adira was right beside him, her face stained black with soot. Her teeth gleamed whiter than ever.

"They're not here to rescue me," Cas muttered.

An amplified voice blared over the screaming crowd.

"Hand over the King and your lives will be spared."

Adira lifted her eyebrows at him.

"Aren't they?" She scoffed, and took his upper arm in a vice like grip. "Let's get you back to the dungeon shall we?"

"Gladly," Cas said. If he was to be held captive, Adira was preferable to Laric. A plague ridden lion was preferable to Laric really. Adira dragged him through the melee. The people were panicked, but most seemed to have the sense to be heading for the exits. Seth and the other guards had set up defensive line behind a knocked over table, the table top was thick enough to block the soldier's arrows, and they were throwing whatever they could get their hands on back towards Laric's army.

No one seemed to be paying any attention to Cas and Adira. Except one man. He stood in the corner of the room, so still Cas had mistaken him for a shadow. Then he caught the glint of an arrow head, pointed not at him but at Adira. The shadow released its arrow.

He didn't think. He barrelled into Adira, knocking her into the ground. The arrow whistled over his head.

"You saved me." She frowned at him. He rolled off her.

"I'm a nice guy." That had been his best chance at escaping. But he never could have lived with himself if he'd let her die.

He stood and found himself face to face with the shadow. Smoke coloured eyes watched him and he stared back. The shadow appeared ageless; his cheeks were smooth like a young boy, yet his flickering eyes spoke of many harsh years. His expression changed just a fraction, and Cas felt a thrill of fear. The shadow melted away as if he'd never been there.

"Let's go," Adira said, her fingers were warm on his arm as she dragged him along. Cas kept looking back, back to where Laric prowled amongst her troops. He saw it when the shadow flickered next to her and hissed into her ear. He'd never seen her look so delighted.

"New orders," she purred. "Kill the King. He's an imposter!"

"I told you they weren't here to rescue me!" Cas muttered, and leapt to the floor behind a table to avoid a knife thrown at him.

"Is it true?" Adira asked, crouching beside him. The whites of her eyes stood out starkly against her smoke blackened face. "Are you an imposter?"

The table cracked as something heavy was thrown into it- an oversized copper pan.

"I'm not an imposter." It wasn't actually even lying.

"This way," Adira said. She ran in a crouch to the far wall, where Seth had set up the blockade. Adira's guards were running out of things to throw. Still, they had done their job; the hall was now empty of children and the elderly. Cas had no idea where they were hiding, but hoped it was well enforced.

"Adira! She wants him. We should give him up and she'll leave." This came from a swarthy man who poked a dirty finger at Cas' chest.

"And have her in charge instead?! " Adira snarled. "We need him."

"She's right, Anup." Seth joined them, throwing a shard of broken plate over the table in Laric's' direction. It hit the woman next to Laric in the shoulder and her next arrow went wild. "The non-fighters have safely reached the bunkers. We need a plan though. We're outnumbered." His voice was strained and there was blood on his shirt. His own or someone else's, Cas couldn't tell.

"Send two men back to the kitchen. Tell them-" Adira started. Her brother apparently knew what she meant without further explanation.

"Good idea!" Seth beckoned two guards over and gave them a short series of instructions. "Sorry about this," Seth said, and grabbed Cas by the collar, lifting him out of a crouch. He was in clear view of the entirety of Laric's' army, and there were half a dozen arrows pointed at him before he struggled out of Seth's grip and threw himself to the floor. The six arrows embedded themselves in a cluster on the wall behind him.

"We needed a distraction," Seth explained with a shrug and a flash of his annoyingly perfect teeth.

"Stay calm, little King." Adira was still beside him. She wouldn't react kindly to Seth's teeth being knocked out. Cas peered over the table. The two guards had made it unnoticed to the kitchen. They picked up an enormous oil drum- filled with gasoline for the stoves- and set it aflame before rolling it towards Laric.

The shadow man noticed it first as it trundled towards his boss. He pulled Laric out of the way- Cas caught a flash of her Skye coloured green eyes- before they disappeared in an explosion of smoke, flames and bits of the bright blue container. Soldiers scattered and screams filled the air.

"Let's get to the bunker," Adira said. She pulled Cas to his feet.

"Wait. I have news!" The voice, female, came from a slim figure pushing her way through the throng of guards.

Cas blinked. He recognised her uniform instantly, though it was so unexpected it took a moment for the thought to form.

A castle maid.

Chapter Twenty-eight

Cas knew her. She was the same maid who had helped Skye, that day she'd collapsed in the corridor. She was a spy. The maid threw him a cold glance and then returned her attention to Adira.

"The King is safely at the castle, gathering his troops to attack us. This *boy* is an imposter," the maid said.

Before Cas could speak, Adira wrapped her arm around his throat.

"That's two people who've accused you of being an imposter." Her breath was hot against his ear. "And I trust Francesca."

"I am the King," Cas rasped. Adira's arm tightened around his throat, sparks filled the edges of his vision. He was outnumbered; Seth stood in front of him, the maid and the swarthy man, Anup, to either side of Adira.

"Get Laric. I want to talk to her," Adira ordered. Anup nodded, and there was a rustle and a thump as he jumped over the table. Three was better than four. Cas kicked out, and slammed his elbow into Adira's abdomen at the same time. His booted feet connected with Seth's chest and sent him staggering backwards. Adira grunted and her grip went slack for just a moment. It was long enough- Cas slipped away, grabbed the knife off her belt and held it to her throat.

He pulled her backwards, away from Francesca, who watched him with narrowed eyes. Seth clambered back to his feet, breathing hard. The patch of blood on his shirt had grown bigger and his face was white.

"Stay back," Cas ordered. An artery pulsed in Adira's neck. He gripped the knife firmly, but he couldn't bring himself to actually cut into the smooth brown skin.

Adira laughed. Could she see the hesitation in his face?

Francesca launched herself towards him, knocking the three of them to the ground. The knife clattered out of his grip and slid away, coming to rest against the wall. Adira was underneath him, and she smashed her knee into his stomach. Stunned and winded, he did nothing as Seth grabbed his arms in a painful lock and hauled him to his feet.

Laric was approaching, stalking towards him. Smoke stained her hair, but not a strand was out of place. The sight of her made his teeth grind together.

Cas struggled to get out of Seth's grip, but his arms were held in such a way that even moving a centimetre made his joints feel like they were about to break open.

"General, thank you for agreeing to talk. My name is Adira. I wish to discuss the accusations you've made about this boy being an imposter."

"Excellent," Laric said. She stood in front of Cas and looked him up and down, a hunter assessing her catch. Cas had never been this close to her before. The resemblance to Skye made him nauseous. Her left arm was shiny and red, burned by the flames from the oil drum. She didn't seem to care. Poor Ander, Tom may have been a traitor, but this woman was an ice queen. "It is as I suspected. His likeness to the King is extraordinary, but this is the imposter whom Tom Candler has been using as a puppet king for many years."

She said Tom's name like it was a swear word.

"The king maker?" Adira asked. She peered at him as well, as if checking for seams around a mask or traces of makeup.

"Indeed. He makes all the real decisions. He is the true enemy." Laric said. She held her hands clasped behind her back, relaxed and poised as though she weren't in a burning building. What was she playing at? She and Tom probably had some elaborate double cross planned out.

"Adira, she's a liar. I am the real king." Cas said. Whatever Tom and Laric had planned, the causalities from a combined attack on the castle would be enormous. "She's working with Tom, not against him." He kept his voice smooth and even, Adira wouldn't respond well to hysteria.

Laric whirled. Her eyes flashed with hatred. Had Cas been able to, he would have taken a step backwards at the force of her glare.

"I would never work with that *vermin*." Cas frowned at her.

"Tell me the truth then little king. If you're not an imposter, then who's back in London sat on your throne?" Adira asked. She used her sugar voice. Her eyes were big and brown and innocent looking. Was there any harm in telling her the truth at this point? Surely things couldn't get any worse for him.

"He's my brother. My identical twin."

Adira laughed; the sound of sugar sprinkling onto the ground. Cas smiled along with her humourlessly. Seth's grip on his arms was loosening; his hands felt cold and clammy, he was breathing fast, and Cas could feel the back of his own shirt becoming damp with Seth's blood. He'd be easy to overpower. Cas just had to wait for the right moment.

"Identical twins? That's the best you can come up with?" Adira said.

"Conjoined actually." She didn't believe him. Adira was still smiling when she turned to General Laric.

"I have a preposition for you," Laric said. "I say we combine our forces and rid this country once and for all of the unwanted monarchy. It's about time someone cared for the people of this country."

Adira's eyes sparkled: that bald-faced lie was exactly what she wanted to hear. Cas worried that she would kneel down and start kissing the general's feet.

"Seth?" Francesca asked. Cas' captor swayed on the spot, his hands losing their grip. Francesca and Adira both took a step towards them, hands outstretched, but it was too late. Seth dropped to the ground like a stone.

Cas ran. He leapt over the table barricade, towards the wall General Laric's' army had blasted open. The room was filled with so much smoke and debris that no one noticed one more figure darting across.

Laric was close behind him, he could hear the graceful rhythm of her boots on the ground. Eyes streaming from the smoke, Cas reached the wall and breathed the icey smog filled air outside with relief. Some of Laric's' army were still out here, waiting on horseback. Cas ran to the nearest one, shoved the rider off and took his place. He spurred the horse into moving.

"Stop him!" Laric yelled. Her soldiers realised what was going on and sprang into action.

Cas leaned down low over his horse's neck. Arrows whistled past him. His horse made an unnatural screeching noise- an arrow had found the top part of its front leg. It reared up and then collapsed, a heap of muscle and dappled hair. Cas lost his grip on the reigns completely and flew several feet. He twisted in mid-air- he had to protect his head and neck. He slammed into the ground, his shoulder taking the brunt of the impact. Pain shot through his arm.

There was no time to think about it. He rolled to his feet and ran. He couldn't move his arm, it hung uselessly by his side. He shoved his way one handed into the overgrown areas off the side of the road. The horses couldn't follow him there.

He needed somewhere to hide. Unintentionally, he'd followed the path Adira had shown him. Ice End road and the old bridge loomed ahead of him. He glanced back. Soldiers had followed him on foot through the bushes; he could hear them hacking at branches as they got closer to him.

Cas ran under the bridge, skidding to a halt on the half-frozen muddy bank. Now what? He didn't dare look over by the wall- he was sure he would see more frozen bodies, still and staring. The river ran through the middle of the archway, it was narrow enough here that he probably would have called it a stream. Sheets of ice floated along the murky surface, cracked and broken. Shadows flickered on the stone under surface of the bridge. His rapid breaths puffed out in front of him, echoing loudly off the walls, the water and the ice.

Tom had taught him to swim. He'd also dived into the moat to save him when thirteen-year-old Cas had overestimated his own abilities. There was no one to save him this time. *Take chances.*

He held his breath and leapt into the river.

Chapter Twenty-nine

The water was so cold it burned. Tiny knives stabbed every inch of his skin. The current was carrying him fast. Cas forced his eyes open. There was light above him and he kicked towards it. His legs were heavy, his lungs already pleading for air. His head broke the river's surface and he gasped in a lungful of frigid air.

He had to get out. He kicked hard towards the bank but the current was too strong; he barely moved. He sucked in another breath, shook wet hair out of his eyes. He couldn't feel his legs. He scanned the banks. *There.* A tree root had grown so large it was sticking out into the river. Cas twisted slightly and the current drove him right into it; the root collided with his chest so hard it made him wheeze. He fought the urge to close his eyes.

He dragged himself over the tree root, shaking with effort and cold. Dripping water, he collapsed onto the muddy bank. His eyes closed, he forced them open again. If he didn't keep moving he'd freeze. Rigid, open eyed corpses flashed though his mind. He had to move.

The river had carried him at least a mile downstream. With any luck, Laric would assume him dead. He tried to move his arm and winced. Something was wrong; his shoulder jutted out at an alarming angle. He clutched his arm to his side and kept walking. He had to keep walking. His thoughts had turned slushy. He had to keep walking, but he couldn't remember why. He collapsed onto his knees, sinking into mud.

"Can I help you young man?"

Cas looked up at the voice. An old man; he'd been sat by the side of the river, holding an odd looking wooden stick. *Fishing,* Cas' tired brain reminded him. The old man came towards him. He passed out.

Cas could hear the comforting sound of a log fire, the soft crackles of the embers and the whoosh of flames. He was freezing. Someone had removed his wet shirt and wrapped him in an old woollen blanket. He tried to sit up and winced as a spike of pain went through his shoulder.

"Easy there, lad. You've dislocated your shoulder." The old man. Cas was lying on the floor, close to the fireplace, in a small hut. His face was caked in dried mud. The old man watched him from a splintering wooden chair. His skin was wrinkled and leathery with age. His hair had once been dark, Cas thought, like his thick eyebrows, but was now snowy white.

"Thank you for your help," Cas said. He pushed himself up with his good arm. "I really need to get back to London."

"You're half dead lad, you won't make anywhere near to London." The old man said bluntly.

"I'm fine." Cas said. He couldn't help shivering, his teeth chattered together uncontrollably. He wanted to make his point by standing up and walking out, but his legs refused to cooperate.

"My wife will be back soon. She was a doctor a while ago. She'll set your shoulder straight for you. How did you end up in the river anyway?"

Cas shuffled closer to the fire, holding the blanket tightly. Why couldn't he stop shivering?

"It was an accident," he replied, "I was riding too close to the river. My horse went wild and bucked me off." The old man raised his eyebrows. Cas changed the subject. "Thank you for your help, um- sorry I don't know your name."

"Marc Bosc," he replied. "And what's your name?"

"Tom." He said the first name that popped into his head.

"Your parents are big royalists then are they?"

Stupid. He hadn't meant to make the old man think of the castle. Tom was considered a royal. The kingmaker.

"I guess they were," Cas said, "They're dead." The orphan card would stop further questions along that vein. Before the old man could offer him a typical platitude, the door opened and a severe looking woman marched in. She was wrapped in an enormous thick fur coat, which she shrugged off and hung up next to the fireplace to dry. Her hair was dark grey with occasional patches of the original brown of her youth. Faded and wrinkled on the side of her neck was the Tommie's gang tattoo.

"Marta, my dear, we have a visitor." Marc said. He leaned back in his armchair.

"I can see that," his wife replied. She looked at Cas with shrewd brown eyes. "Where did you find him? He looks half drowned." Her accent was foreign, Eastern European maybe.

"By the river. He collapsed in front of me. Dislocated his shoulder."

"Let's see," Marta said, and yanked the blanket off Cas' shoulders. He felt her eyes linger on the scar on his chest, before moving to his shoulder. Her fingers prodded over the malpositioned bones and he bit his lip. "Do you want some whiskey?" she asked. "For the pain?"

Cas was tempted to say yes. Tom had never let him try whiskey. *A king must always be in control of his actions and words.* He shook his head- he had to get back to Skye and Ander as quickly as possible.

"Your loss," Marta said. She placed one hand on his aching shoulder and with her other pulled and rotated his elbow. It felt like she'd shoved a garden rake into this armpit and twisted it around. The fingers of his free hand gripped the blanket so tightly he thought it would rip. The inside of his cheek bled he bit it so hard, but he wouldn't scream. There was a pop, a crunch of bone against bone, and then Marta released him.

He grabbed his shoulder- the bones were no longer jutting out-and let himself breath again. That *hurt*. His eyes watered.

"I need to get to London," he managed to say. His voice wasn't as steady as he would have liked.

"I need a bigger house and a lot more money," Marta replied. She shrugged. She unwrapped a thin scarf from around her neck and fashioned a sling out of it. She was gentle when she manoeuvred his arm into it.

"Please. It's a matter of life and death."

Her eyes flickered down to his scar again. Did she know? How could she possibly know? She glanced at her husband, who gave her the slightest of nods.

"We have a horse. He's old but he's fast."

"Thank you! I'll pay you back, I promise." Cas leapt to his feet. Or he tried to; it was more of a slow edging up the wall until he was upright.

"You should regain your strength first," Mark said. Cas spotted his jumper, hanging over the back of a chair and pulled it over his head one handed. It was too painful to try and get his injured arm into the sleeve, so his left arm stayed in the sling, creating an awkward bulge in the fabric.

"Where's the horse?" He didn't have time to argue with them. He'd make it to London. He had to.

"Out in the shed," Marta said. "She's ready to go."

"I won't forget this," Cas said, walking to the door. He shivered slightly as soon as he moved away from the fire.

"For God's sake. Take this." Marta threw her thick coat over his shoulders. "Get out of here before we change our minds about letting you go."

Cas nodded and opened the door. He had to force himself to take the first few steps into the cold. The wind whistled in his ears, and he wasn't sure if he imagined Marc's final words.

"Good luck, Your Majesty."

Chapter Thirty

Ander woke up with a start and sat bolt upright, damp with sweat. The edge of his dream lingered- a castle on fire, smoke staining the sky- and it took a minute for his breathing to settle. He was still on the sofa- he must have passed out after Skye left. *Skye.* He could still taste the sweetness of her lips, still see the look of horror on her face when he'd told her Cas had feelings for her. Ander was sure there was a special place in hell for people like him; who kissed their brother's girlfriends whilst said brother was being held hostage.

He had to get Cas back. Then he'd teach himself to be happy for his brother. Ander rubbed his face with his hands. It didn't help, he could still feel it, the ghost of her lips on his, the heat from her flushed cheek against his face.

Someone rapped politely on the door.

"Come in," Ander called. His leg hurt too much for him to want to get up and check who it was. What if it was Skye? He wasn't sure what he'd do if he saw her.

A spikey haired young man stood at the door. They'd never met, but Ander knew this was Cas' personal assistant, Tae. He looked even younger than he did in his file photo.

"You're wanted in the throne room, Your Majesty."

"I'll be right there," Ander said. Tae nodded and shut the door again. What a polite young man. If Ander overslept at rebellion headquarters, a junior recruit would have been tasked with pouring a bucket of ice cold water over his head.

He needed a change of clothes; these ones were blood stained and filthy. He hopped to the walk in closet and picked black trousers and a black jumper. Black was an intimidating colour. He re-tied the bandage around his thigh, awkwardly pulled the clean trousers on and had just tugged his T-shirt off when Skye walked in.

He wasn't normally shy, but the way Skye stared at his chest made blood rush to his cheeks. Her eyes were red rimmed; either she'd been crying or hadn't slept at all. Or both.

"It's a mirror image," Skye said.

"What?" He was surprised his voice didn't croak.

"Your scar. It's not identical to Cas'. It's a mirror image, a reflection." She reached forward as if to trace its outline, but her hand dropped like a stone before she touched him. Ander quickly pulled the clean T-shirt over his head. Would she ever look at him without seeing Cas? Would anyone? "How's your leg?"

"It's getting better." If she didn't mention the kiss, he wasn't going to either. "We need to get to the throne room."

Skye nodded, and followed him out into the corridor. They walked side by side. Ander was hyper aware of the distance between them; a few centimetres of air felt like a metre of concrete. His fingers itched to hold hers.

"I still haven't been to speak to my father," she said. She didn't look at him, but stared straight ahead of them towards the end of the corridor.

"One crisis at a time," Ander replied. "I can't promise it will be easy to deal with Tom once Cas is safe, but it will be easier."

The corner of her mouth crept upwards in the hint of a smile. She still didn't look at him. It was a relief to reach the throne room and be ushered to the podium at the front, where Orla stood waiting.

"Your Majesty," she said, "The troops are ready to be deployed at your command."

"Good." Ander turned to Tae, who'd appeared as if by magic at his side. "Ready my horse. I'm leading the soldiers to Nottingham. Skye will be my regent whilst I'm gone."

Cold fingers grasped his upper arm.

"I'm coming with you," Skye said. Her green eyes met his, her lips pressed into a thin line. Never had she looked so much like Laric; fierce and beautiful all at once. He should order her to stay behind; her illness would slow them down, would put her and others at risk. But she'd never listen, and he'd rather have her by his side than sneaking along behind.

"Fine," Ander said, "Shafiq will remain behind as regent."

"Your horse is already ready, Your Majesty." Tae said, and gestured for them to follow him. Efficient and polite, Ander thought, this guy deserves a promotion.

In the courtyard, the army had assembled. They were an impressive sight, all stood to order in neat little rows. There weren't nearly enough of them though. Ander had always thought the royalists would win against the rebellion through sheer numbers. He suspected he'd been wrong.

Two horses awaited them, saddled and bridled. Skye leapt onto hers like an athlete, graceful and quick. Ander clambered onto his like a ton of bricks. He stared out at the ranks of soldiers. This was when he was meant to make some inspiring speech, about honour and bravery. He didn't feel honourable or brave, and instead simply nodded at the gathered army. He didn't have to turn to know that they were following him.

Word of the planned attack had spread fast, the London streets were busier than Ander had ever seen them. People had braved the smog and the cold to watch the soldiers pass.

"Long live the King!" An elderly woman shouted as they passed.

Not everyone was so complimentary. Several people tried to spit at him. He didn't envy Cas. Training in the rebellion had been hard but he'd been judged fairly, rewarded for his triumphs and punished when he should have tried harder. These people blamed Cas for everything.

"How does Cas put up with this?" Ander muttered. His jaw ached from forcing himself to smile at the public.

"Cas is-" Skye said, and hesitated. Brave? Selfless? Amazing? "Clueless." It was the first negative thing he'd ever heard her say about his brother.

"What?" She'd always worshipped the very ground Cas walked on.

"I adore Cas, you know that." She swallowed and a pink tinge appeared along her cheeks. She looked up at him. "He's an optimist. He only ever sees good. Maybe it's my father's fault; keeping him sheltered all these years."

"I thought that, when I first arrived," Ander admitted. "But he surprised me. You know he's been sneaking out of the castle, hanging out with gang leaders, trying to find a cure for you?" He thought she'd be delighted, instead she frowned.

"See, that's exactly what I mean. He can't ever imagine things not turning out well. What if there isn't a cure? What if Laric wins? What if you hadn't stopped trying to kill him? Cas still thinks like a little boy- that good will always win."

"He'd be a pretty crappy king if he didn't think he could well for his people."

"I know." She sighed. "I just want him back."

Ander nodded. Her horse was close enough to his that he could have reached out to touch her. He kept his hands carefully on his reigns. Cas and Skye would get their happy ending. He'd make sure of it.

"Ander, look!" He jerked his head upwards and saw a figure on horseback. The figure was bundled in fur, a hood covering his face. "It's Cas, I know it." Skye shot forwards before he could reply.

Ander forced himself to wait before following her. He held his hand up, stopping the army behind him. Tae galloped forwards for instructions.

"Wait here," Ander said, "I don't want to spook this guy. He might have information we need."

Tae nodded his head in assent, though his eyes darted towards Skye in concern. Ander spurred his horse forwards, towards the lone rider, who'd stopped his horse and clambered down. It was Cas; pale and shivering, but the flash of his blue eyes was unmistakable.

Ander slowed his horse and watched Skye approach Cas. She leapt down from her horse, her chest rising and falling rapidly, and into Cas' side. Cas hugged her with one arm and kissed the top of her head. Skye lifted her face to Cas'. Ander's heart stopped, cramped painfully in his chest. Their faces were so close together… what if?

Skye buried her head in Cas' shoulder. Ander let relief wash over him as he approached. Cas looked awful; smoke stained and dirty; his left arm tucked limply by his side.

Even so, Ander's head began to pound. He stopped five feet away and didn't dare get any closer.

"We've got to get the army back to defend the castle." Cas said. "Laric and Adira have combined forces and they're on their way." The rebellion alone would have outnumbered them. This was not good news.

"Are you OK?" Ander asked. His own words came as a surprise. He wasn't usually the sentimental type.

"My shoulder hurts and I really need a hot bath." Cas said, "But yeah, I'm OK."

"Good." Ander said, even as his headache intensified. "Keep your hood up. Stay at the back. I'll lead."

Cas nodded.

"It suits you," Cas said.

"What?"

"Being king."

Chapter Thirty-one

Cas is back. Cas is safe. Skye repeated the words in her head over and over again until she could let go of Cas and not worry that he'd disappear.

"How did you get away?" she asked. They were lagging behind the army, which Ander was leading at break neck speed. Skye could see him, a lonely figure right at the front. He'd told them an attack was imminent.

"Laric attacked- I think she thought I was Ander- I got away in the confusion." His teeth chattered when he spoke. The skin on his one exposed hand holding the reigns was a nasty shade of blue grey.

"Cas, I," she started. I, what? *I kissed Ander. I love you both. I let my father be locked up. I'm afraid my mother is a monster. I wish you'd be more careful.* "I'm glad you're back."

"What, no lecture?" He smiled at her.

"No lecture." She took his ice cold hand. There was no awkwardness; it was effortless like holding her father's hand when she'd been a small child. "Dad's been thrown in jail."

"I'm sorry." The brightness of his eyes dulled. "I mentioned him to Laric you know. She's a great actress- really has the 'I hate Tom' thing down." He stared at her, "You look like her."

Skye felt the tiniest thrill of pride. She looked like her mother! Cas let go of her hand to pull his cloak more tightly across his shoulders. He hadn't stopped shivering.

"We need to get you warmed up, Cas." The castle wasn't far now.

"I know." His breath rose in a puff of white in front of his face. "Jumping in the river in the middle of winter wasn't one of my better ideas."

"I'm not even going to ask," Skye said.

"That's a shame, cause it's a riveting tale of heroism and bravery."

"I expect nothing less." His chest puffed out at the compliment.

"We're almost there, Skye. I'll take the secret passage through the crypts in."

"I'm coming with you," Skye said immediately. She couldn't bear to have him out of her sight. Besides, he looked as though he might collapse.

"Someone might notice you're-"

"I'm coming."

"Fine. Come on then." He jumped down from his horse and waited to help Skye down. She took his hand and slipped down. After an encouraging pat on their backsides, the two horses continued to follow the army in the distance.

The secret passage was hidden at the base of a large oak tree. She'd only been through it once before, when Cas had first told her about it. Then, she'd been giddy with excitement; Cas had trusted her with the secret, and the two of them had been alone in the dark tunnel. That had been before she'd gotten sick, before Ander, before her father's betrayal.

The damp cold air made her breathless.

"I told you shouldn't come this way," Cas said, "It's too dusty." His voice echoed oddly in the tunnel before being swallowed up by the damp walls. He stopped walking and slipped his arm across her back, supporting her.

Tiny streams of light filtered in from the roof. She could see the outline of his face, the shape of his chin, the slight curl of his hair. She knew exactly where his mouth was; that his lips would be pressed firmly together, because that's how he looked every time he was worried about her. If she tilted her head up, and turned ever so slightly, she could kiss him. *He's never going to notice* Ander's voice said in her head. *He has feelings for you.* And then Ander's anguished face popped into her mind.

"I'm OK," she said, "Let's go."

Cas didn't let go of her, and led them at a slow place through the crypt and up the stairs. Skye popped her head out of the door and checked the corridor was empty, then nodded at Cas to follow her. Her breathing had returned to normal, and she tried to pull away from him.

"Don't," he said, "You're warm." His face was grey under the hood.

"I'm not your personal walking heater." She stayed close to him until they reached his room and he collapsed onto the sofa. The fire was already lit and she topped it off before going into the closet to find him clean, warm clothes. She chose black, to match Ander.

"Here," she said, and tossed the pile of clothes at him. Already, colour had returned to his skin.

"Thanks." He pulled his jumper off and tossed it to one side. He winced as he took his arm out of the sling underneath.

"Fell off a horse," he explained. He got his arm into the clean top with gritted teeth. Skye retied the sling around his neck. Her fingers paused there for a moment, the soft patch of skin between his hairline and the top of his collar. There was a knock on the door and she dropped her hands to her sides. She was uncomfortably warm.

"Come in," Cas called.

"We don't have much time," Ander said, walking in. "Scouts have spotted Laric and Adira; they're just North of the river, heading towards us."

When he spoke, Ander stared at the patch of air in between Skye and Cas. He blinked rapidly; his fists were clenched by his side. The chip was working again.

"We need to-"

Tae came into the room without knocking. That was unusual for him, as was his dishevelled hair and breathlessness. His hand remained on the door knob and his jaw dropped open as he took in the sight of both twins. Ander dragged him into the room and shut the door.

"Your Majesty," he said. He kept glancing between the twins, obviously confused about who to address. "Tom has an urgent message for you, he said it's very important."

Cas stood up. He looked at Tae. Skye flinched at his expression. She'd never seen Cas look like that. Ruthless. Powerful.

"Don't breathe a word of this to anyone," he said. Tae nodded, his eyes wide. Tiny beads of perspiration broke out on his forehead. "Thank you for delivering the message. You may go," Cas said in his normal voice. He clasped Tae on the shoulder and the assistant left.

"What?" Cas asked, because Skye was still staring at him.

"You're a scary bastard, that's what," Ander answered. Skye glanced at him gratefully but his eyes slid quickly away.

Cas shook his head.

"One of us should go see what Tom wants," he said. He didn't look like he was about to volunteer.

"I'll go." Skye said. She'd put off the conversation with her father for long enough. She had to know.

"Good, that's probably for the best. You'll be safe down in the dungeons," Cas said. For just a moment he gave her the crooked grin, and her heart fluttered. Then, Ander was next to her. He squeezed her hand with cold fingers.

"Stay safe," he whispered, and kissed her cheek. His lips were as soft as she remembered. He opened the door for her.

"You too," she said to both of them and stepped out into the corridor. It was an odd feeling, walking down a corridor she'd known all her life and feeling more terrified with every step she took. Around every corner she expected to see soldiers. As she passed windows she expected an arrow to come flying through and sink into her chest. And every step brought her closer to her father, the liar, who might finally tell her the truth.

She met no one until she reached the old stone steps leading to the dungeon.

"He's been asking for you Miss Skye," said Harry. The prison warden had been standing guard at the dungeon steps since before Skye could remember, and he was now as gnarled and withered as the oak branch he was using as a walking stick. His green eyed gaze was clear and he looked at her with sympathy. Skye didn't smile back. Harry was old enough to remember her mother; he probably knew the truth. It dawned on her that all the adults in the castle had been lying to her for all her life.

She stepped past him and made her way down the steps. She took measured breaths, watching them mist in front of her. Maybe that happened inside her chest as well, and her lungs were clogged with icey white haze.

Her father was the only one in the dungeon. He sat at the back of his cell, leaning against the wall. He looked thinner than she remembered, his hair tangled. He looked up at the sound of her footsteps and stood up, his face close to the iron bars.

She stood far enough away that he couldn't reach out and touch her.

"Skye," he said. There was no emotion in his voice when he spoke. There hardly ever was. He could have been calling for his dog.

"What did you have to tell us?" Maybe she could be as cold as he was. It had to be in her genes after all.

His eyes flickered but his tone didn't change.

"Laric. You have to tell the boys: she knows the secret passageways. All of them. They need to post guards."

She looked at him with disgust. He was still lying. Still pretending to care.

"Why bother?" she snarled. "You've probably already told her to expect guards. Why are you still lying, Dad?"

"Skye," Finally there was a hint of something in his voice. Desperation? Pleading? He held on to the bars. His fingers were bone white.

"How could you betray them like this? And me?"

"I didn't. I would never. Certainly not for *her*." Some barrier had snapped. He sounded angry and regretful and bitter.

"*Her?* She's my mother! At least admit that much!"

He looked back at her like she'd sprouted wings and tentacles. He stared at her for a moment, then spoke,

"She's not your mother, Skye. If you don't believe anything else, believe this."

"I don't believe anything you say. You've li-"

Someone grabbed her from behind. Thin, long fingers wrapped around her mouth, cutting off the rest of her sentence. She was dragged backwards. Her attacker smelt of perfume, sweet and musky. A female. She struggled but the woman's grip was like a vice, and Skye had to stop to catch her breath. It was even harder when she could only breathe through her nose.

"Let go of her." She heard her father's voice. It shook.

"I don't think so, Tommy." The voice of her captor purred. Laric. It had to be. "Killing your daughter would be the perfect revenge."

Cold metal pressed against her throat. Skye felt the sharp sting of a blade and screamed.

Chapter Thirty-two

"Do you want to wear the disguise or shall I?" Cas asked.

"Forget it," Ander said. "People will only see what they expect too, just put your hood up."

"You're probably right." Cas reached up with his good arm and pulled his hood low over his face. He'd finally stopped shivering, though his whole body ached like he was recovering from a bad bout of flu. "We need to get going."

"Yeah." Ander reached into his pocket and pulled out the box of pills Dr Bonnington had given him. He swallowed two. "To your health, brother," he said, washing them down with a cupful of water.

Cas wasn't sure that was a good idea, but it was too late to argue the point so he just pulled the door open and they set off down the corridor at a jog. Orla would be waiting for him in the throne room, ready to give the army final instructions. That's where they needed to head.

"Wait, Cas," Ander pulled him to a stop. "Look." He turned him to stare out of the stained glass window. Soldiers had filled the courtyard; knives flashed, arrows flew, fists connected with flesh. The coloured glass Cas was looking through turned everything red.

"We need to get down there," Cas said, and turned to go.

Ander held him back.

"No." His words came out slurred. His eyelids drooped. "She's not there. She never arrives after her army. Never."

There was no doubt that *she* referred to Laric. Ander was right, she was distinctive in a crowd and he couldn't see her. Where the hell was she?

Ander rubbed his eyes with his hands. What had those drugs had done to him?

"She's gone to the dungeon, Cas. I'm sure." Cas stared at his brother. His chest rose and fell steadily as if he were just about to fall asleep. His grip was still vice-like on Cas' forearm. "She wants Tom." Ander said.

"Ok, let's go." If Ander was wrong, he'd just abandoned his army, his people… but if Ander was right, Skye could be in serious trouble. He ran, and Ander stumbled along next to him like a drunk.

He found Harry unconscious at the top of the dungeon steps. The old man was bleeding from a gash in his temple, but there was a strong pulse at his wrist.

"She's here," Cas said. *Skye.* He took the stairs down two at a time, sending little pieces of stone flying off the crumpling steps. He stumbled near the bottom and half fell, half jumped to the ground. He sprang to his feet. His breath caught in his throat.

Skye's face looked up at him, white in the dim lighting. General Laric held her in a headlock, a knife to her throat. It was startling to see them together; as if someone had held up a slightly distorted mirror next to Skye's face.

Behind them, in the cell, Tom pulled on the metal bars as though he could break them with his bare hands.

A knife pressed into Cas' side. Laric hadn't come alone.

"Why, hello little King." Adira. She narrowed her big brown eyes at him. "Or are you the imposter?"

Where was Ander? He'd been just behind him on the stairs. He hoped his brother had a plan. Cas' mind had gone blank. He ignored Adira and addressed himself to Laric.

"You can take Tom. Just let Skye go," Laric laughed. She laughed so hard her hands shook and the knife bit into Skye's neck. A bright red drop appeared on Skye's skin. He forgot about Adira's knife. It scraped across his skin as he tried to rush forwards. Adira grabbed him, this time with the knife at his neck, and he was forced to stop. Skye's eyes widened across the room. There was a white hot line of pain across his stomach where the knife had cut him, but it was shallow.

"Have you not taught this boy anything? So much talent wasted." Laric looked at Tom when she said this. At that moment, Cas could have killed her with no remorse.

"Let her go, Sophie. Please. You can do anything you want to me." His expression was blank. His eyes had dulled to the colour of ditch water.

"Cas!" Adira was distracted by Ander's voice. She turned her head towards the noise and it was enough for Cas to break free, shoving her to the ground. Simultaneously, a small stone flew like a bullet into Laric's temple. It startled her enough to release her grip. Cas darted forwards and grabbed Skye, pulling her back with him. He reached for the knife in his belt and held it out in front of them. Ander held his own knife up on Skye's other side.

The three of them stood facing Laric, who grinned, and Adira who picked herself up off the floor looking annoyed. Cas glanced down at the cut across his abdomen, making sure it had stopped bleeding.

"See? I raised the cleverer twin." Laric said to Tom. The woman was insane.

"Twin? But I thought you said-" Adira's eyes narrowed. Laric had lied to her and she was starting to figure it out.

"Either way the monarchy needs to be abolished. Both these boys are pretenders to the throne." Laric cut Adira off with a pressed lip smile. She looked at Ander. "Ander, my perfect little soldier. You've delayed this long enough. Kill the boy and we will take our rightful place in the castle."

"We? I'm not your puppet anymore." Ander glared at her, raised his knife. He wasn't slurring his words any longer. She watched him with her head cocked to one side. Cas watched Adira, she was getting angrier by the second.

"Remember, this is all for your own good." Laric said. "Kill the usurper." She said the phrase precisely, over pronouncing every syllable like it was some kind of password.

Ander stiffened. His eyes glazed over. He pushed Skye to one side without a word. Once, years ago, Cas had visited a farm in the south. The farmer owned a fluffy golden haired dog. Cas had enjoyed playing fetch with it, until the farmer had spotted a fox in the field and ordered the dog to attack. Cas' four legged friend had turned into a monster. That was what Ander looked like now.

"Ander?"

His brother didn't respond. Cas wasn't sure he could hear him. He backed away as far as he could.

"What have you done to him?" He heard Adira ask.

"Years of conditioning. Along with the chip. He won't stop until Cas is dead." Laric sounded eager. Cas didn't dare take his eyes off Ander to look at either of them.

The rough stone wall was cold behind him. He had nowhere to run.

"Ander, please."

Ander lifted the knife and stabbed down. Cas ducked out of the way. The knife scraped along the rock wall; the noise made his hands tingle unpleasantly. Skye screamed: he had to protect her. He thought he saw Laric reach for her, but they were lost from view as Ander grabbed him by the arm and threw him to the floor. He clutched his injured shoulder in agony, and forced himself to roll to his feet.

Ander had lost his knife. His empty hands were clenched into fists, one of which came flying towards Cas' jaw. He side stepped and held up his own knife, hoping it would scare Ander off. His brother didn't notice. Cas kicked at Ander's injured leg, but Ander grabbed his foot before it connected.

Cas stared up at the ceiling, the back of his head throbbing.

Ander's face swam above him. His brother's fingers wrapped around his throat. The edges of Cas' vision faded. The knife was still clenched in his sweaty grip- he could save himself. Could he hurt Ander enough to disable him without killing him? Could he even bring himself to do it? He couldn't see anything but darkness.

His brother's weight pressed down on him; he couldn't get enough air into his chest. He could feel Ander's heart pounding alongside his own. He had a bizarre thought; if their scars lined up, would they join together again?

Far away, a girl screamed. *Skye*. Cas lifted the knife and sunk it into the soft flesh in between his brother's ribs.

Chapter Thirty-three

"Grab the girl," Laric ordered. Adira twisted Skye's arm behind her back. Ander had acted as though he hadn't even recognised her. Now he had Cas pinned to the ground by the throat.

"If we're to continue working together, I want answers," Adira said. There was anger in her voice. She didn't like people being controlled, that was obvious.

"Isn't it obvious? Laric wants power. That's all she's ever wanted. She'll betray you like she betrayed us." Skye spoke quickly. She couldn't take her eyes of the twins on the ground. Cas was about to lose consciousness. Ander looked empty.

"I didn't ask your opinion." Adira twisted her arms further. Skye screamed.

Across the room, Cas clambered to his feet. The knife clasped in his shaking hand was coated in blood. Ander, sprawled on the ground, didn't move. Bile rose at the back of Skye's throat. She'd never seen that look on Cas' face before; as if some dead thing had climbed into his skull and was looking out through his eyes.

"I'll kill you myself!" Laric screamed. Her composure vanished. She clawed at Cas' face like an animal. "You killed him!" Her nails left angry red lines on his cheek.

Cas dropped to his knees, as if he didn't care whether he lived or died. His knife fell out of his grip. Laric reached for it but Adira got there first.

"Skye!" Her father's voice. "Let me out." She was free, Adira had released her. She followed her father's instructions without thinking, tossing him the key from where it hung by the staircase. "See to Ander!" He ordered, fumbling with the lock.

Ander. She ran to his side. He was breathing, short shallow gasps. There was a rush of blood to her brain; Skye could think again. She pressed her hands to the wound in his side, trying to stop the blood flow. He groaned but remained unconscious.

"He's alive," she said. Tom and Laric were circling each other and didn't seem to hear her. Knife in hand, Adira watched them. Who's side was she on now? Cas crawled next to Skye and held his brother's hand.

"Give up Sophie," Tom said.

"I will never give up. Not after what you did." Laric replied. She pounced on him, her open palm jabbing upwards at his chin. He spat blood out of his mouth and threw a punch at her temple. She ducked and came up behind him, kicking with a booted foot. He grabbed her leg and threw her onto the floor. She rolled up again, kneeing him in the stomach.

It was like watching Cas and Ander fight that first time in the stadium: two people who had sparred so often they knew the other's moves before they'd even made them. They moved in the same way, fluid and agile.

"You can hate me all you want. How could you do this to them?" Tom was angry. *Never fight angry. You'll make mistakes.* That was the golden rule he'd taught her.

"I'm making Ander a king!" Laric punched him in the stomach.

"You made him a murderer!" Tom blocked the jab aimed at his ear.

"He's the one lying there with a stab wound, half dead!" Spit flew out of Laric's' mouth. She was angry too. Upset. In her own weird way, she cared about Ander. Skye was sure.

"Ignore me," she whispered into Cas' ear, for he was still moving as though in a trance. He nodded, his blue eyes wide and watery.

"He's dead!" Skye wailed. Tom flinched, but Laric seemed to implode.

"You take everything from me!" She shrieked. She became a wild woman. She showered Tom in punches, opening a cut along his cheek and making his nose bleed. She forgot to keep her guard up. His next swing caught her in the temple and she dropped like a stone.

The room was quiet. Adira handed Tom the knife and stepped back. He stood over Laric, the knife gripped loosely in his hand. Blood dripped from his face onto the ground; the noise was almost deafening. Shadows flickered behind his eyes. He threw the knife to one side.

"You, go get some help." Tom pointed to Adira. She looked at his bloody face, at Laric unconscious on the ground, the pool of blood and Ander's side. She nodded and marched up the stairs. "Skye, are you sure he's-" Tom choked on the words.

"He's alive," Skye replied. "I said it to distract her."

"We should kill her," Cas said. His voice was low; his eyes still dead.

"Cas, I'm sorry, I can't." Tom said. *Can we ever really hate the people we once loved?*

"Cas, she's my-"

"For the last time, she is not your mother." Tom said. His eyes softened as he looked at Skye and Cas, and then at the woman on the ground. "She's my sister."

Chapter Thirty-four

Years earlier

"Sophie, please can I come too?"

"No Tommy, you're too little." Sophie zipped up her hoodie. She pulled on fingerless gloves she'd fashioned for herself. The ruins would be cold, but she still needed to be able to climb.

"I'm only one year younger than you!"

"It's dangerous Tommy. When you're as big as me and Ken then you can come." Ken was her best friend. It didn't matter that she was the gardener's daughter and he was the King's son- they were inseparable.

"Are you ready?" Ken asked, sauntering into the room. He could never just walk.

"Are you?" His skinny limbs were poking out of a baggy T-shirt and shorts. Even inside, she could see goose bumps on his pale skin.

"I'm toughening myself up. A little cold never hurt anyone."

Tom nudged her with his elbow.

"I might not be as big as him, but at least I'm not as stupid!"

"I heard that!" Ken glared in her brother's direction.

Sophie frowned and pulled Tom out from where he'd hidden behind her legs.

"It is pretty stupid."

"Fine, but when I die in battle cause I was too busy shivering, I'll only have you two to blame." Ken pulled the jumper she offered him over his head.

"And when you don't die of pneumonia, you'll have us to thank." She threw her arm around his shoulders. "I'll happily accept a knighthood."

Ken clambered to his feet and punched Tom in the arm. Lean where Ken was stocky, at some point in the last year Tom had grown taller than the prince. Sophie had to look up at both of them. Still when they sparred, she *always* won. Her little brother was too predictable, and Ken was too slow.

"Come on Sophie," Ken called. "Now that your brother has tired me out you might actually have a chance to beat me."

"Making excuses already are we?"

Ken grinned at her as she faced him in the arena. Her stomach clenched in an oddly pleasurable way. That had been happening a lot around Ken lately.

"Ready. Set," Tom counted them in. "Fight!"

Ken leapt at her. His bigger weight almost sent her toppling to the ground, but she side stepped and placed her hip in exactly the right place to catch him in the stomach and double him over. Then it was easy to flip him and pin him underneath her, her forearm pressed against his throat.

Her face was close to his. His eyes were blue; she could see herself reflected in them as if they were the clear waters the Highland lakes they visited every spring. His upper lip was swollen, bruised from an earlier fight. What would it feel like to touch? Her heart raced.

"And Sophie wins…. Again!" Tom said. Sophie leapt up. She'd forgotten her brother was even there.

"One day…" Ken said. Were his cheeks a little flushed too? It was probably from the exercise. She had to pull herself together! He was her friend, her best friend, but that was all. "I'm gonna beat you." He took her hand and pulled himself to his feet. His face was close to hers again. She swallowed hard.

"I doubt that." Tom. She took a step backwards, let out a breath she hadn't realised she'd been holding. Tom caught her eye, looking worried.

"You can't beat her either," Ken said. He wiped his forehead with his sleeve. "Go on, it's your turn."

"Tomorrow. I forgot, Sophie, Dad wants to see us." Tom took her by the elbow and escorted her out of the training room. As soon as they were out of earshot, he pulled her to face him. "What are you doing?"

"Nothing! What's your problem?"

"Sophie, I can see the way you look at him! He's never going to notice."

"I don't know what you're talking about." Sophie was a good liar, the words came out smoothly. But her brother knew her too well.

"He's the Prince, Soph. He can have anyone he chooses."

"So what, I'm not good enough for him?"

"No that's not what I mean." Tom sighed. "I just don't want you to get hurt."

"Mind your own business, Tommy." She shoved his hand off her shoulder and stormed away.

"Sophie," Ken called. Sophie shut the door behind herself and sat beside him on the sofa. He took her hand. Her heart raced- it always did when he touched her. Even with blood shot eyes he looked handsome in his black suit and tie. "I still don't believe father is really gone."

Sophie said nothing. Ken needed her to listen. He rested his head against hers; his over long hair tickled her cheeks. It was painful to be this close to him; she felt the heat of his skin as though it was a blazing furnace.

"I'm so glad you're here Sophie." He lifted his head. She fell into his lake blue eyes easily. He was so close. And moving closer. His hand was warm around the back of her neck and the side of her face. His mouth pressed against hers. His lips tasted of the sugared cakes they'd been serving at the funeral.

She'd imagined this moment over and over in her mind. He'd never been crying, but otherwise it was… *perfect.*

"Sorry. I don't know what came over me." He mumbled and pulled away. Sophie couldn't speak.

The door burst open. Tom walked in, the top button of his shirt undone and his tie loosened. There was lipstick on his cheek.

"Are you guys OK?" He shoved himself in between them on the sofa and didn't wait for an answer. "I only just managed to get away from your crazy Aunt Sanchia. She kept pinching my cheeks and telling me how handsome I was. Funerals make people do all sorts of crazy things." His words clung to the air like icicles on an winter morning.

"Who is this guy anyway?" Sophie asked. She pulled at the collar of her uniform. It was stiff and scratchy and she resented being made to wear it.

"For the last time, the ambassador from France." Ken frowned at her. "Stand up straight!" He sat primly on his throne. Sophie stood to his right hand side as was expected from the captain of the guard.

She rolled her eyes, longing for the days when it had been just her and Ken, exploring the castle. Now they spent all their time in meetings and writing agendas. Neither of them had ever mentioned the kiss again, though Sophie thought about it often.

Ken's advisors were telling him to get married. The thought made her feel sick. This ambassador from France was probably here on behalf of some French Princess or Duchess or noblewoman.

Sophie snapped to attention as the hall doors were pulled open. The ambassador entered at the head of an elaborately dressed entourage and Ken gasped. His pupils dilated, his mouth hung open, Sophie could practically see the drool dribbling down his chin.

Stood before them was the most beautiful woman Sophie had ever seen. Her hair, thick and smooth, curled around her head like a crown. Her features were slender and delicate; her eyes shone like emeralds. When she smiled her teeth sparkled- she was young, likely not yet out of her teens.

"Greetings from France. I'm ambassador Cirrcadi. Please call me Celine."

Sophie reached for her spare saddle, inhaling deeply before tucking it under her arm. She liked the smell of leather. A ride would help clear her head. And keep her away from Celine. She was a nice enough girl, but the way Ken looked at her, the change in his voice when he said her name, made Sophie want to- *stay calm,* she told herself. She uncurled her fingers.

Voices approached the stable and Sophie ducked behind the partition. She didn't want to speak to anyone right now.

"I'm the King- I really shouldn't have to carry your stuff."

"As my King, you should make sure all your horses are sane and well trained. You poorly trained horse led to what I'm fairly sure is a broken arm." Tom. Had he hurt himself?

"You tried to jump an 8 foot brick wall." Ken sounded angry, and Sophie heard a pile of equipment clatter to the ground. She half stepped forward.

"If you're mad at Sophie, you just need to tell her." Tom's voice, low and soothing. "We both know that's what's really bothering you."

Sophie stayed behind the partition. If she squinted, she could make out the boys through the gap between the wooden panels. Ken threw himself down onto a hay bale.

"I just don't understand why she won't even give Celine a chance," Ken said. Tom, holding his left arm in his right, sat down beside him. "I honestly think they'd get on. But Sophie is just so cold all the time. Celine's really making an effort and all she's getting is the death glare."

That was unfair! Sophie had been perfectly civil. She just didn't like the French girl. Ken wasn't finished.

"I just really need them to get on. Because I think I'm in love with Celine. I'm gonna ask her to marry me. Sophie's my best friend, I want her to approve."

Blood trickled down Sophie's wrists from where her fingernails had dug into her palms. Silent tears dripped down her cheeks.

"Oh." Tom said. In the gloom, through the narrow gap, she couldn't tell if he was smiling. "You really have no idea."

"No idea about what?"

Don't tell him. Please. She wanted to move forwards, make a noise, stop this conversation, but she had frozen.

"Sophie loves you."

There it was. The truth. Sophie had known it for years, but she'd never said it out loud before, not even to herself. And now her brother had painted it bold and bright for Ken to see. Blood was rushing so loudly in her ears she almost missed his response.

"Well of course, you know I love her too. That's exactly why-" Tom shook his head. *He'll never notice.* It was spelled out in front of him and Ken still didn't see it.

"That's not what I mean. Sophie *loves* you."

She saw light glint off Ken's enlarged pupils.

"She-? But she never, I don't understand. How do you know?" There was a creak in his voice, a tear, like what was happening in her chest right now.

"It's obvious. She stares at you. Her face flushes every time you touch her, even just a pat on the back of her hand." Her brother's expression was still hidden the gloom. "I warned her not to fall in love with a king, and she did it anyway." He was angry? It's not like she had a choice.

"We kissed once," Ken admitted. "But she never said anything, I thought she'd only done it to comfort me."

Sophie's heart leapt. He remembered the kiss!

"Do you love her?"

Ken was silent for a long moment. His head was bent down, his face shadowed.

"Not like that. When I'm with Celine, I feel alive. With Sophie, I feel safe." He sighed. Sophie wished she could see his face clearly. "I could marry Sophie. We'd be happy." Did he sound wistful or sad? But he wanted to marry her? A bubble grew in Sophie's chest. She would have flown right up to the ceiling had she not been holding onto the wooden beams, her face pressed against the crack.

Then her brother drove a knife through her heart.

"You can't marry Sophie. You'd regret it and you'd both be miserable. Marry Celine. She's the one you love." He spoke as if it were simple, a perfectly balanced equation.

Sophie stood up. Somehow she expected them to look different; the boy who didn't love her and the brother who'd betrayed her. Ken was still Ken, young and adorabley rumpled looking. Tom was still her little brother, green eyed and brown haired, like looking into a more chiselled mirror.

They both jumped like they'd seen a ghost.

"He's right. Marry Celine. She'll be a good Queen." The words tasted like ash in her mouth.

"Sophie I-" Ken was half way up to his feet. She had to get away, she couldn't look at him.

"I can't stay here." She opened the stable door and burst out. It was still early afternoon but dark clouds made it seem much later. The air smelt of iron and rust; there was a storm brewing.

"Sophie wait," Her brother chased after her. His hand dropped onto her shoulder. She shrugged it off. "Sophie, you have a life here. Where will you go? You're being ridiculous."

She grabbed his broken arm and twisted it as hard as she could. There was a satisfying crunch. He doubled over in pain, clutching his forearm. His eyes watered. He had cried easily when he was small; Ken had teased him for years. Thunder rumbled above them. It started to rain; cold, fat raindrops sent shivers down her spine.

Ken caught up to them. He placed his hand on Tom's shoulder with concern, but he was looking at Sophie. Staring at her like she'd grown horns.

"Sophie, please. You're my best friend. You can't leave-" He pushed wet hair back from his forehead.

"You're the King. I'm the gardener's daughter. We never should have been friends in the first place. And I was so stupid to think we could ever be anything else."

Leaving the two boys she loved most in the world, Sophie ran. Her boots squelched in the mud, water saturated her clothes and sprayed off her as she moved. She ran until the castle was a hazy speck on the horizon and her chest seared with pain. She fell to her knees in the mud by the riverbank, breathing hard, whistling each time. That must be the sound of heart break, she thought.

Sophie stared at the castle. Once, it had been her home; a welcome site after a long journey. Now it was her target.

"Are you ready for this?"

"I was born ready," Holly said. She tossed her long blonde hair and winked, pretty even in the ugly castle uniform. Holly had found Sophie just over a year ago, breathless and going through garbage to try and find something to eat. Taking pity on the skeleton girl, she had taken her home and fed her in secret like a stray dog.

Eventually, Holly's father discovered the girl living in his daughter's closet. He was a ruthless man, a gang leader and anti-monarchist, but fair. He listened to Sophie's story. He plotted her revenge. She told him all of the King's secrets, fuelling his plans for a rebellion, and in return he was trying to find a cure for the illness that was plaguing her. He had all the medical gang members working on it, and so far the inhalers had been a massive step forwards.

If she'd been well, she knew it would be her going instead of Holly. She clasped her friends shoulder.

"Good luck."

Holly hefted the heavy backpack onto her shoulders and walked away into the night. The backpack was full of explosives. She'd take the secret passage into the castle, plant the bomb and return without anyone noticing.

Celine, and her unborn child if rumours were to be believed, would be killed. And Tom, the traitor. A knot tightened in her stomach. Sometimes, when she thought of him she saw the little boy who'd cried easily and hidden behind her legs. Instead she forced herself to see the man in the stable, smiling in the dark as he told Ken to marry someone else.

Ken. He would be killed too. Her breath hitched in her throat. That had been the part of the plan she liked the least. Holly had convinced her it was unavoidable, her father wouldn't take no for an answer. Her eyes watered. She squeezed them shut. She opened them again. His face, pushing his hair back in the rain, had been pasted to the backs of her eyelids since the day she left.

Sophie waited. And waited. It had been too long. Something had gone wrong. She sucked in a breath from her inhaler. There was no Holly and no explosion. She must have been captured. As dawn swept across the castle Sophie stood stiffly and trudged back to headquarters. There was an emotion in her chest she didn't quite register. Was that bitterness? Anger? Fear? Or just relief?

Holly's father wouldn't be happy.

Today, Sophie would finally rescue Holly. Five months had passed before Holly's father had approved of one of Sophie's rescue plans. Five months! His own daughter, captured, and it had taken five months to authorise a rescue. Part of her admired that. He didn't let emotion get in the way.

He'd stuck a poster to her wall:

*"We are but helpless Pieces of the Game He plays
Upon this chequer-board of Nights and Days
Hither and thither moves, and checks and slays"*

Know your place, he said, and accept your destiny. He was a cold man. Sophie wouldn't have wanted him as her father, but he was an excellent teacher and strategist.

She stashed her inhaler carefully inside her boot and strapped a knife to her belt. He'd planned a distraction, a riot across the river, whilst Sophie snuck in and got Holly out.

She collected a horse from the stables and rode out to the castle. It was easier to ride than to walk, but she was still breathless when she reached the river bank. She took a puff of her inhaler. The entrance to the secret passageway was in sight, just the way she remembered it. *I've got a secret to tell you,* Ken's voice said in her head. She could still see the excitement in his face, young and smooth at sixteen.

Lost in her memories, Sophie almost missed the shadows flickering at the base of the oak tree. Someone was coming out.

Tom. He looked older, his features sharper. He'd cut his hair short. He was laughing, dragging a girl by the hand. How could he be so happy?

"Come on, or we'll miss the boat!" He said to the girl behind him.

She giggled, pulled him back for a kiss, and Sophie froze. The girl gazing adoringly at her brother was Holly.

Sophie stuffed her hand into her mouth to stop her scream of rage. Her muscles trembled. The couple moved further away. Had Holly betrayed her too? No. There had to be some other explanation. She was probably just playing along until she could be rescued.

Sophie followed them.

Two days later, she was exhausted. They'd travelled on foot, on a boat- Sophie had had to leave her horse behind- and then even further on foot. Holly was an excellent actress, she stared at Tom, held his hand, even flushed prettily. Sophie had to fight her nausea at the sight and wondered how Holly was tolerating her repulsive brother.

The couple wondered into a copse of trees and Sophie crouched a few metres away, hidden behind a thicket of roses. The flowers were in full bloom; their scent was everywhere.

"It's beautiful, Tom." Holly said. She stared out at the blue lake, glinting in the sun. The air was clearer this far North, the sky almost blue instead of grey. "But why are we here? You know Ken needs you right now."

"There's something I need to tell you," Tom said. "There's someone Ken needs even more than me. She's been missing for almost two years now. I thought," He looked around at the trees, the lake, the blue sky. His wretched expression looked out of place in the scene. "I thought she might be here. Last ditch attempt. We used to come here when we were kids, you see. Me and my sister. Did I tell you I had a sister?" He'd been looking for her. Something in her chest loosened, threating to spill over.

Her throat felt tight but she didn't think her inhaler would help.

"Tom." Holly breathed. "I'm so sorry." She grabbed the front of his shirt with both hands. Her fingers looked shockingly pale and small against the dark fabric. "I didn't expect this to happen. It was supposed to be easy. In and out."

"What?" The look on her brother's face was ugly. He took a step back from Holly, pushing her hands away from him.

"The day you found me, collapsed at the bottom of the stairs. I didn't fall cleaning. I fell trying to plant a bomb in the castle." She paused for a breath and continued, "I know where Sophie is. She's been working with me and my father, trying to- to get revenge. You have to understand, she was heartbroken."

Holly had betrayed her. Had betrayed her own father. All for the pretty smiles of the wolf she'd once called her brother. Her ears rang, but she could still hear Tom's words.

"Please, you have to tell me where she is. I need to find her."

Sophie stepped out from behind the bush. The cloying scent of roses clung to her skin.

"I'm right here."

"Sophie!" Holly exclaimed. "How on earth- You know what it doesn't matter. I think you've been wrong about your brother. He didn't mean to hurt you."

"He fools a lot of people with that pretty face." Sophie said. "I don't blame you. We can kill him now, together, and return to your father. I won't tell him about your lapse."

Holly's face turned the colour of ice.

"Sophie," Tom croaked. "I'm so sorry." He approached her with his arms outstretched. Sophie tightened her grip on her knife.

"You ruined everything. You were so jealous of me becoming queen that you convinced Ken to marry someone else."

"What? No!" He was only a step or two away from her. "I knew Ken didn't love you. And if you're honest you knew it too. Not the way you wanted him too. You both would have been miserable."

"You didn't even come after me!" He stepped closer and she slashed out with the knife. He hissed in pain, glancing down at his torn sleeve and the cut underneath. Holly let out a little scream.

"I couldn't find you. I looked for you everywhere! The searches had to be secret, obviously. We had to tell the court you were dead!"

His eyes on the knife, he took a step forwards. "Please Sophie, come home."

"I can't go back there." Her chest ached. The whistling started. She couldn't let him see this weakness. "Stay. Away. From. Me." She couldn't speak.

"Sophie, what's wrong?" He sounded so concerned she almost believed it was genuine. Her breathing was far too quick. The trees span around her. She swayed, the knife dropped, and her brother caught her.

"Sophie you're not well. You need to come back to the castle. The castle medics-"

Sophie tried to pull away from him but couldn't; it was only his arm that was keeping her upright.

"Where is it?" Holly demanded. Knowing instantly what she meant, Sophie pointed at her boot. Holly retrieved the inhaler and shoved it into Sophie's hands. She breathed it in slowly.

Tom's expression had gone blank. He did this when he didn't want anyone to know what he was thinking. The arm holding her up felt stable and secure, and she hated how safe she felt next to him. He'd taken everything from her! Ken, her home, any semblance of a normal life, and now Holly. She pulled away, bracing her hands on her knees but able to stand on her own.

Tom opened his mouth to speak but all that Sophie heard was a low growl. It came from behind her brother, and all the hairs on her body stood to attention. Tom span around, looking for the source of the noise. Something large and furry flew through the air and leapt on him.

A wolf. White and grey fur. Big blue eyes. Long fluffy tail. Wolves had once been extinct in Britain, but soldiers had brought them back to use as guard animals. They'd been quietly roaming the highlands since the Last

War. It was a beautiful animal, were it not for the fact it's yellow jaws were clamped around her brothers throat.

He struggled in vein, the animal was too strong. He couldn't pull it off him. He was losing blood; the wolf's muzzle was stained red. Holly looked too shocked too move, her hands shaking by her sides.

Sophie could save her brother. She could let him die. In that split second of indecision Sophie saw her mother's face. She'd died when they were very young. Sophie had almost forgotten the last words she'd said to her daughter but they came back to her now, '*Look after your little brother. He needs you.*'

Sophie threw her knife. It buried itself in the wolf's side. It released Tom with a howl and staggered away into the forest. She hoped it would be enough to scare of the rest of the pack.

Tom was unconscious, his neck was badly cut. Blood oozed, staining the ground under his head. He might not live.

"If he wakes up, it's better that you say it was you who saved him," Sophie said to Holly.

"But-"

"I don't ever want to see either of you again." Sophie walked away, leaving her brother bleeding on the ground and her best friend trembling in fear.

Holly was pregnant. She was trying to hide it with a baggy jumper, but to Sophie it was pretty obvious.

"What are you doing here?" Sophie demanded, "If your father catches you-"

"We need you to come back, Soph." Holly whispered, though she knew full well that all the rooms in headquarters were sound proofed. She'd developed a nervous habit of jerking her head round to look behind her every few seconds.

"You know I won't come back."

"Celine is dead. My father's last attack killed her."

"Ken?" He never left her side.

"He's alive. He needs you Sophie. Please come back."

Her heart leapt at the thought of seeing him again. It had been almost three years. He might look different. He still wouldn't love her, but if Celine was gone then at least she didn't have to watch him with anyone else.

There was a sharp rap at the door.

"Hide!" Sophie hissed. But the door opened before either of them could move. A tall pale haired man walked in. His uniform jacket identified him as a General, as did his stiff gait and perfect posture. He wasn't thrown even for a second by seeing his daughter.

"Holly." He glanced down at her abdomen, at the wedding band on her left hand. "You've betrayed me." He turned to Sophie. "Arrest the traitor."

Sophie hesitated, but Holly had already held out her hands, ready to be hand cuffed.

"Father, I'm sorry. I hope you can forgive me."

"I will never forgive you. Betrayal is the worst crime of all. The penalty is death."

Holly didn't baulk. Her father had trained her well.

"Sir, she's pregnant. We can't just-"

Her heart pounded against her chest and her mouth had gone dry. The general would kill his own daughter and unborn grandchild to make a point. She didn't doubt it. Why had Tom sent her here? The coward! He should have come himself.

"Did you know about this?" The general asked. The tone of his voice never varied.

Sophie had always been a good liar.

"No, Sir. She just turned up. I was extracting as much information as I could before raising the alarm. I believe she's been seduced and brain washed by Tom Candler."

"My daughter is far too clever to be brain washed." The general said. He nodded at Sophie to proceed with the hand cuffs. "I don't kill the innocent. I will wait until your child is born and then your sentence will be carried out."

For four months Sophie racked her brains each day trying to think of a way to get Holly out of headquarters. Security was tight. Guards wouldn't be bribed. She was too out of breath. Holly was too heavily pregnant. Anything she thought of would have failed.

She cursed her brother. He'd sent his pregnant wife here. He hadn't even tried to get her back.

Holly's child, a baby girl, had been born yesterday. The general claimed that he had her delivered to the castle safely. Sophie had no way of knowing if that was true. She dreaded what would happen to Holly now.

The hospital wing door opened automatically as she approached, the General's re-fashioned millennial technology in action. Holly sat on a leather chair. Her face was pale, there were bags under her eyes and drips in her arms. That was expected after childbirth. The bandage around her head was unusual.

The General stood behind his daughter, as expressive as a stone wall.

"Thank you for joining us," he said.

Holly smiled at her. Just a hint of her dimple appeared.

"I have learnt some interesting things, Sophie," the general continued. "First I did a little experiment. I placed a chip into my daughter's head- millennial technology. Now she can only ever speak the truth. You have also betrayed me, though to a lesser extent. You knew Holly was a traitor and kept it hidden. You'll be punished appropriately."

A thrill of fear went through Sophie's chest. She clenched her inhaler in her hand. She hated using it in front of the general, showing weakness, but she was so terrified she might have to.

"I asked Holly what she most afraid off. Do you know what her answer was? I would never have guessed. But perhaps you would. *Being attacked by a wolf.* And then the whole story came out.

This then is your punishment. You will take Holly back to the Highlands. You will tie her to a tree and not release her until she's been ripped limb from limb by wolves."

Sophie could do nothing but stare at him. Her mouth hung open but she had no strength in her jaw to close it.

"If you refuse, I will send Umbra to take the King from his bed at night and leave him for the wolves. Then I will kill Holly myself. So you would be sacrificing your dear Kenneth simply to spare yourself the heartache of killing Holly yourself. The choice is yours."

She didn't doubt the general meant every word he said. She wanted to vomit. Could she watch Holly being ripped apart and not intervene? Holly had saved her life that day she'd found her rummaging in the bins. She was the only one to come back for Sophie. But…she'd also betrayed her by choosing her brother. That still hurt.

If she didn't kill Holly, then Ken would be killed. Ken, the best friend of her childhood, her first love. He'd chosen Tom too.

"I'll make it easy for you. Remember Holly can only tell the truth." The General turned to his daughter. "Holly, if you were given this choice, who would you choose to kill; Sophie or her brother?"

Holly didn't hesitate.

"I would kill Sophie." Her eyes were glazed. She'd probably been drugged. Still, her answer was clear.

"I'll do it." Sophie said. The General smiled. His teeth were yellow and sharp. Just like the wolf.

Sophie tied the final knot and stepped back. It was only mid-afternoon but it was already darkening. Her breath formed a cloud of grey smoke and drifted upwards, mixing with Holly's on the way. Holly wouldn't have many more.

"I'm so sorry." Sophie said. She'd said it over and over again. Never in her life and she sounded so pathetic. But she couldn't help it, she'd never felt so helpless. If she didn't bring back the remains of Holly's body, the General would kill Ken. And then hunt down Holly and kill her anyway.

Holly had said very little on their journey, spending most of it in a semi drugged sleep. Sophie pulled out her knife. She cut Holly's forearm- the scent of blood would attract the pack- and the other girl didn't make a sound.

Sophie spoke without deciding to.

"Do you forgive me?"

Holly finally showed a reaction. She smiled. Sophie would never forget that dimpled cheek.

Sharp transition

"I forgive you," she said. Sophie moved away. Her face was wet and frozen. She thought Holly said something else, but it was lost in the howl of the wind. *Forgive him.*

Ken was dead. Sophie felt nothing. That wouldn't last long; her grief was stored behind a dam in her mind that would burst at any moment. The General had finally succeeded in killing the King. He had set the bomb himself. Now he was missing, and Sophie was trapped in the burning castle. She'd followed the General to try and stop him, but she'd only made things worse.

She made her way to the crypt, choking on dark smoke. Her brother waited at the crypt entrance, almost as if he'd been expecting her. Sophie didn't try to run. If he wanted to kill her he would catch her easily. She couldn't fight him, not now that her breathing was so bad.

"Was it you? Who set off the bomb?" he asked. His eyes were red. The wolf had left a nasty scar on his neck. She shook her head. If she spoke, the dam would burst. "But you helped him…" Fresh tears streaked down his face. He still cried easily. "Ken is dead, along with his son." She couldn't cry in front of him, so instead she became angry.

"Finally your dreams of being king can come true."

He moved faster than she'd expected, pulling a dagger off his belt and holding it to her throat from behind. She'd taught him that move.

"I should kill you now," he hissed. She wished he would. "You killed Ken and Ander. And Holly." The hand holding the knife shook ever so slightly. "But you saved me from the wolf. And Holly begged me never to hurt you." He released her. "For her, you get one chance. If you ever come near the castle again, I swear I will kill you."

Sophie was too numb to care. She crept down the stairs without looking back at her brother. When she reached the courtyard, it was warm. Fires still blazed in patches. Bodies were strewn across her path. Sophie ignored them; they were all dead.

Then she heard a whimper. A child was crawling out from under the rubble. He'd hidden inside a thick wooden wardrobe; it had protected him from the worst of the blast and the subsequent fall. The child was crying, curled up into a ball.

Sophie was not a monster; she couldn't turn her back on an injured child. She picked her way across the debris towards him, grabbed his shoulder and turned him over.

Her heart stopped with a jolt. She choked back a scream. It was Ken! The mop of dark hair, the startling blue eyes. No. Ken was dead. And Ken was now a man. This was a boy, barely ten years old. His son. It had to be.

Sophie stared at the boy. He stared back for a second, and then his eyes rolled backwards and he slumped forwards, unconscious. He was bleeding from a cut across his eyebrow. He was small, all skinny limbs and narrow shoulders and smooth cheeks. Sophie felt a sudden overwhelming protectiveness. She picked him up, cradling him like a baby.

She would raise him. He would be smart, and brave, and loyal. His father would be proud. And when the time was right, he would remove Tom and take his rightful place on the throne, with Sophie by his side.

Chapter Thirty-five

Tom finished speaking and Cas' ears filled with silence. He stared at his godfather. Tom hadn't betrayed him. He clung to that- everything else had fallen apart.

How had he missed this? Skye looked like her father. She had his green eyes- eyes he shared with his sister. His sister- General Laric- *Sophie*- who had been to Ken what Skye was to Cas. Somehow their relationship had disintegrated to the point where Sophie had hated Ken enough to risk his death.

He stared at the back of Skye's neck, kneeling in front of him to keep pressure on Ander's wound, and vowed that would never happen to them.

"We need to get him to the infirmary," Skye muttered. "He's lost a lot of blood. And he's breathing oddly."

Cas didn't want to think about it. If his brother died…. His hands shook. He forced himself to look down. Skye was right, when Ander took a breath in only half of his chest seemed to be moving.

"We need Dr Bonnington," he said and was surprised by the forcefulness of his own voice. "Tom, you deal with Laric. Just put her in a cell until we work out what we're going to do with her. Skye, help me get Ander upstairs." As he spoke, Adira and two dozen of her soldiers poured down the staircase. She'd helped them out earlier, but that didn't mean she wouldn't turn on him now. This was a perfect opportunity for her to take the throne for herself.

"Adira, can you send someone to fetch Dr Bonnington? He works at Tommie's." She met his eyes for a second, then turned and snapped an order at one of her soldiers. The young man nodded curtly and disappeared back up the staircase.

"There's still a battle going on outside." Adira said, "They need to know Laric has been defeated. They need to hear from their King." Their King who had missed the entire battle. Cas knew his people were dying out there.

Adira was testing him. Who would he pick? His people, or his brother?

"I need to stay here until Ander is safe," he said, without hesitation. *Until I know I haven't murdered my brother.* She gave him the smallest of smiles. He had to send someone in his place. Skye was out of the question; she was holding on to Ander as if he was a grenade that would explode if she released her grip. Tom then. His godfather looked tired, his face set into an emotionless mask. But news of his imprisonment had spread, and many people would have now worked out that Laric was the sister he'd lost so many years before. They wouldn't trust him.

"You talk to them," Cas said to Adira. "Give them one of your inspiring speeches. Tell them everything. I'll be there as soon as I can."

"Of course little King," Adira grinned and swept up the staircase. Her soldiers followed her.

Tom dragged Laric into the cell he'd vacated and locked her inside.

"I don't think we should be here when she wakes up," he said. "Skye?" He touched his daughter's shoulder. "Let's get him upstairs." Tom grabbed one of Ander's arms and Cas grabbed the other. Together, they carried him up the stairs and into the first empty bedroom they came to.

"I'll make sure the doctor knows where to find us," Tom said, and left the room.

Alone with Skye, Cas couldn't help the words that poured out of his mouth.

"Skye, I'm so sorry. I can't believe I- I should never have, if anything happens I'll never forgive myself." His voice choked and he stopped speaking.

"You had to. He would have killed you." Her voice was grey. What if she left him like Sophie had left his father so many years ago? He had to do something. She stared down at Ander, pushed his hair back from his pale forehead. Cas tugged her round by the shoulder to face him. He leant down and kissed her, clumsily bumping noses. She inhaled sharply against his mouth.

Her arms tightened around him. She broke the kiss and instead buried her head against his neck. Her cheek was wet with tears. He clung onto her until she stopped shaking.

He wanted to make a joke- something about not being that bad a kisser- but the words wouldn't come out. She pulled away from him to check on Ander, placing two fingers against his neck to take his pulse.

It seemed like hours later when the door opened and Tom came back in, followed closely by Dr Bonnington. A pretty, dark haired nurse was carrying several medical bags.

"Out of the way. Let me have a look." Bonnington said, and pushed Cas and Skye to either side. He pulled aside the makeshift bandages and Cas caught sight of an angry, bubbling red wound. He'd done that to his own brother. The room swayed.

He was dragged out of the room by the hand. Skye.

"Let's give him some space to work," she said. Cas nodded. He felt numb, his brain wasn't working. She sat down by the door, her back against the wall. Cas wanted to sit beside her, to hold her hand and wait together to see if Ander would be OK. He couldn't- his people were counting on him.

"Cas, go," Skye said. She already knew what he was thinking. She knew him better than anyone. "I'll make sure he's OK." She didn't offer to come with him.

"Thank you," he said. He left her sitting on the cold stone floor and ran back to the dungeon. He needed Laric. He found her stirring on the dungeon floor. A bruise was forming next to her left eye, dark purple and out of place on her immaculate façade. She noticed him and blinked a couple of times, still not completely conscious.

"Ander?" Her voice was hopeful.

"Wrong." Cas didn't tell her Ander was alive. It was better she stayed devastated. He pulled out his knife. It was covered in Ander's blood and he made sure she could see it. "Get up," he ordered. "Put your hands on your head and stand back."

She did so, meekly, not meeting his eyes. Cas suspected it was an act. She was a dangerous woman. He unlocked the cell door, let it creak open.

"Let's go," he ordered. She stepped out of the cell. He kept the knife pressed against her back, one hand holding the collar of her jacket. He wished he'd tied her hands, but forced her up the stairs anyway.

"Where is his body?" She asked like she didn't care. He could see her hands shaking and knew that she did.

"That's not your concern," Cas replied. He was being cruel, he knew that. His father had loved her. Tom loved her. Even Ander loved her. But Cas despised her. She had made him stab his brother.

They reached the front entrance. He pushed Laric out first and then followed her into the cold. Snow fell from the grey sky; tiny pellets of ash and ice. He almost slipped as he stepped forwards.

It was chaos. There were people everywhere, hacking and clawing at each other, slipping on blood and ice. Soldiers in rebellion green, soldiers in the black castle uniform, commoners wearing jeans and jumpers. They were wild. He had no idea how to make it stop. Explanations weren't going to sort this out.

What had happened to Adira? He spotted her- her face was rapidly reddening as a rebellion solider wrapped his arms around her throat. Before Cas could take a step towards her, Seth appeared at his sister's side and took the soldier out with a rock to the temple.

"Are we just going to stand here?" Laric asked. She showed no reaction at seeing the soldiers fighting on her behalf.

"Shut up." Cas dug his knife into her back.

One of the soldiers in green- a curly haired girl, no older than Skye- heard Laric's voice. She looked over, pointed and screamed:

"The imposter king has General Laric imprisoned!"

Oh crap. Why hadn't he thought this through? Cas gripped the knife harder. He was still in control. Even if several rebellion soldiers had noticed him and were advancing towards them. Out of the corner of his eye he saw Laric's shadow soldier- Umbra. There was likely an arrow pointed at him right now.

"Call off your army," Cas demanded. "No one else needs to die."

Laric moved. She was fast- faster than Ander, faster than Skye. She twisted out of his grasp, turned and faced him. The knife was still in his hand, but it was useless. He was outnumbered. Laric's soldiers had gathered around them like moths to a flame. They formed a ring around their General. Laric held up a steady hand- it was a clear signal. She wanted to deal with this herself.

Cas saw Orla watching from across the courtyard, ready to give an attack order. He gave her a small shake of his head. In this, he agreed with Laric- they would deal with this themselves. Winner takes it all- as the old saying went.

"Tom told us what happened to you," Cas said. "I know you loved my father." She stared at him and said nothing. "Give up. You have nothing to gain here. This isn't what he would have wanted."

"You talk too much." She hit him, an elbow to his ear that he didn't see coming. He lifted the knife to defend himself, but it was no longer in his hand. He'd dropped it. Laric kicked it away, each of them left with nothing but their fists and their rage.

Cas kicked out at her, She grabbed his foot, but he was ready for it. He used his momentum to bring his other foot up and smash it into her nose. He landed hard on his back, winded. She clutched at her broken nose, blood gushing freely.

Cas jumped up to his feet. Laric grabbed his arm and threw him over her shoulders like a rag doll. He winced as he slammed into the ground- he heard a crack that might have been one of his ribs. He struggled to his feet. He had to beat this woman. She had hurt everyone he loved.

He tried to punch her. She grasped his wrist and twisted. He was on the floor again. Her booted foot pressed against his chest, sending waves of agony through broken ribs.

"I would have trained you better," Laric said. Someone handed her back the knife. She pressed it against his throat. Cas stared at her. If he was about to die, he could pretend her eyes were Skye's.

The knife disappeared from against his throat. Laric stepped back. She held out her hands, palms up.

"I surrender," she said. Toneless. Without hesitation, her soldiers dropped their weapons and held up their hands. They were well trained.

One hand pressed to his chest, Cas clambered to his feet.

"Why?" he managed to say breathlessly.

"He would never forgive me," she said. Cas didn't know which *he* she meant. Ken? Tom? Ander? Maybe all three. Castle guards approached and tied her hands. They looked at him for instructions.

"Dungeon." He could only manage to say one word at a time. The guards began to lead her away. Tae appeared out of nowhere. He threw Cas' arm around his shoulder, helping him stay upright.

"Come on your Majesty. Let's get you-"

"Sophie!" Cas called. Her head jerked but she didn't turn back. "Ander's alive." She still didn't turn back. But he saw the curve of her shoulders relax; invisible weights lifting away.

Chapter Thirty-six

It hurt to breathe. Ander kept his breaths shallow. Where was he? He'd been in the crypt with Cas and Skye. And Laric. She'd said something. He couldn't remember much after that. He was lying flat on his back, staring up at a stained white ceiling. He tried to sit up, but a searing pain in his chest sent him straight back down.

"It's about time." Cas appeared above him, looking pale and drawn.

"What happened?" Bracing himself, Ander pushed himself into a sitting position. The left side of his chest was covered with bandages. A plastic tube sneaked out from under them and into a fluid filled bucket on the floor. Was that coming out of him? It bubbled when he breathed.

"Well, it's a long story. Do you want the good news first or the bad news?" Cas sat back in his battered plastic chair. They were in a hospital ward. Cas was the only person not occupying a bed; there was barely enough space for his chair. Ander wondered how many rules his brother had bent to be allowed to stay.

"Bad news."

"I had to stab you. I'm sorry. I punctured your lung and your chest started filling up with air. That's why you've got that drain in. But don't worry, Dr Bonnington says you'll be as good as new."

"What's the good news?" Ander didn't want to know what he'd done to force Cas to stab him.

"Two bits of good news actually! Firstly, we captured Laric. She's in the dungeons right now. Secondly, Bonnington got the chip out of your head. So now you'll only want to kill me when I'm particularly charming."

Ander touched the back of his head. There was a fresh bandage there. A weight lifted off his shoulders.

"How did you capture Laric?"

Ander listened as Cas told the whole story. Laric had loved his father. And he hadn't loved her back… Skye. He had to get Cas to tell Skye how he felt. And then he'd bury his own feelings so deeply they may as well not exist.

"Where's Skye?"

"Skye's with her Dad. They had a lot to talk about." Cas looked away when he said her name.

"Cas, after hearing Dad's story, don't you think it's about time you tell Skye how you feel? I won't let you be that blind. She loves you."

Cas opened his mouth and hesitated, then spoke.

"I kissed her." Ander fought hard to keep his expression neutral. The pain in his chest worsened, and his breaths became more shallow. Cas didn't notice. "I got so scared that she would leave. I just did it. And it was nice, but-" He shrugged. "It was like there was something missing. I mean, the timing was a bit crap," His voice trailed off into nothing.

Ander had nothing to say. There was something missing? What did that even mean?

"Your Royal Highnesses, you have a visitor if you're feeling up for it," the ward clerk said as she approached. She pushed her glasses back up on to her forehead as she spoke, her eyes flickering between the two of them.

"He's not ready for visitors, Laura" Cas said, "Tell them to go back to the castle and wait. I'll see them later." The ward clerk flinched at the force of his voice.

"No, it's fine. Send them up," Ander said. He didn't want to be alone with his brother and have to talk about Skye.

"But-" Cas started. Ander glared at him until he nodded at the ward clerk and she walked to the door, trembling from head to foot.

"I thought you were the nice one," Ander muttered.

"I am the nice one!" Cas said. He tried smiling at the ward clerk as she passed. Her eyes widened and she practically ran back to her desk. Adira, who'd walked in three steps behind her, gave her a puzzled look and then turned to face the twins.

"Hello little King. Kings." She grinned down at them and Ander was reminded of a viper. Cas sat up straighter in his chair. "That looks nasty." She pointed at the chest drain. "My brother Seth had to have one of those too. I swear he still bubbles when he laughs." Ander hoped she was joking.

"What's going on Adira?" Cas's voice sounded deeper than normal.

"I need to know what your plans are. The people are uneasy. There's no ruler. Laric' army is lurking, leaderless, I suspect they're waiting for your little identical sidekick to come back." She jerked her head in Ander's direction. "Your people in the castle are pretty peeved about being lied to all these years. Every time your dear godfather tries to placate them they swear at him. And my people, well, we're still hoping you'll both abdicate. You need to do something before we have a full scale riot on our hands."

"Just give me until tomorrow. We'll think of something." Cas said.

"Don't disappoint me little King," Adira said, and ran her finger down Cas' cheek before strolling away. Cas blinked, and stared at her until Ander waved an arm in front of his face. This was not good.

"She's dangerous, brother."

"I know that," Cas said, and held up a bandaged hand.

"You don't love Skye, do you?" Ander asked. He wasn't sure what he wanted the answer to be. If Cas loved her, the two of them would be happy. If Cas didn't, then she'd be miserable. Unless he could win her over…overtime… maybe.
over time

"No I don't." Cas sighed. "I just don't want her to leave." He shook his head. "We need to decide what we're going to do. I don't think anyone would deny we can rule jointly now. I'll ask the council and Tom and-"

"Cas," Ander hadn't said this out loud before. He'd never even admitted it to himself. "I don't want to be King."

"What?"

"You heard me. I don't want to be King. You can do it." He tried to sit up straighter, sending an agonising pain through his chest. He sank back against the pillows, breathless, his hand pressed against the bandage on his chest.

"Ander, it's our duty, we have to-"

"Don't you see Cas? We've been pieces," Ander said. He had realised something and he wanted Cas to understand. "Like in General Laric poem." He'd had it memorised for years, and he recited it for Cas.

> *"We are but helpless Pieces of the Game He plays*
> *Upon this chequer-board of Nights and Days*
> *Hither and thither moves, and checks and slays"*

His brother looked blank. "She said it meant that we're all helpless, pieces on a board, trapped in our destiny and one way or another we'll all end up dead. She wanted to discourage us from getting any ideas. We were her soldiers, her pieces on the board, and she'd move us anyway she pleased. And that's what we are Cas, I'm black and you're white- identical but not- and all our lives people have been moving us. Our father, General Laric, Tom." Ander gripped his brother's shoulder. Cas watched him with an odd expression. "General Laric was wrong Cas. The world is not black and white. We don't have to stay in the boxes. It's time to tip the game board over."

They had been pawns for far too long.

"What do you propose we do?"

"I won't be King. I wouldn't be good at it." Ander said, "But if you want to rule then you should."

"I don't want to make the people pawns either. But I think I could help them. I want to help them. So… I'll arrange a vote. The people can choose; to have me as their King, or to return to the old way of an elected leader."

Ander nodded. Cas was good at this. Away from Laric's sharp ears, rebellion soldiers had often talked about elections. How good it would be to have a choice.

"I think that's fair."

Footsteps approached from the far side of the ward.

"Your Majesty, I think it's time we took that chest drain out," Dr Bonnington said. He smiled in a way that made Ander nervous. "Don't worry, it doesn't hurt." He snapped some gloves on to his hands and approached with a tray of instruments. They looked sharp.

"You're not filling me with confidence here." Ander grimaced as Dr Bonnington peeled back the bandages.

"Cas, why don't you go round the other side and hold your brother's hand?"

"Uh- yeah OK." Cas stumbled over to Ander's right hand side. He was a pale shade of green, and his hand was sweaty when he gripped Ander's.

"Are you OK?" Ander asked.

"Yep, just fine." Cas ducked his head down, leaning on the side of the bed.

"Just going to cut the stitches out," Dr Bonnington said. Ander couldn't help looking down. It was so odd seeing something sticking out of his chest. "Take a breath in, then breathe out and hold."

Ander did as asked. With a weird tugging sensation Dr Bonnington pulled the tube free. It was smeared with blood. It was probably for the best Cas wasn't looking.

"Here, hold this," Dr Bonnington said, and pressed Ander's hand to a new bandage over the hole. He taped it down.

"Thanks," Ander said. "Can I get out of here now?" He didn't like being here. It reeked of death and decay. And reminded him how close he'd come to dying.

"Absolutely not! You need rest and monitoring." Bonnington muttered under his breath as he walked away.

"Cas?" His brother was still face down against the mattress. Ander poked him in the head. "It's done, let's go."

"Go?" He still looked green. Ander was sure he hadn't heard anything that had been said in the past few minutes.

"Yeah, they need the space." That was true- directly opposite him a boy with a broken arm and a younger girl with a nasty looking rash were laid horizontally across the same bed. "Can I have your jacket?" He didn't have anything else to wear.

"Sure," Cas said, unzipped it and handed it to Ander. Ander pulled it on. Moving hurt even more than breathing. He had to close his eyes for a moment and force himself to continue taking breaths. "Are you sure Bonnington said it was OK to go?"

"Of course," Ander lied, and forced himself to his feet. Once he was upright it wasn't too bad. If he kept his hand pressed tightly to the wound, didn't breath too deeply, and concentrated on moving as few body parts as he could, then he could walk.

He walked side by side with Cas off the ward.

"I've got the bike down in the tunnels," Cas said, "Grant picked it up for us."

"The motorbike?" Ander couldn't keep the dread out of his voice.

"Yep!" Cas grinned. Ander wondered how they could be so alike and yet so different. Stairs weren't good, the slight bump of putting his foot down a step sent a spike of pain through his chest. He gritted his teeth, half paying attention to his brother's inane chatter. It was something about engines and horse power and Ander nodded as if he understood.

"You have no idea what I'm talking about do you?" Cas said when they reached the ground floor.

"What?" His thoughts had drifted to Skye. What would he say to her? Was it selfish or decent to tell her Cas wasn't interested?

"You are just like Skye. She barely listens to me when I talk about engines either... You'd think I talk too much or something."

"I'm in love with Skye."

There was a long pause. Ander realised he'd said the words out loud. He wanted to kick himself, but he was already in enough pain. Cas stared at him like he'd grown an extra head. He frowned.

"But you were telling me I should tell her I love her."

"I wanted you to be happy. I could see how Skye felt about you from the start, I didn't want to get in the way of that. I don't want to get in the way of that. I don't know why it even came out of my mouth."

His chest ached, distinct from the sharper well defined pain from the wound. He'd once read about a difficult to pronounce medical condition where you literally died from a broken heart. He wondered if that was happening to him.

"You should tell her." Cas said.

"But-"

"I kissed her because I was scared. It was stupid." Cas stared at the ground. "She pulled away. Whatever feelings she had for me, I think they've changed." He shrugged and approached the motorbike, kicking away the stand. He grinned at Ander. "You wanna drive?"

"No thank you." The last time he'd driven that thing he'd gotten an arrow through his leg. Not his most pleasant memory. He climbed up onto the bike behind his brother and held on as they shot into the tunnel.

He was so tired his eyes were drifting shut despite the wind blowing hard into his face. He must have fallen asleep, or passed out, because they were on the bridge over the moat. A half-moon hung low over their heads, bright despite the swirls of smoke drifting across its surface.

"Should we make a grand entrance?" Cas yelled.

"Don't we always?"

Instead of stopping at the entrance, Cas drove on, speeding the motorbike along the stone floors and causing several people to leap out of their way. He skidded to a stop in the throne room, leaving skid marks over the gold plated tiles.

The sudden deceleration sent a bolt of pain through Ander's chest, but it was entirely worth it to see the councillors mouths drop open. He and Cas leapt of the bike simultaneously and stood shoulder to shoulder as soldiers and council members gathered around them. They'd even managed to splatter Shafiq's white shirt with mud.

"That's how you make an entrance," Cas said, and grinned.

Taking a long time to come to the end. The action has been over for a while now

Chapter Thirty-seven

"Dad, I'm not sure I want to see her again. She killed my mother!" Skye said. She was already out of breath, struggling to keep up with her father's long legged stride. He noticed, and slowed down, a concerned frown appearing in between his eyebrows.

"She insisted that she wants to see us both if she's going to tell us where to find the cure," Tom replied. "And don't forget she also saved my life." He nodded at Harry, still sporting a bandage around his forehead, as they passed the prison warden and descended the dungeon steps. He approached the metal bars of Laric's' cell. Skye stayed close to his side.

"Sophie, we're here like you asked. What did you want to say?" His voice was perfectly even. Laric was curled up at the back of the cell, her back to them. At Tom's voice she stretched like a cat and climbed gracefully to her feet. She stood close to the bars and her face caught the light from the lamp Tom was holding.

It was odd. She'd hated and feared Laric for as long as she remembered. Now, when she looked at her all she could see was her father. The same green eyes. Same slightly upturned nose. How had she never noticed?

"In the lab at my headquarters you'll find the cure. Once only injection. The old general imported it from Australia, where they've gotten one of the old genetics lab running. There's no guarantees, but it worked for me." Laric shrugged.

"Thank you," Tom said. His voice was still even, but the air filled with unsaid words. Skye could never tell what he was thinking.

Laric was even harder to read. Skye tentatively smiled at her. She looked back at Skye and the layer of steel in her expression cracked. Her eyes filled with tears, and her hands shook as she gripped the bars.

"You have her dimple." Laric wiped at her eyes and turned to Tom. "I am sorry you know, Tommy. For the way it all turned out."

"So am I," Tom said. They clasped hands through the bars. The light caught their faces at an odd angle, so they were each half in light, half in dark. "The council may grant you leniency."

Laric scoffed.

"Excuse me, Sir." Harry's voice called from the foot of the steps. "I've just been informed that the King – Kings- have returned."

Skye's heart leapt. Kings- Ander was back!

"Go ahead, Skye." Tom said. "I still have things to discuss with my sister."

"Ok, thanks." She hugged her father quickly and nodded at Laric. She climbed the stairs two at a time, taking them as fast as she dared. Ander had been unconscious the last three times she'd seen him. She needed to hear him speak, make sure he was OK.

She burst into the throne room. A motorcycle lay on its side in the middle of the room, a small amount of smoke coming from its exhaust pipe. No one paid it any attention. The twins stood side by side, shaking hands with a long queue of battle survivors. It was amazing to see them together, identical but not. Cas was bright and fierce, Ander pale and perceptive.

Cas spotted her first. He pushed through the line of soldiers and pulled her close. For a moment, Skye thought he would kiss her again. His breath was warm against her ear.

"Take chances, Skye." He kissed her cheek and released her. He winked and flashed her the crooked grin. There was a part of her heart that would always belong to Cas, and she smiled back at him.

He stepped back, and prodded Ander forwards. Her heart fluttered at the sight of him, the perfect chipped tooth grin. *Take chances.* Cas and the entire throne room were watching. She didn't care. She threw her arms around Ander's neck and pulled him down to kiss him.

His mouth formed a smile under hers. A nearby wolf whistle made her break away, and she felt heat rush to her cheeks.

"Skye, I love you." Ander said. His blue eyes drilled into hers. Flushed cheeks brought colour to his otherwise pale face.

"I love you, Ander." It was true. Cas was her best friend, but Ander was…something else. Everything else. She kissed him again, quickly. The crowd had grown bigger and was watching their every move.

Ander turned to face them. He held her hand, and Cas joined them and took her other hand. The crowd was waiting for something. Adira was there, near the front, watching with hooded eyes and a sly smile. On the far side of the room, there was a flicker of shadows, Umbra, Skye assumed.

"Ladies and gentlemen," Ander began. He wasn't as used to large crowds as Cas, but he spoke well. "I, Ander, son of the late King Kenneth, relinquish all my rights to the throne."

There was an explosion of noise, especially from the far end where the majority of Laric's' army were waiting. Skye looked from Ander to Cas in surprise. There was no way Cas would let his brother give up the throne. He wanted them to rule together. But Cas didn't look surprised. He gave Skye's hand a squeeze and lifted his other hand to silence the crowd.

"I, King Cassander, rightful heir and ruler will be making a decree." Cas said. What was he doing? Surely he wasn't actually going to abdicate? Adira was, well, a little bit nuts. "I will remain King until a vote can be held. You, the people, will decide if I should remain King, or if a new leader is to be elected. All adults will be entitled to a vote." His eyes swept across the audience to include everyone, even the shadow.

"What just happened?" Skye stuttered as they turned away from the crowd. The noise was overwhelming; her skin felt like it was vibrating.

"I believe it's called democracy." Adira. She stepped up onto the podium, and Cas turned to face her.

Skye could almost feel the tension in the air between them, as if they were two poles of a magnet. "Nicely done, little King." Adira winked at him and left, melting into a crowd of her own followers.

Cas stared after her, until Ander poked him in the side.

"I keep telling you she's dangerous," Ander said. "Be careful."

"Cas is never careful," Skye said. She wasn't jealous, which was a pleasant surprise. Cas smiled at her.

"Come on, we've got a lot of work to do."

Chapter Thirty-eight

Cas had avoided his godfather as long as he could; surrounding himself with meetings and councillors and soldiers. This was the last place he'd expected to find him, sat alone at the base of the tower in the ruins, lit only by faint streams of moonlight.

"What are you doing here?" Cas asked. He held up the flashlight. The bright white light made Tom seem even paler, and Cas could suddenly see why people might think the ruins were haunted.

"You've been avoiding me," Tom said.

"How did you know I would come up here?" Cas asked. It was the middle of the night. No one had seen him sneak out. He hadn't even told Skye and Ander where he was going.

"You're more like your father than you think." Tom said, "This is where I found Ken hiding, all those years ago after Sophie left."

"I'm sorry. I never should have doubted you," Cas said. The conversation was now unavoidable. His guilt spilled out, an inky black stain between himself and the man who'd raised him. When his father had died, Cas had been unable to sleep for days, convinced he could hear ghosts and monsters in the walls. Finally, Tom had agreed to stand guard at the foot of his bed, a knife in hand. That was the first time Cas had felt safe.

"I should have trusted you with the truth," Tom shrugged, looking up at him. That was unusual. Cas had always had to look up at Tom.

"I hope I've done the right thing," Cas said. "Giving up the throne."

"You did what you thought was right," Tom said. "You've given people a choice, and you've put them ahead of yourself. As a royal advisor, I wish you'd consulted with the council first." He stood, and held out his hand for Cas to shake. "As your godfather, I couldn't be more proud."

Cas took his hand and pulled him in for a hug. He didn't need Tom to stand guard at the foot of his bed anymore. But it was good to know he would if Cas asked.

Ander had to hurry. The results of the vote were being announced in the next hour, and Cas wanted him to be there. Before the shift of power, he had to see General Laric. A new leader might demand her execution. It might even be appropriate. But he still had to see her.

"I really can't tell which one you are… but go on through, Your Majesty." The old prison guard gestured him past. Henry or Harry, Ander couldn't really remember.

"Thank you," Ander said as he moved past. He took the stairs slowly; his chest still ached and he struggled for breath if he moved too fast, though he was improving every day. His empathy for Skye's illness had amplified, and as soon as this vote was over he was going to go to headquarters and get the cure for her himself.

"Ander." General Laric voice came from within the cell before Ander had even reached the bottom of the steps. He approached the bars, stood close to them. He wasn't scared of her, not now.

"How did you know it was me?" He watched her, leaning against the stone wall of the cell. Her hair had come undone from its immaculate bun, instead framing her face with dark brown waves. It suited her.

"I raised you. I just know."

"Cas is giving the people a vote. I gave up my rights." He wasn't sure what he expected her to say. Would she be angry? Upset?

"Good," she said. She smiled. It was the same smile she'd worn when he'd climbed a forty foot wall for the first time. "Power ruins us all. I wanted it so badly I was willing to kill my own brother, my niece, my best friend." She sighed. "I was willing to let you, my innocent little boy, the son of the man I loved, become a murderer. I'm a monster Ander. And I'm so sorry I almost turned you into one too."

Her words triggered a memory in Ander's mind.

'She's a monster. You should burn it and stop thinking about her.' Tom. Young and haughty, he crossed his arms and glared at Ken across the room. Ander was hiding from Skye in his father's closet and they'd walked in without warning. He was trapped.

"I can't, not ever. She'll always be her." He held up an old photograph. Faded and grey, Ander caught a *glimpse of a skinny boy and a girl with fingerless gloves, laughing arm in arm in front of the ruins.*

"Who's that?" Ander asked, unable to contain his curiosity any longer. He burst out of the closet. He had never seen his father cry before.

"I forgive you," Ander said. He meant it. In her own way, she had done her best for him. "My father never forgot you. I hope you know that."

"I know," she said, and leaned back against the stone wall, closing her eyes. She wouldn't want him to see her cry, so Ander left.

The throne room was already bustling when he arrived, and he had to push his way forward to the front where Cas was standing waiting for him on the podium. He held a sealed envelope, the results of the vote contained inside. They had been double and triple checked by representatives of all of the three main factions; the royalists, the rebellion and the commoners.

As Ander reached his brother's side the audience fell silent. They already knew what Cas had been waiting for. The corner of Cas' mouth lifted.

Cas opened the envelope, breaking through the wax seal with his thumb. He pulled out the paper inside and stared at it for a full minute. Ander twisted his brother's arm so he could see the result. He turned to the audience.

"Ladies and gentlemen, let me present to you my brother, the newly elected King of England."

Turning back to his brother, he winked and knelt on the ground. Behind him, there was nothing but stunned silence and the shuffle of hundreds of feet. As one, they knelt before their king.

Great plot

I don't like the blurb at the back. Gives too much away + too wordy.

~~Now~~ In the midst of civil unrest a mysterious stranger appears to challenge the king. ~~Who is it?~~ for his throne, for his ~~life~~ love and maybe even his life ~~for his love~~. Can deeply suppressed secrets ~~be~~ that span across decades be finally detangled before the realm is ~~finally~~ utterly ~~lost be~~ destroyed?

Something like that

Printed in Great Britain
by Amazon